BLAMELESS

a novel

BLAMELESS

Lisa Reardon

 Random House ■ New York

All rights reserved under International and Pan-American Copyright Conventions. Published in the United States by Random House, Inc., New York, and simultaneously in Canada by Random House of Canada Limited, Toronto.

RANDOM HOUSE and colophon are registered trademarks of Random House, Inc.

Book design by Mercedes Everett

Library of Congress Cataloging-in-Publication Data
Reardon, Lisa.
Blameless: a novel / Lisa Reardon.
p.   cm.
ISBN 0-375-50405-2
1. Children—Crimes against—Fiction. 2. Women—Psychology—Fiction. 3. Bus drivers—Fiction. I. Title.
PS3568.E26825 B57   2000
813'.54—dc21   99-055524

Random House website address: www.atrandom.com

Printed in the United States of America on acid-free paper

2   3   4   5   6   7   8   9

First Edition

For Mick Weber, with love

Acknowledgments

Thanks to Jennifer Rudolph Walsh for performing her many miracles. Thanks also to Courtney Hodell for her patience, persistence, and wisdom.

I am grateful for the technical assistance given by Mr. Dennis LaBelle, prosecuting attorney of Grand Traverse County. Others who supplied needed information include George Hicks, Hunter Hicks, Pat Neely, and the people at Munson Medical Center in Traverse City. Any factual errors are the result of my carelessness alone. Thank you to Shawn Hirabayashi and Milan Stitt for their helpful responses to early drafts of the book.

I wish to thank Myra Colon, Michael Udolf, and Patricia Walter for giving me a place in which to grow. Thank you also to the group members of the Adolescent After School Program, who have shown me how joyful that growth can be.

Author's Note

Kassauga County, Lake Kassauga, and the town of Riverton are fictional places set in northern Michigan.

BLAMELESS

1

"Oh my God," she cried. "Oh my God," with heaving, gasping, snot-filled sobs.

"It's all right, Sharon." I pulled my visor down low over my face. People up and down the beach were looking at us. "It has a happy ending."

"Oh Jesus!" Two tears raced one another down her cheeks.

"What's the matter with her?" asked a voice by my left shoulder. I lifted my visor and looked up. Julianna stood over me dripping lake water all over my towel and staring at Sharon who continued weeping into her hands.

"Hey Juli-Wuli," I said. "How's it going?"

"Going all right." Julianna's eyes were pale hazel to the point of yellow, and tilted up at the corners. She wore a ragged old fishing hat with a white band around it that she'd found earlier in the summer and hadn't taken off since. She was twelve years old on that Sunday afternoon in August and, like all girls before puberty erupts, she seemed indestructible.

"Is she sick?" she asked, still watching Sharon.

"She's reading," I answered.

"Wow." Julianna turned on her heels in the sand and scuttled back to her grandma twenty feet away. Nana was large and soft with a grandmotherly braid wrapped around the crown of her head. Her swimsuit was modest with a pleated skirt sewn in. Upper arms swayed when she handed Julianna her plastic bottle of 7-Up. I wanted to be pressed to that bosom, enfolded in the old-woman smell of Jean Naté or lemon verbena. I closed my eyes and felt the sun on my arms. Sniffles continued on my right.

"You okay, Sharon?"

"No," she said, trying to catch her breath. "I'm not okay."

I handed her a mini-pack of Kleenex out of my bag. The sun was relentless. My skin was tightening like a baked chicken.

"Come on," I told her. "Let's get in the water."

"Let me finish the chapter," she said, blowing her nose. It was *Middlemarch*, the scene where Dorothea goes to her rival Mrs. Lydgate and reassures her as to Will's affections. I made a mental note to buy more Kleenex. Sharon had insisted that an afternoon at the beach would be just the thing to cheer me up, take my mind off the upcoming trial. I lay on my stomach, chin in my hand, and gazed at the prickly woods beyond the edge of the beach. The leaves on the trees were nibbled and torn, the squirrels nicked and ragged from playing too rough, flowers had had their nectar sucked dry by the hungry bees. God, I hated these dead August afternoons. When Sharon closed the book we headed for the water.

"You coming in?" I called to Julianna.

"Nah," she hollered back. Now she and her mother were playing badminton while Nana dozed. They played without a net, just hitting the birdie back and forth, counting to see how many volleys they could make before it hit the ground. Her mother was younger than me. She nodded to me the way you do to someone you only know by sight. A tanned little boy ran past, leaving a trail of Cheese Doodles from the snack bar farther up the beach. They sold hamburgers, hot dogs, even nachos. When I was a kid they had licorice chains, candy cigarettes, and wax lips in the glass counter at kid-eye level. My favorite was the giant diamond ring made of solid Sweet-Tart. To this day I gnaw on my index knuckle when I'm tired or anxious, almost tasting the sugar that melted pink or blue or green on my numbed tongue.

Sharon and I walked down to the water and waded in. The lake was warm at my ankles, chilly at my knees, freezing at my thighs. I dove into the water, my skin shrieking and gasping with the shock. My head came up and I breathed in the hot sunshine. Sharon bobbed up about ten feet back. She was not a strong swimmer. I took first place at the state swim meet in Lansing for the one-hundred-meter butterfly in classes B, C, and D. Sharon's head appeared, disappeared in the small waves. I stretched out into a leisurely backstroke, letting myself move with the lake. Noise was drowned out by the rhythmic hum of water beating on my eardrums. No laughter or yells from the beach, just peace and oblivion. My body undulated with the waves as if the lake were a rolling crib in which I lay. Sleep crept across the waves and held out its arms to me. I drifted into them longing for rest. In the middle of the afternoon I was safe. It was the nights that were dangerous, nights that had been invaded all summer, my sleep torn up like old dishrags. Other people had dreams that slid in over their windowsill; I had the Night Visitor.

It had been nearly a week gone by with no sign of trouble until last night. I awoke quietly, no thrashing around or crying out. I opened my eyes and there I was in my bed as though something had delivered me there wide awake and alert. I was pinned, arms and legs paralyzed. I could only take small, shallow breaths because he was on my chest pressing my lungs into the mattress. The Night Visitor was a gargoyle made of crumbling gray granite. He crouched on me, gripping my ribs with his cold stone toes. His face was kept hidden in shadow. I saw the knuckles on his granite clawed hands, the scaled elbows, the dull matted texture of his back when he turned this way or that as if I were no more than a ledge upon which he sat, not a living thing; as if I were not there at all.

Frank was at the corner of the bed, stretched out, asleep. His fur was tinged with the moonglow gliding in the window. The cup and saucer were on the nightstand where I'd left them. Familiar shadows clung to each other in the corners of the room. Outside the window the usual trees stood dark and silent. But inside, the Night Visitor shifted his stone weight and breathed slowly. It was pointless to struggle, cry out, beg, or threaten. There was nothing to do but lie wide awake in the silence of deep night and wait for him to go away.

I don't know how long he stayed. Time stopped, thought stopped, the beating of my heart stopped, while he continued to crouch with numbing indifference. I waited as weeks and years went by, broken by swift-sharp pictures that flashed and were gone. Like old snapshots they appeared then disappeared, there but not there. A door opening, but then gone before I could discern was that her foot? Yes, the same toe poking out from the same old hole in her sock. And later, a close-up of her face. I lay there, growing old, watching.

Then no more pictures. He was lifting himself off me, slowly slowly, because stone moved at an eternal pace. He dissolved into the shadows outside the window. My sheets were clammy from icicle sweat. I waited for a count of one hundred, although he rarely returned the same night. Then I got up, went to the kitchen, and switched on the light that hung over the table. The clock on the stove said 4:52 A.M. I returned to the bedroom for my robe and wool socks to mitigate the harsh reality of the kitchen's tile floor. The threat of impending cold reigned high at that hour. Pockets of October chill were lurking in the dark of an August night. I grabbed a Stroh's out of the fridge to help me back to sleep. Picked up a stack of *National Geographic*s from the couch and dropped them onto the kitchen table. If anything were standing outside the window near the woods, at the dark line where the trees met my yard, they would see a window; inside the window a warm island of light encompassing the kitchen table, a woman sitting alone with magazines scattered around her. The birds were starting up already, singing a greeting to the day that had not yet arrived. A single car went by out on Route 108. It wouldn't be long until the purple blue crimson pink gold of the sunrise.

Something grabbed my foot and yanked me under the waves. Water closed over my head and rushed up my nose. I kicked myself free and reared up into the sunlight.

"Gotcha," Sharon said.

"You asshole." I blew lake water and snot out of my nose. Tried to breathe with soggy lungs.

"It won't kill you," she said, playfully slapping her palms flat on the water. Crack, crack, crack. I lunged upward and braced my hands on her shoulders, laughing as I pushed her down into the water. She backed out of my grip and bobbed up again several feet away.

"Come on," she said. "Let's head back in."

We were parallel to the buoys marking the edge of the swimming area, the cutoff point that separated swimmers and motorboats. We were out more than fifty yards.

"If I hadn't grabbed your foot, you'd have floated all the way across to the marina." The marina was on the other side of the lake. I looked across the water as a big speedboat jetted by, leaving a wake that bobbed the pontoons like a row of gleaming metal ducks. That's where I'd been headed when Sharon pulled me back. How long had we been in the water?

We both swam for shore: Sharon in a clumsy freestyle, me in a steady breaststroke. It felt good to stretch out and move, arms and legs reaching, pulling me through the water. Moving like an animal gives the illusion of control, as if you have some say over what you will or will not do, as if it's as simple as killing what you will eat, mating when ready, and dying when something larger, faster, hungrier gets you. The muscles in my thighs pushed against the waves as I strode toward the shore. Sharon was a few feet ahead. She was shorter than me, slimmer. If it were a bare-handed contest then and there, I could have had her in a choke-hold in two seconds flat. I doubt the thought had ever occurred to her. Wondered why it had occurred to me.

By seven o'clock Sharon had packed up and gone home. In

the waning hours of the afternoon I opened my book and continued Jacqueline Susann's *Yargo* for the fifth time. The lake was
dark, lifeless. The sun was just about to give up on the day.

Off to my right Julianna's mother was telling her to put on
her T-shirt and sandals, time to go. Julianna ran top speed for
the lake, bound on getting in one more dip before she left. She
was three feet from the water when her mom looped her up in
a one-armed hug, twirled her around once, and set her down
going in the opposite direction. Julianna kept running like she
didn't notice the change in direction. She ran fast toward me
and landed like she was sliding into home plate. Sand fantailed
all over me.

"You're funny," I said over her laughter, shaking sand out of
my book before I swatted her with it.

"The Merc's looking good," she said. My black '65 Mercury
was parked behind us, shining and spotless. She'd been over to
the cottage that morning, scrubbing the hubcaps while I hosed
down the hood.

"Juju, let's go." Her mother had one hand on her hip, one
hand shading her eyes, shaking her head at me to say, "Can you
believe this kid?" I smiled back and murmured to Julianna,
"Better get moving."

She stood up. "See you later, sweet potater."

She walked pigeon-toed back to her blanket, clucking like a
chicken, diving down to retrieve an item here and there, flapping her elbows occasionally. I shifted my sunglasses up off my
nose, rubbing the bridge where two red welts showed what bad-
fitting sunglasses could do. Closed my eyes, let the book fall
off my knees, pages muffling through the sand. I was tired. I
dropped the sunglasses into place. Julianna was walking to

their car, no longer clucking like a chicken, but singing a song in fake French.

"Ooh ooh, bee bee, ju mu tu pooh. Ooh ooh, bee bee, I love you-ou!"

Julianna waved good-bye as their Cutlass crawled away through the parking lot. The beach was near empty. A few small, spidery children screamed and splashed thirty yards down the lake, too young to mind the first evening chill. They sounded far away, years away. The beach that was so warm earlier, teeming under flip-flops and naked feet, was now damp and chilly. Behind me the tops of the pines caught the sun's last rays. They flamed gold against the cooling blue sky like silent candles blowing over the black and bottomless water.

I was expected at Mom's house for dinner. I picked up *Yargo*, dog-eared the left page and, snapping it shut, shoved it into a ragged old beach bag made of unbleached canvas. It was nubby and speckled with a faded red, white, and blue design of the Statue of Liberty: "1776–1976 United States Bicentennial," it said. I rubbed my feet back and forth on my towel to scrape off the sand, and slipped on my Keds. They didn't slip on like good old Keds ought to. They were still new and I hated them. Yanked on my cutoffs, grabbed my green pullover windbreaker. This time of year in northern Michigan, it cooled off a lot after sunset. I snapped the towel hard a few times and threw it over one shoulder, the Bicentennial bag over the other. I walked up across the sandy weeds until I hit firm blacktop. Checked all four tires on the car, hard as nuts.

The Merc knew the way to Mom's house. I relinquished control over the steering and shifted back against the seat, letting the car stretch out and run. Tomford Road was bounded on either side by shallow sand ditches and a wall of fir trees that were tall, dark, annoyed by the road snaking through their midst. Once in a while, in a storm or on a wild August night, one would tear its roots up out of the sand and fling itself down across the road. Brown trucks came with snarling saws to dismember the fallen one and cart it off to God knows where.

I rode silent and steady along the asphalt. The sun had gone under for the night, taking with it the long, blue shadows. There were hundreds of deer in the trees. I could feel their eyes on me, velvet, long-lashed, and blinking. A handful of crows kicked up a cold caw-caw and flapped out of the trees as the Merc rolled by. No other noise, just the hum-hiss of car tires on the pavement, the occasional pop of a pebble shooting out from under the rubber. In the distance the cars on Route 108 did a whish and fade, whish and fade. It was that time of day.

The Merc slowed down when we came within view of Mom's yard, and coasted past the cast-iron squirrel sitting on top of the Brickham's mailbox. Mr. Brickham next door had three fingers missing off his right hand. Used to scare me and Amy to death to peek over the ragged fence and watch him raking leaves. Dad had warned us they had a rabid dog locked in the basement that had bitten Mr. Brickham's fingers off, so we'd better stay the hell out of their yard or else. I snapped off the headlights as the Merc crept into the driveway. Got out and stood watching fireflies in the backyard. It was still light if you were there outside. If you were in the kitchen with the light on and you were looking out, then it was already dark. A subjective time. A couple of bats frenzied past, swooping down in a jerky arc to snag a mouthful of mosquitoes. I remembered when Dad hung mousetraps in the trees one summer, thinking it'd kill the bats. Carl laughed until he cried when he saw the old maple full of traps set with dead flies.

Standing outside the garage, watching the bats swifting and darting, both Carl and Dad were far away. Dad died seventeen years ago come January. Lungs and liver gave out simultaneously. And Carl was remarried seven years ago in early June. Amy had worn silk apple blossoms in her hair. And all of us bridesmaids, we each carried an armful of the same. All lined up like taffeta ducks in a shooting gallery, Sharon said at the time. What a day that had been.

I could see Mom in the window, in the warm yellow light of the kitchen; tall and raw-boned with breeder's hips. Dad had called her his homestead bride, for no reason we could discover. Even after he died, Mom would only say, "You know your father." She was fixing dinner, chopping something and talking to Sharon over her shoulder. Boy, she was talking up a storm. Halted chopping every once in a while to wave the knife sharply in the air, stabbing a point. Behind her I caught a flash of dark blond; Sharon reaching into the cupboard, taking down plates for the table. Mom looked at her watch and frowned, looked out the window into the dark. She hadn't heard me pull up, couldn't see me standing there. I wished I could stay out there all night watching my life from a distance, but it was too chilly and I was hungry. The kitchen was bright and dry and warm, and supper was almost on the table.

I stepped through the side door into the mudroom. Pulled off my Keds, bracing heel against toe, heel against toe. There was an open archway from the mudroom to the kitchen. I could hear everything in there.

"Hello," I announced my arrival.

"About time, Mary," said Mom. "Starting to worry." She went on, not waiting for an answer. "Stacy and Ruther are coming tonight."

"Hmm."

"They're bringing back the linens," she said. Linen table-cloths from Stacy's baby shower.

"Okay," I said, tossing the Bicentennial bag in the corner.

"I can hear you," said Mom, appearing in the archway with a large metal spoon in her hand. "It won't kill you to be nice."

"I'm always nice." I pulled the pullover up and over.

"It's the *way* you're nice," she said.

Stacy was twenty-seven, Sharon twenty-eight. I was creeping up on thirty-five in the fall. Once Stacy's kid arrived I would be the crazy old maiden aunt.

"Bitter is not a pretty quality," Mom continued.

"I agree," I told her.

"It's not as if you didn't have your chance," she added. . . . *And blew it* echoed silently over our heads.

I stepped to the window above the sink. Like the night before, I tried to imagine anyone out there looking in, seeing me framed in the yellow square of light. Did I look safe? Sharon handed me some silverware, which I carried over to the table.

"All newlyweds are a little complacent," Mom went on. "You have to forbear a little. She'll grow out of it."

"Well, she's certainly growing," Sharon said, folding napkins and tucking them crookedly under my carefully laid forks. "No doubt about that."

"She's your sister. Don't forget that," Mom said.

"How could we?" I replied.

"Why don't the two of you be quiet?" Mom had that edge to her voice. We shut up. Sunday supper was mashed potatoes with hamburger gravy and Brussels sprouts on the side. Sharon talked about work up to the Sleazebag Inn. It was really the Sleepy Bluff Inn, part of some cut-rate discount chain. Business was booming now at the height of the season. After Labor Day Sharon would be on unemployment until the Christmas rush over at North Country Crafts.

"Are you playing this week?" she asked me. Women's fast-pitch softball. I was a left-handed first baseman.

"No, saving myself for the tournament," I answered.

"If they'll let you come back," Sharon said carelessly.

"How's your shoulder?" Mom asked. I'd broken my collar-bone last February. I rotated my arm at the table, shrugged my shoulders a few times.

"It'll be all right," I told her.

Over coffee and leftover angel food cake Sharon talked about the skirt and jacket she was sewing. "It's from an old pattern, from the fifties. I have to go up two sizes, things were cut so small then." She drained her coffee mug and looked at me. "So for the moment, I'm a size twelve like you."

I bit back a reply, reminding myself that Marilyn Monroe was a size fourteen. Sharon sewed like a maniac. She'd made a dozen sleepers and rompers for Stacy's baby. She'd hand-stitched the trim, and I had embroidered a series of baby animals on the front of each one. Baby monkeys, elephants, lion cubs. Between the two of us, we worked for months on those things. Gave them to Stacy for the shower.

"These are homemade?" she said, holding them at the tips of her fingers as if she were inspecting them for uneven seams, unclipped threads. "That is so thoughtful of you both," she smiled. "Heirlooms."

She went into orgasms when she saw the pram from Ruther's mother. It was navy blue with lots of silver trim to match the $900 crib she'd picked out. Stacy didn't work outside the home. Ruther worked a lot of overtime at his dad's Ford dealership in Kalkaska.

We were on our second cup of coffee, the angel food cake a pleasant memory beneath our belts, when Mom said, "What about you, Mary?"

What she meant was, "What have you been doing with yourself?" Sunday dinner with Mom and Sharon usually ended the same. What has Mary been doing with herself? I was spared the need to answer by headlights in the driveway and then car doors slamming and footsteps on the back porch. A quick knock and then a round, pregnant belly waddled into the kitchen, attached to Stacy, who was followed by Ruther, whose face reflected a self-satisfied smugness whenever he looked at his wife. "Look what I did with my very own dick!" he seemed to say. Stacy looked surprised to see me, as if I weren't there every single Sunday night for dinner, as if she were the only one who visited.

Mom went into the front room with the newlyweds while I cleared away dessert plates. Sharon stayed to help. I told her to go on into the other room; I was just going to rinse the dishes and I'd be right there. I rinsed each plate, each coffee mug, each fork and spoon. Wiped my hands on the linen towel and folded it neatly across the sink. Thought about coasting the Merc silently down the driveway. I'd be halfway home before they missed me.

"... and you should see them, Mom," Stacy was saying as I entered the living room. "They are so pretty, just above the window like a valance."

"I'll come over and have a look," Mom told her.

"Window treatments," Sharon said to me, catching me up on the conversation. Good old Sharon, who tried.

"You could probably make them." Stacy turned to Sharon. "Out of pine boughs and pinecones and some berries or something. You're good at that sort of thing." Stacy shifted in her seat on the couch, directing her belly straight at me like all ten guns in a firing squad. "How is it going?" she asked.

"I'm fine, Stace."

"I'm glad," she said.

"Thanks."

She exchanged a quick glance with Mom. I had been the topic of a recent discussion. "Well, time to go," I said to the room.

"Can't you please stay awhile?" Stacy asked, exasperated.

"Don't go already," said Mom. Sharon kept her mouth buttoned, rolled her eyes.

"We hardly ever see you," said Ruther.

Mom came back to the mudroom. "I wish you'd at least make an effort."

"I did," I said as I went out the screen door.

I had a hell of time backing out around Ruther's fake Jeep without nicking the Merc. The ride home was cold with the windows down, but I was too annoyed to roll them up. Chilly dark blew through hollow bones by the time I hit my back door. Didn't bother turning on any lights in the cottage. The moon poured in the windows; I could see well enough to start the bath and strip. Clothes flung themselves into the basket in the bedroom closet. Home, home, dear old home. In the semidark I saw the old disintegrating quilt thrown over the back of the sofa, the soft cotton worn to threads. There on the counter was the toaster cover I had embroidered, robins singing on a branch of dogwood, cheerful good-morning singing while I made my coffee. I was naked in the dark, surrounded by my things, safe in my home, lit by the moon.

Then I was in the tub. Sweat filmed on my forehead from soaking in water a little too hot. I had the window open an inch. A corner of the curtain shuddered, swayed, and the cool air slid over the windowsill. It curled down toward me and glided like a lover's hand around the back of my neck. The hot/cold heaven was dangerous, wild, like someone might catch me feeling good, alone in the dark, and then I'd catch hell. Through the window I could see the half-moon soar through wisps of clouds. Outside the crickets hummed and pulsed. There was no other sound except the distant howl of a logging truck flying down Route 108. I closed my eyes and breathed in the sweet sound.

The phone rang. I jumped hard. Water splashed up the side of the tub and over onto the bath mat. Jesus goddamn Christ, who was calling on a Sunday night? I rose out of the water. Goose pimples erupted as the second ring tore a jagged hole through the evening. I grabbed a towel and dripped out to the kitchen. Picked it up on the third ring.

"What."

"I'll call back later, when you're done," said Amy.

"Oh hey." I was cradling the phone against my shoulder, rubbing everything hard with the towel. "What's up?"

Amy sighed, "Oh hell, I don't know. We went to a barbecue last night over to Suzanne's place. We're starting to put together the Beer Tent."

"Hmm." I was dry now, but still naked and cold. I stretched the phone cord and lunged for my bathrobe hanging on the bedroom door. Missed. "What'd you do today?"

"Nothing. Carl went over to Harley Sherman's. Helping him put a new roof on the garage. He's not home yet." Amy was left alone to shift for herself on a Sunday night, probably bored. "I'm bored."

"Why don't you call over there?" I grabbed the broom from next to the sink, stretched the phone cord back again toward the bedroom.

"I did," she said lightly. "No answer. And I wish you'd get an answering machine. I tried you all night."

"No."

"It's a hostile thing, not having an answering machine," she said. "It's openly hostile." Amy was my best friend. She loved phrases like "openly hostile."

"Nothing's so important that it can't wait." I'd taken a swing with the broom at the closet door and managed to knock the bathrobe onto the floor. Now I was dragging it across the floor toward me.

"What are you doing?" she asked. "You're panting."

"You want to come over here? We could get drunk and make popcorn balls."

"I would except I got my hair wrapped in tinfoil." Amy did her own hair color. Very complicated. I sat in her kitchen one night and watched her. We killed eight beers between us before she was through. I picked up the robe, shook it hard a few times to clear off any cat litter or other crud from the floor.

"Has Sasha had her kittens yet?"

"No," Amy said in a sinister tone. "She's about to explode."

"Check your dirty-clothes basket. You don't want to chuck 'em in the wash by mistake."

"Those damn wild dogs had her treed out behind Gillespie's barn."

"Someone ought to start hunting those things." I wrapped the robe around me, wrestling with the cord and receiver. Blessed, blessed warm and dry. "They're like giant rats."

"I wish you'd stop weight lifting or making the bed or whatever it is that you're doing," she said.

"Sorry." I grabbed the kettle off the stove and filled it in the sink. Softly, so Amy wouldn't hear me.

She said, "What'd you do today?"

"Went to the beach—"

"Why didn't you call me?"

"—with Sharon."

"Oh." There was no great warmth between the two of them.

"Had dinner over to Mom's. Stacy dropped by." I placed a tea bag in the old rosebud teacup that belonged to Grandma Culpepper.

"How's she look?"

"Ready to explode."

"Jesus," she laughed. "We're surrounded by breeders. Oh, hold on." There was a pause and then, "He just pulled in. I'll talk to you tomorrow."

"Night." Click.

I pulled the plug in the tub. The kettle started to whimper, then wail. I poured my cup of tea and carried it through the dark cottage to my room. Returned the bathrobe to its hook and disappeared into a flannel cloud of nightgown. The folds puffed out as the hem fell over my head to the floor like Wendy in *Peter Pan*. Little Miss Mother. Sharon made the nightgown for me. It was white with a small pattern of violets scattered through the flannel. There was lavender ribbon at the throat, and again at the cuffs. In that nightgown nothing could happen to me; I was impregnable. The thought brought a little smile as I lifted back the blankets and propped up the pillows. Sipped the tea that was supposed to help me sleep through the night, rested my head back, and let the calm take over again. When I set the cup and saucer carefully on the nightstand Frank leapt up onto the bed with a tiny cat grunt. He was carrying Sock Buddy in his mouth.

"Where've you been?" I scratched a few times on the back of his neck and settled under the blankets. He stuck a cold wet nose in my ear for an answer, walked in one full circle along the perimeter of the bed, and settled in a brown and gold ball against my leg. He was purring so hard I could feel him vibrating through the covers.

"Good night, Frank." We were both home and safe where we belonged, no better feeling in the world. Maybe I would be able to sleep longer than a few hours. Amy came to mind, her phone call. She'd been calling around to see where Carl was. I imagined my phone ringing and ringing earlier, me not here to answer it. What had she been thinking?

2

Monday I arrived at the municipal building at 9:30 A.M. sharp. The day had not yet heated up. I sat in the parking lot with the windows rolled down on the Merc and let the morning breeze bat a lock of my bangs back and forth. I was a half hour early. Sipped black coffee out of a paper cup and opened up the bag from Howard's Bakery. Jelly doughnut, gone in four bites. I balanced the cup on the dashboard and used a napkin to carefully brush the powdered sugar off my lap. The dress I was wearing was new. I'd gone alone a few days before to pick it out at Lehmann's in Traverse City.

"Think of this as a dress rehearsal," Melanie had said, no pun intended. "A dry run of the real thing." The dress was simple. Not the small floral print that Melanie had suggested, but a pale yellow linen cut in clean lines. "Nothing severe," she'd warned.

I could never pull off the look she was aiming at; a soft, plump, moist-speaking sort of person who collected Hallmark figurines. "I'm not interested in the real you," Melanie had said when I balked. "I'm interested in showing the jury what they want to see."

The round face of the Merc's clock nudged me at 9:50. I rolled up the windows, crank, crank, crank, leaning far across the front seat to reach the passenger window, wrinkling the linen. Piled my keys and wallet onto my notebook and walked across the parking lot. The breeze wafted up my bare legs like chilled perfume.

I walked in through double glass doors and the breeze had to wait outside. Went down wide corridors with low ceilings and fluorescent light, like an endless basement filled with hundreds of thousands of old, useless files. I pressed the efficient little elevator button and worked at untying the knot of muscle between my shoulder blades. *Ding!* I stepped in and deliberately took my time pressing the button. I got off on the third floor. My heels clicked hollowly, cheaply, along the corridor. Lots of suits crisscrossed my path, male and female. They had the faded faces of career county employees. When I entered the prosecuting attorney's office I got the same feeling as the first time I'd been there back in February, and the time after that, and after that as well. Irritated.

"I'm here to see Melanie Mahoney," I told the guy at the desk. He was a young man, a very young man. I couldn't remember his name, something soft and plump.

"Miss Culpepper?" he asked, raising his eyebrows unnaturally high.

"Ms." Not to be a bitch about it, but give me a break.

"Have a seat please," and the eyebrows plunged downward again. I flipped through *Newsweek* and *Michigan Living* before Ms. Mahoney came out to the waiting room. She was all smiles and bustling energy. She had dark hair that stood out in cork-screws all over her head, pale skin, gray eyes. "Mary, how are you?"

"Fine."

"Would you like some coffee or anything?"

"No."

"Take messages," she instructed the very young man behind the desk. I followed her quietly down the hall, like I was going to the dentist, or the principal, or my own death. Though we'd gone through my testimony two or three times over the course of the spring and summer, she still plucked and poked at me. An hour later, Brandon or Matthew or Jonathan brought in a pitcher of water and poured me a glass; my friend for life. The yellow linen dress was limp and crumpled even in the air-conditioning.

"Just a few more questions," Mahoney assured me. "Had the other two kids indicated any problem when they boarded the bus that morning?"

"No."

"And did you have any reason to suspect that there was abuse taking place in the house?"

"No. None."

"Well," she said, slapping her pen onto the desk and looking at me closely. "Almost no deviation whatsoever."

She went on with last-minute instructions for the witness stand. The dress would do fine, keep my chin down, cry if I felt the need, wear earrings.

"I don't own any earrings."

"Borrow a pair. And a necklace as well," she said. "Something with flowers."

I jotted these things down in my notebook, along with a note to send her a bouquet of flowers when the trial was over. She wouldn't get the joke. I doodled carnations, snapdragons, a couple of sweetheart roses.

"The start date is next Wednesday," she said. "As a key witness you're going to have to keep yourself available." I could feel her excitement, her confidence bristling as she led me out of the room. I secretly christened her Mad Dog Mahoney. "If there's anything you want to add to your story, now's the time to tell me," she said.

"Like what?" I asked. I was tired, hadn't slept the night before.

"Like anything new you may have suddenly remembered." She was walking along quickly, leading me back to the very young man. "Any extra information that you forgot to mention before."

"I've told you everything I'm going to remember," I said, matching her stride for stride.

"It would help me if I had evidence of prior abuse," she said for the hundredth time. "I'm sure you know that."

"I'm not the lawyer," I answered. "I just drive a bus."

"People don't kill their kid out of the blue. There had to have been previous injuries." I didn't answer, just looked at her and waited. She continued. "You saw Jen Colby every day through the school year."

I replied, "She was a perfectly normal kid as far as I could see."

She stopped abruptly and there we were in the lobby, back where I'd started.

"I'll talk to you next week," she said, and disappeared. There was the very young man with his eyebrows up to his hairline in silent question. I stood clutching my notebook, staring back at him.

"We'll be in touch," he said.

I left the office feeling guilty, like I was getting away with something. The elevator sank me back to the main floor, and I headed for the exit. To hear Mahoney talk, Patricia Colby wasn't guilty or innocent, just a person we were putting the screws to. I didn't like the idea of prosecutors and defenders, like this was a football game and I was Mahoney's star quarterback. After next week it would be over and my dealings with lawyers ended forever.

I opened the double glass doors and stepped out into the glare of the morning. It had heated up while I was inside. A couple of suits stepped aside as I headed for the Merc. "Excuse me, miss," said one.

I pulled out and away, using a sugar-dusted napkin to wipe the sweat from my forehead.

▪   ▪   ▪

A few days later I stopped by Mom's in the morning after dropping off a few bags of old clothing at the First Presbyterian Church. Mom wanted some things from Kmart so I drove over there with her. I needed a new carafe for my coffeemaker; I'd rammed mine against the sink while rinsing it. That's three I'd lost that way. So we were in Kmart and there was Julianna and her mom standing in front of the plastic no-scratch spatulas.

Julianna was using an ice-cream scoop as a microphone, interviewing passing customers as they moved up the aisle.

"And you, ma'am, what did you come to Kmart for today?" she said in a Dan Rather voice.

"Please, I don't have—I don't know." A large, toothy woman smiled. "I get stage fright," she said, and pushed her cart away. Julianna got a fit of giggles and her mother smiled.

"Are you coming?" Mom asked, over by the toaster ovens.

"Just a minute," I told her. I looked purposefully at the tongs, strainers, pickle spears, pretending I was a stranger. Julianna inched over to me, ice-cream scoop poised, playing along.

"What brings you to Kmart today, miss?"

Miss. I loved that. Without taking my eyes off the shelves in front of me I muttered, "Frog tongues."

"What?" She was surprised, but kept the microphone in position.

"Frog tongues." I looked at her. "You know. For salad toppings." Her mother heard this. She gave me a smile.

"Frog tongues?!"

"Yes." I picked out a carafe, hefted it under my arm.

"No such thing, lady."

"Been eating 'em all my life."

"Interesting." She pointed at an imaginary camera. "Can you give us your name please?"

"Eleanor Prudhomme," I said into the ice-cream scoop.

Julianna giggled when I mentioned Eleanor's name and punched me in the arm. The first time I met Eleanor was one morning last April, when the weather had turned warm enough for bike riding. The bike had been a Christmas present and Julianna told me all about it on the bus when Christmas vacation was over. As soon as the weather warmed up, she rode over to show it off to me.

"See, it's got this odometer, counts the miles," she said, spinning the bike tire until the counter clicked over. "I'm riding to the North Pole this summer."

We sat on the front porch of the cottage while she took an atlas and a large map of Michigan out of her backpack.

"Okay, see, it's seventy-seven miles from here to Mackinac Bridge. Then another forty-two until I hit Canada." She scratched at her ankle and flipped open a small spiral notebook to a page filled with numbers. "At the rate I'm going now it'll only take me six weeks to blow through Ontario." She unfolded a page torn out of the atlas. Showed me highway routes and mileage up through Manitoba. "Once I hit the Arctic, I figure I can ride across the ice floes. I'll have to figure in the currents, and a little zigzagging, maybe storms and stuff." She was talking fast, explaining it all to me. "But I figure if I average twenty miles a day, I'll hit the North Pole by October first."

That first Sunday morning in April she helped me wash the Merc, using a wooden brush to scrub the tires and hubcaps while I cleaned the hood and roof. Once the car was sparkling on the outside we refilled the bucket with Tide and fresh water, and she washed her bike while I dragged the vacuum out and finished the inside of the car.

"Where are you now?" I asked, continuing our earlier conversation.

"Well, I just started four days ago, and I only have a couple hours after school before supper." She rubbed her cheek against her shoulder to wipe off some soap suds. "So I'm just a mile south of St. Ignace."

"You got a name for that bike?" I asked, taking Windex to the windows of the car. Julianna was scrubbing each spoke with an old washcloth.

"Eleanor," she said, patting the front tire like it was the muzzle of a horse. "Eleanor Prudhomme."

"That's a name and a half."

"I read it in a book, *Eleanor, the Biker Babe.*"

"You did not."

"I swear to God. I'll loan it to you if you want." We worked for a while in silence. "When you gonna drive our bus again?" she asked, keeping her eyes intent on her work.

"I don't know." It was a beautiful day in April. Birds were chirruping and swooping around the newly budded trees, just as they had that day last February, that false spring day when the last snowfall had melted and the next hadn't yet hit. Would it would be this hard every spring to come? "I don't know," I said again.

Julianna stepped back from the bike and inspected it for water spots. She rubbed a towel along the handlebar, uncertain whether to say any more about it. "You ever gonna drive our bus again?"

"I don't know."

"I don't know what I'd have done if it was me," she said finally, shaking her head like she'd probably seen her grandma do a hundred times. I concentrated on the side mirror, sprayed the Windex, rubbed. Satisfied that the bike was perfect, Julianna lay down on some dry grass and snapped the towel a few times in the air. She said, "Anyway, the guy they got driving now is a real turd."

"Yeah?"

"He makes us call him Mister Elliott. He's not much of a talker." Frank had been lying on the back porch steps, ears flicking in the breeze. Now he trotted across the grass and tried to catch the corner of the towel as Julianna waved it back and forth. "What kind of car is that?"

"It's a 1965 Mercury Monterrey with the breezeway window option." I tore off a fresh paper towel.

"What's a breezeway?" Julianna asked.

"The back windshield goes down."

"No way. Are you kidding?"

"Push a button, down it goes." I wiped my hands with the towel, turned the key halfway, and pushed the button to show her.

"Damn! Can I have a ride in it?"

"Not today," I told her. "And don't swear."

"But sometime, maybe?"

"Sure. Here." I yanked a couple of bucks out of the pocket of my shorts. "That's for helping."

The next week I gave her the promised ride in the Merc, stopped at the Little Skipper for a root beer float. After that Julianna got in the habit of dropping by every Sunday morning. We'd wash the Merc and Eleanor Prudhomme, sing along to country music on the stereo: Iris DeMent or the Carter Family. Julianna filled me in on the gossip I was missing.

"Roger Hufford got his boot stuck on the bus between the seat and the wall and he cried like a baby until Mister Elliot yanked him loose."

She told me about her dad, who couldn't come to the beach because he worked on the weekends, but he was home on Tuesdays and Wednesdays. She talked about school, about going into seventh grade, which meant junior high that fall and no more riding my bus with the little kids. Some days she talked about boys. Troy Martin in her class sent her a postcard from the Black Hills where his grandma lived and signed it "Love, Troy" and what did that mean? But most days she talked about Eleanor Prudhomme and their trip north through the wilds of Canada.

Back in Kmart, Julianna was juggling the ice-cream scoop with one hand. "We're going to the Dairy Dip on the way home. Wanna come?"

"Your treat?"

"I ain't got two pennies to lay on a dead bastard's eyes," she said, looking pleased with herself.

"Where'd you hear that?"

"My Uncle Ted." She looked around for her mother, who was disappearing into the hardware department. "I gotta go. Maybe I'll see you up there?"

"Maybe."

"Maybe yes or maybe no?"

"Maybe maybe." I turned up the aisle to see Mom looking at me with a stack of sixty-watt lightbulbs held in one arm.

"Who were you talking to?" she asked me.

"Friend of mine." I hated it when she got that disapproving tone.

"How do you know her?"

"She's a kid from my bus," I said. "Her name is Julianna."

"What a curly-cue name," she said, arranging the lightbulbs neatly in the cart. She wouldn't look at me. I wheeled us into the pet supplies and loaded up with two five-pound bags of Kleen Kitty. I kept my mouth shut as we went through the checkout

line. Mom threw an issue of *People* on the counter, then added
Woman's Day on top of it. "Summer Dessert Delights," it promised. On the way out of the store, a newsstand caught my eye.
The headline jumped out at me: COLBY TRIAL SET BACK. I stopped
in front of it. Mom turned to see what kept me, so I hurried after
her. Even after all these months I couldn't get used to seeing it
blurted out like that for everyone to see.

I had been torn from a soul-restoring sleep at 8:30 that morning by the phone ringing. Assuming someone was dead, I
lunged for it. "Listen," said a moist voice in my ear. "They've
pushed us back, so forget about next week." I was silent, trying
to figure out who and what. "Hello?" the voice said.

"Yes," I said. "I'm here."

"We'll be issuing a new subpoena—" Oh. It was Mahoney.
Yes. The trial, the testimony, the dead girl. Jen, Jenny, Jennifer.
"—a few weeks from now."

"Fine," I said shortly. A few weeks? And I had thought it
would all be over after next Wednesday.

"August thirtieth," she continued. "You might as well note it
in your calendar right now."

I wrote it down on a Little Caesar's Pizza napkin lying near
the toaster. After I hung up the questions sprouted like crocuses, but I was damned if I'd call her back.

Now the story was back in the paper. More headlines, more
pictures of Jen on the front page. I followed Mom out of Kmart,
trying to forget all my questions, all the answers written in
black and white back there on the newsstand. We piled the bags
in the trunk of the Merc and I pulled onto Chessman Road.

"Mom," I started. She cut me off with a little open-handed
slap on the armrest.

"I will learn to keep my mouth shut," she said.

"What?"

"Nothing," she said. Then, "I'm sorry."

I half wanted her to explain the problem, half wanted her to continue to avoid the subject. "I'm not supposed to talk to kids now?"

We drove awhile. Sunshine dappled over the windshield, first shading, then blinding me. "Of course you can talk to kids," she said finally. "You're going to have to sooner or later."

Meaning when school started and I was behind the wheel of that bus again. I kept my eyes on the road. Could feel Mom making the effort not to say anything more. An ambulance sounded in the distance; silence inside the car. I pushed the button for the back windshield, took a breath.

I couldn't stand it. "What?"

"I didn't say anything," Mom answered.

"And you're not saying it very loudly."

We turned onto Tomford Road, which followed about three miles to the house. A mile past the house, you hit Lake Kassauga; another couple of miles, my place. Mom looked over at me once we were out of traffic.

"I love you, Mary," she told me. "Nothing could change that." A mantle of cold settled over my shoulders like a squid.

"What makes you say that?" I asked, glancing out at the fields that butted up against the woods. Two deer stood out in the distance.

"Because you're having a hard time and you won't let anyone help you." Poor Mom, at a loss.

"It's getting better."

"You look exhausted."

"I'm going to take a nap when I get home."

"Are you taking those pills that Dr. Morisseau gave you?" she asked. Good old Dr. Morisseau, who'd been our family doctor for a hundred years.

"No."

"Aren't they helping?"

"They make me dopey and stupid," I told her. "I wake up all cotton-headed."

She didn't say anything to that. Dr. Morisseau gave her the same pills so she could sleep those first few months after Dad died. She was cotton-headed twenty-four hours a day.

"Have you thought about seeing that person over in Cadillac?" Meaning, that shrink.

"I don't have money for that sort of thing." Meaning, I don't need a shrink.

"You don't want any help," she said finally, out of patience.

"I'll think about it." And I would. I would think about all of it, once I was out of that claustrophobic car with Mom hogging up all the air so I couldn't get a goddamn breath. I caught a flash of a turtle sunning himself on a half-submerged tire in the ditch, unconcerned with the conversation taking place in the black car that sped past. Joe-pye weed was growing tall and straight along the road, never had to worry about sleeping. Amoral weed.

I helped her unpack the groceries, then pulled out and headed back toward town rather than home. I rolled past a billboard, a grainy photograph of a fetus in the womb: THIS IS A CHILD, NOT A CHOICE. And below that, "Paid for by citizens of . . ."

A lot of strong feeling on that score around here. Stopped at the Blue Light Amoco on Main Street and asked Harold Tucker if he had time for a tune-up in the next week.

"You having any problems with her?" he asked through bared teeth. Harold always looked like he just banged back his first whiskey of the day and the aftertaste was killing him. He had worked on our family's cars as long as I could remember. He'd been an old drinking crony of Dad's, but drunk or sober, he could make an engine sit up and sing.

"No problems," I told him. "But it's been six months."

He squinted at the Merc, scowled at a Wagoneer up on the lift, at the gas pumps, the pile of tires by the fence, at his hands.

"If it's no emergency then," he said, "can you wait 'til Friday?" We set a time, which he wrote down in a small greasy notebook. "How's everyone?" he asked, tucking the notebook in the pocket of his coveralls.

"They're good." I picked up the Kalkaska paper as if an after-thought.

"You say hello to your mom, then."

"I will."

I paid for the paper. His eyes fell on the headline. "Damn shame about that," he said.

"Hmm," I replied.

"They shouldn't ought to torture the poor woman." He shook his head, the grimace deepening. "Any idiot could see it was an accident."

I kept my eyes on the Dairy Dip sign across the street. A giant vanilla cone smiled back at me. Harold pinched his chin and said, "Well there, did I go and put my foot in it?"

"It's okay," I said. "Mind if I step across the street?"

He stepped under the Wagoneer, glaring ferociously at its muffler. "Yeah, leave her there," he said. "She's all right."

I left the Merc for the moment and stepped to the curb. Now that the paper was in my hand, I felt furtive. I folded it in half, tucked it carefully under my arm, and crossed the street to the Dairy Dip. A small band of flies rose up in greeting as I stepped to the window. An impossibly young girl stood on the other side, biting her nails. They had been gnawed halfway to the cuticle. She saw me looking at her hands and whipped them behind her back.

"Can I take your order?" she parroted.

"Vanilla cone with a chocolate dip." I wanted to apologize for staring at her hands. Just shutting up would be better. The sweet-greasy smell of the Dairy Dip wafted all over me. A disastrous grape Slushie sprawled at my feet, half dried into a sticky puddle. The girl reappeared, holding my chocolate dip. She'd put on little plastic gloves to cover her torn up nails. My heart dropped a few inches at the sight, sorry that I'd made her feel ashamed. She slid the little screen door to one side and carefully handed the cone out to me.

"Dollar sixty-five, please."

I handed her two dollars. Couldn't think of any way to apologize without making things worse, so I told her to keep the change. There was one picnic table. I flopped the paper down on it and had a seat at one end. Tore into the waxy chocolate, careful not to let any break away and fall to the ground. I worked on getting the melting ice cream under control before turning my attention to the paper. There was the headline that I'd seen as we came out of Kmart. Below it, a school picture of Jen Colby, the same picture we'd all seen in every paper in the state by now. A thin-shouldered six-year-old beamed back at the camera, an average happy kid. People wouldn't be so shook up about this trial if she'd looked haunted or terrified. But there she was smiling away, about as normal a kid as you could hope for. My eyes drifted down to the article itself.

Patricia Colby was to face charges of second-degree murder at the trial scheduled to begin next week at the Kassauga County Courthouse. However, a motion from the defense has postponed the trial until August 30. Mrs. Colby is accused in the bludgeoning death of her six-year-old daughter, Jennifer Colby, on February 8 of this year. Her ex-husband, Brian Colby of Manistee, was granted temporary custody of the surviving children, ages nine and ten.

At the bottom of the page, a small article on efforts to reform the child protection agencies in Kassauga County to avoid any more "needless tragedies" in the future.

I dropped the paper and chewed on my knuckle. Jen Colby wasn't more than a month or two old when her parents were divorced amid mutual accusations of infidelity. It was a big stinking mess and the whole town heard about it. Opinions were divided as to who was really at fault. But everyone agreed at the time that Pat Colby was an excellent mother.

"I don't know how she does it," Nancy LaFarge had said. "I know for a fact he's not sending child support half the time."

Now Brian Colby had custody of the older two, and Patricia Colby was accused of deliberately hitting her six-year-old daughter with a cast-iron skillet hard enough to kill her. Mad

Dog Mahoney was going to use my testimony—how I'd found her, the condition of the body—to put a woman in prison. I had to get up in front of a jury and tell a story with no happy ending and no clear conclusions. Shapes approached and sat at the other end of the picnic table.

"Hey," said a voice to my right. "Did you get your frog tongues?"

I looked up and there Julianna sat behind starry sparks from rubbing my eyes too hard. She and her mom were sharing a banana split. Patricia Colby probably brought her kids to the Dairy Dip a time or two. I pushed the paper away as if to protect them from contagion. Julianna's mom read my face and broke into the silence.

"Don't bother people, Julianna."

"It's not people, it's Mary," Julianna said.

"I'm Doreen," her mom said to me, our first formal introduction.

"Mary." Mouth full of vanilla, I had to talk with an underbite.

"Listen," Doreen said. "If she ever bothers you, send her on home." Julianna rolled her eyes, as if she could ever bother anybody.

"It's all right." I took a large bite of the cone and gulped it down. Instant blood vessel constriction followed. My brain beat like congo drums.

"Mary's the bus lady," Julianna reminded her. "That's her car I told you about across the street."

"Nice," said Doreen, admiring the Merc.

"My Uncle Ted has a 1967 Corvette convertible," Julianna informed me. "From before I was even born."

"He let you ride in it?" I took another bite of ice cream. More conga drums inside my skull. My poor brain had frozen down to the size of a pea.

"Me and Donna rode on the back of it last year in the Labor Day Parade. We dressed up like we were Miss Kassauga County and he drove us in the parade. Donna's gonna win the pageant this year and she'll still let me ride on the back with her. That's what we're gonna do, aren't we, Mom?"

"That's the plan," Doreen said.

"Who's Donna?" I asked.

"My cousin," Julianna replied. "That was about the grossest thing I ever heard in my life, frogs' tongues." Julianna scraped up a spoonful of hot chocolate syrup, dividing her gaze between it and me. "Except for Tyler Claybank picking boogers and eating them in the lunchroom."

Her mother dropped her spoon into the banana split and held her head in her palm, but she didn't scold Julianna or tell her to shut up.

"That's pretty gross," I agreed.

"It was on a dare," Julianna explained.

"I'm sorry about that," Doreen said simply, nodding toward the paper. "About that girl."

I was about to give some bland remark about what a shame, when I realized what she meant. She was sorry for me. My face flushed hot. In seven months no one had said that. Outrage, worry, curiosity, but no straightforward sympathy like this; after all, I wasn't the one who'd been killed. But here it was now like a little bird, and from a woman I hardly knew.

"Thank you," I said. I ate the last of the cone and wiped my hands with the paper napkin. I couldn't meet her eye.

"Hey, I'm exactly halfway through the Northwest Territory," Julianna said.

"You're making good time."

She nodded, pleased. "I found a Holiday Inn with a pool. Nobody even knows it's there except me. I'm taking a day off to swim and relax."

I stood up to go. "I gotta head home and relax myself," I said, holding the paper behind my back like a guilty secret.

"Nice talking to you," said Doreen, which struck me as kind of sly and funny. Julianna had done most of the talking.

3

The first game of the Riverton Women's Fast-Pitch Softball Tournament was the third Tuesday in August. I was ready to play at last. I pulled the Merc into Everett Park and grabbed my mitt out of the backseat. Warmed up throwing the ball back and forth with Nancy LaFarge, shortstop for Dudley Hardware. I played for Marion's Bar & Grill, the type of bar where you could bring the kids for a burger on a weeknight. Playing for Marion's Bar & Grill meant that Marion supplied the money for our uniforms: a T-shirt with the bar's name and logo on the front, our number on the back. A little goodwill and some cheap publicity all summer. And Marion got to coach, which meant she hung around at first base and gave us hell between innings.

There were eight teams in the league. New businesses in town wanted to add teams so they could be sponsors too, but we kept it to eight. There'd been an uproar last year when

Joe Turlane, who bought NAPA Auto Parts, tried to bribe the Lake Crest Café team into switching sponsorship. This year had been relatively quiet and scandal-free except for the usual complaints over Toomey Sherman's lousy umpiring. But just as there have always been eight teams in the league, so Toomey has always been the women's umpire. No one but him would take the job.

Nancy was throwing wide and high so I could practice catching with one foot planted. I snagged the ball and hefted it from the glove into my left hand. It felt good letting it rip, throwing wild grounders or low line drives at Nancy's knees. My shoulder rippled like a horse. I couldn't wait to get a bat in my hands, take a swing at the ball, smack that son of a bitch until the seams unstitched.

The 5:30 sun was sending sparks off the metal bleachers. A handful of people sat back with their elbows resting on the seat behind them, legs stretched out on the seat below, caps pulled down low to keep the glare out. Visiting back and forth, folks waited patiently for the game to start. Later those bleachers would be full for the men's game: wives and girlfriends, kids and old men, married couples on a tight budget. Didn't cost a dime to sit and watch softball all night, visit with friends, let the kids run all over Everett Park like a pack of wild cats.

We beat Dudley Hardware easily. I got a solid double and two RBIs. Not bad for a first game. People welcomed me back without making a big stink about it. The shoulder felt fine. All in all, it was okay.

For the men's first round Sizemor Septic was playing the Red Robin Truck Stop. Carl played for Sizemor, so when our game was over, Amy, Sharon, and I stayed to watch, along with

Suzanne O'Dell who was engaged to the pitcher for the Red Robin team. The bleachers were filling up. Sharon headed off to get a chili dog from the concession stand.

"Get me a lemonade, will you?" I called after her.

"I'm not your maid," she called back. I climbed to the top of the bleachers where there was less socializing, more ball game watching.

"Nice hit," I told Suzanne. She had a perky nose with dainty little bumps at the tip. Always wore her red hair back in a French braid. But she could smack a ball. Hit a homer in the fourth inning worth three runs.

"Thanks," she said, kicking clods of dirt off her sneakers. Suzanne looked like she'd be chatty and birdlike, but no. She worked in the Allstate insurance office here in Riverton. They covered pretty much everyone and everything in town. Suzanne was in a position to know a lot of private information, which made it doubly fortunate that she wasn't a talker. When Allstate paid out Dad's life insurance years ago, I wish it'd been close-lipped Suzanne who'd cut the check. As it was the whole town knew why I had to work after school at the bait shop.

"Mary, you got any Chap Stick?" Amy asked. I dug down in my sock, pulled out my Carmex, handed it to her. She and Suzanne were discussing who had volunteered to do what for the Beer Tent this year. The Beer Tent was the central feature of the Riverton Labor Day Festival up at the Kassauga County Fairgrounds. It was the event of the year when it came to getting drunk and making an ass of yourself. I closed my eyes and listened to Amy divvy up names and chores. There was a coolish breeze kicking up from the river, flipping a strand of hair against my forehead. I watched the men warming up on the field. One man in particular, Number 34, had a great set of shoulders. I'd been eyeballing him all summer from a safe distance. Pulled my visor low for some privacy and watched him. There were kids screaming and laughing in the playground, the noise a constant underscore. I looked over in that direction. From where I sat it looked like hundreds of small bright bodies swarming and swirling around the swings, the teeter-totters, the slide. Among them maybe half a dozen women. Not nearly enough to watch them all.

I chewed on my knuckle and looked over at the Merc. It seemed tiny sitting out there at the end of the parking lot. In two minutes I could be fired up and headed home where it was quiet. I saw Sharon's dark blond head bobbing through the crowd, coming back from the concession stand. Over her head the sky was immense, clouds sweeping like the wings of a gigantic owl. I gripped my knees and blinked. I saw a bedroom closet, the door half open. . . .

"Hey," Sharon called up to me from behind the bleachers. The top wasn't all that high, maybe six feet. She held several small bags up to me. "Grab these," she said. "I'm climbing up." I took out my lemonade. It excavated its way down my throat. "What's the matter?" she said under her breath as she settled into the seat beside me.

"Nothing."

"You look upset."

"I'm not."

"Okay." She reached in her bag and pulled out a chili dog smothered in onions. I concentrated on the players in the field. Looked for that particular width of Number 34's shoulders, how the muscles tapered down to the small of his back. There he was in left field, where he'd been all summer. He snagged a fly ball for the second out. Jesus, I wanted to sink my teeth into those shoulders.

"What are you looking at?" Sharon wanted to know.

"Would you get off my ass?"

"Fine," she said through a mouthful of chili. She turned away to Suzanne and said, "Careful. Mary's in one of her moods."

Amy shot Sharon a look and then glanced at me, silently asking, did I want to go for a walk? But I gave her a smile, everything okay. The breeze blew a prolonged gust, carrying the smell of rhubarb. Me and Amy were ten years old out behind Grandma Culpepper's house, picking rhubarb to make pie and eating half of it as we went along. It tasted sharp, bitter and tangy like guilt. Sharon and Stacy came running from around the garage.

"We want some. Can we have some?"

We shoved them away, wouldn't give them one goddamn bite of that rhubarb. I pushed Sharon hard enough so she fell straight down on her butt and got a grass stain on her new purple and white gingham shorts. I could hear her crying as Amy and I made our way up the path to the cow pasture, taking the last of the rhubarb with us, Grandma's pie forgotten.

"Crybaby!" I called back to Sharon. Stacy stood over her with a hand on her shoulder. United in their hatred, they watched me and Amy disappear to the frog pond where we pulled the petals off buttercups and told each other's fortunes to see who would escape Riverton first. Amy was going to live in Paris and I was going to astronaut school.

Next to me, Sharon was popping the last of the chili dog into her mouth.

"Sharon," I said.

"Hmph?" She turned to me, ignoring Suzanne in mid-sentence.

"Remember that time when Amy and I were picking rhubarb behind Grandma's house?"

Sharon took a sip of her Pepsi and said, "God, will you forget about that?"

"Forget what?"

"How many times are you going to say you're sorry?" she asked me. "I told you, I don't remember it. I was three."

I looked at Sharon. "Stacy remembers," I finally said.

"Look. I forgive you. I forgave you the last four times you brought it up. And for the time you pushed me out of bed for snoring and broke my thumb. And the business with the pansies. I forgive you for that too."

"What pansies?"

"You dug up all of Mom's pansies by the roots and gave them to your teacher. Told her I did it."

"No I didn't."

"It doesn't matter," Sharon dismissed me. "I've forgiven all of it."

All of it. As if I'd abused the shit out of her every day of her childhood. Amy was on the seat below me. She'd caught every word. She lit a cigarette, shaking the match long after it was out. She handed the pack over her shoulder toward me. I smiled and told her no thanks. I had quit smoking seven years ago, but Amy never failed to offer me one, like a secret message: "I'm on your side."

Between the fourth and fifth innings I went to the concession stand for more lemonade and bumped into Julianna. I wasn't surprised to see her there. She'd told me her dad played, and I'd seen her around the park all summer.

"I was putting miles on Eleanor and thought I'd stop and see what's shaking." She wore a T-shirt and cutoff shorts. She had flipped up the brim on her old red fishing hat. We ended up at a picnic table nearby, sharing a sloppy joe and chips.

"You ever want to get married?" she asked suddenly.

"Not now, no."

"But ever?" she asked. "Like ever in a million years?"

"If I met the right person, sure." I pulled my visor up to get a better look at her, see what was up.

"Yeah, but are you a lesbian?"

"No." This wasn't the first time I'd had this question tossed at me. Julianna chewed on the inside of her lip for a while, not eating. A loud cheer came up from the bleachers. "Are you?" I asked her.

She let go of her lip and heaved a long sigh. Pushed her fishing hat back on her head, as I just had with my visor. She lifted her eyebrows and looked at me.

"I don't know," she said.

"Haven't decided?"

"Well, I haven't even kissed anyone yet." I dumped our plates and napkins in the trash. Half a dozen bees hovered around the barrel, looking for trouble. "It would be okay if you were a lesbian, though," Julianna said to me. "We'd still be friends."

"Thanks," I said. "Same goes for you."

"Even if they sent me to reform school for it?" She slapped away a bee and waited for me to answer. God, she wasn't kidding.

"Even if they boiled you in oil for it," I said.

She laughed. "I gotta get Eleanor home before dark, or Nana kills me." And she was gone.

Back in the bleachers Sharon and Peg Monroe were arguing who had the best ass on the Sizemor Septic team, Carl or Harley Sherman. It was a fine August evening with a stiff breeze that kept the mosquitoes from landing. Kids ran under the bleachers, screaming to one another. Jen Colby's thin shoulders came to mind, as if I could see her running beneath my seat, tearing around with all the others. Thought of Julianna, trying to decide if she liked boys or girls. Had she hit the Arctic Circle on her bike yet? Nothing could hurt that girl. If anyone raised a hand to her, she'd hit them back harder. Maybe spend months plotting her revenge. She was one indestructible kid. The breeze blew. Out on the field, Number 34 was up to bat. Christ Almighty, he had a great set of forearms. First pitch was way outside. He stepped back, tapped one shoe with the bat, and took his stance. The ball came fast and smacked him on the hip. This shit had been going on all summer with the Red Robin team. Peg Monroe's boss had a cracked elbow thanks to this pitcher. Number 34 threw down the bat and came at the guy, pulling his batting helmet off as he ran. He landed a punch on the pitcher's jaw before the umpires closed in. The crowd in the stands was up and cheering. Number 34 was thrown out of the game, though everyone knew the other guy had it coming. It wasn't the first time Number 34 had fought on the field. He was so quick, the punch was always landed before anyone saw it coming. He went into the dugout to collect his mitt, limping and laughing. His laugh was mean and careless and the sexiest thing I'd heard in years. I watched as he left the dugout and headed to the concession stand. Lost sight of him at the Budweiser booth. I forgot about the children screaming and running, about Sharon and Amy and everyone else. Something about that man made everything all right.

▪   ▪   ▪

Later that night Marion's was full, the winning team bringing the crowd home with us. The front and back doors were propped open, getting a nice cross-breeze through. Above the talk and laughter I could hear Etta James on the jukebox wailing "Steal Away." The sound of it made me restless and peevish. We had a euchre game going at one of the far tables. I dealt out the hand and flipped the top card. Jack of clubs. Carl grunted, pleased. On the surface we could still be taken for the couple we'd always been, before the divorce. I took a long pull of my Stroh's. This was easy. This was the good old days. I could do this in my sleep. Carl gave me a smile. Amy was in a booth up front with Suzanne O'Dell and a couple of others, sipping a gin gimlet and tilting one eyebrow like she did when she was feeling rakish. Her laughter leapt up and somersaulted over the heads of everyone there, landing on the table between us. Carl slapped the ace of diamonds on it. We took all five tricks for two points, beating Jeff and Sharon easily. Jeff left the table to get us another round. He was Amy's younger brother. I'd known him since he was little enough to run around naked at the beach. I took another pull from my Stroh's. It fizzed and kicked at the back of my throat.

"Go find out if the kitchen's still open," I told Sharon.

"Go yourself."

"I'm the winner. My ass doesn't leave this chair until we lose."

"What do you want?" she asked.

"Hamburger with bacon."

Sharon headed over to the bar to find Marion. Peg Monroe flopped down in Jeff's seat and started shredding his napkin. "I got next," she said absently.

"We're undefeated," Carl warned her. She snorted and waved one hand. Went back to shredding the napkin.

"How's your mom?" I asked.

"Up and around," Peg said. "Driving me crazy." She tossed the napkin confetti over her shoulder to dismiss the subject.

"Who's your partner?" Carl wanted to know.

"Hell." She looked around the room. "I don't know."

I looked around the room as well, wondering if Jeff was heading back this way. I heard a gunburst of laughter at the end of the bar and there was Number 34, the one with the wide shoulders and the quick fists. He and two of his teammates were talking loud and knocking back shots of something. *Jesus Moses, that was one good-looking man.*

"Hey, Denny!" Peg shouted toward the bar. "Come on. I need a partner."

A voice came from one of the Sizemor players. "What are you playing?"

"Euchre," Peg hollered. Moments later a hairy hand placed a Pabst Blue Ribbon on the table, and a body dropped into Sharon's vacant chair. It wasn't Number 34.

"Where the hell is Jeff with our beer?" I asked no one. "Christ, did he drive over to Cadillac to get it?"

Peg was peeling the label off my empty Stroh's and rolling the bits of paper into spitballs. Carl and Denny nodded at each other like men do. I brushed away Peg's spitballs. She started a fresh pile without comment. Jeff came out of nowhere and set a cold beer in front of me. I snuck another look at the bar. Number 34 was still there. He glanced over at me. I turned back to the table and stared stupidly at my cards. A handful of red. *Whoa, those eyes.* This wasn't the first time he'd caught me looking at him. Shit.

"What's the matter with you?" asked Carl.

"Nothing." Something was the matter with me. Carl looked like a stranger, like a foggy memory of someone I used to know. I held the cold bottle to my forehead.

"What's the matter?" said Peg. "You got hot flashes?"

She and Carl thought this was funny. She dealt and flipped up the nine of hearts. I told her to pick it up.

"You're drunk," Carl said to me.

"Pick it up."

Denny leaned back in his chair, smiling. Peg added spitballs to her beer. Marion slid a burger with bacon onto the table. It was loaded with ketchup, mustard, a fat slice of onion. I sank my teeth in. Denny was eyeing his cards, eyeing me. Carl led with a king of clubs. Denny followed with the queen. I had to decide whether Carl needed help or not. Peg had left off with the spitballs and she was yanking on her upper lip.

"Hey Peg," I asked quickly. "You got the ace?"

"Huh? Yeah," she said, so I slapped down a trump.

"What the hell?" said Denny. "What the hell was that?"

"What? What?" asked Peg.

Carl said, "You can't ask her what's in her hand!" He hated it when I pulled that shit. He pushed back his chair with a patronizing shake of his head and walked off to the bathroom, ending the game. I drank my Stroh's. To hell with him. As I brought the bottle down to the table, Number 34 was smack in my line of vision. He and his buddy had moved to the table just behind Carl's empty seat. He'd been watching the game, saw my stunt with Peg, and now he was looking at me like I was a steak cooked to order just for him. I looked back. My heart swelled up to twice its normal size and bared her claws.

"I want that!" she howled, banging her head against my sternum and pointing at Number 34. "Give me that!"

My heart had a will of her own. She had named herself Loretta, God knows why. Loretta wanted to grab Number 34 and maul him, eat him, spit him out, and devour him all over again. She was so big, the room couldn't contain her. A wave of power and recklessness soaked me to the bone. I smiled at him. He scratched the side of his chin with a lazy thumbnail and smiled back at me. Loretta's hair stood on end.

Amy slid into Carl's empty seat and said, "Hey Peg." She smiled at me, setting her drink on the table with an emphatic gesture. "Who won?"

"No one," I said. "Carl had a little fit."

"I had lunch with Rebecca Whitehurst yesterday." She took a match to her Virginia Slim, waving it out with six shakes of her wrist. She offered me the pack, which I declined with a smile. "She said to tell you hello."

"Hmm." I shifted in my seat. Amy was blocking my view.

"What are you looking at?" she asked, and turned around to see what she was missing behind her. I immediately leaned close to Peg, as if in deep conversation. "Sorry about the ace, Peg."

"No problem." She had been mesmerized all this time, adding salt to her beer and watching the head revive. Out of the corner of my eye I saw Amy turn in her chair and look at Number 34. Her shoulders straightened, posture improved, as if by instinct. God, she was amazing.

"Good game tonight," I said to Peg.

"What happened to Angie?" she scowled. "That's what I want to know." Angie was our pitcher. She walked eleven women that night.

"She stank," I agreed.

Peg heaved a long sigh. After a moment she said, "My mother's driving me up a goddamn wall."

Amy turned back to me. "Who's that?" she asked quietly.

I was deep in conversation with Peg. "Who?"

Suddenly Van Halen was singing "Jamie's Crying" full blast on the jukebox. Amy had to lean over the table and shout in my ear. "That guy you were staring at."

She cocked her head in his direction, just enough so I caught a glimpse of him checking out her ass. It was quick and subtle but unmistakable. Beneath the scraping of my chair I heard her voice. Was she saying something to me or to him? I saw the front door wide open and headed for it. Still had the bottle of Stroh's in my hand as I stepped out onto Main Street. Something crept out from beneath my tongue, sharp and sour. It trickled down my throat. I couldn't swallow.

4

Outside the bar, the night had grown sweet and cool, more like late spring than late summer. The Merc was parked in back of Marion's, but I was in no hurry to go back there. I walked down Main Street, past the Dairy Dip and the First Presbyterian Church. Turned up Second Street and wandered uphill through the dark toward the edge of town. The breeze out there was chilly. It would be an early fall, no doubt about it.

I came to a tiny ranch house at the end of Second Street. Stood looking at it in the bluish moonlight. In all the years since I lived there, it seemed to have shrunk and died. I'd been nineteen years old, living alone for the first time, renting the place for cheap. Carl and I were just dating then. The front porch had an awning over it now, and porch furniture. Back when I lived there, it had been bare concrete with a simple low railing. It was odd to look back to a time before my marriage, before my divorce, before everything that came after that. It was as if I had leapt backward over fifteen years and landed face-to-face with the person I was back then. I looked at the porch, at the empty place where I once sat on a January night fifteen years ago, bleeding through my nightgown and feeling more alone than ever in my life. I could see myself huddled under a frozen sky. But it was as if it were someone else, not me at all, sitting there waiting for Amy, afraid she'd never come.

I remembered sitting in the doctor's office in Lansing earlier that day. I had traveled far from home for the appointment, found a doctor through a friend of a friend who lived downstate. They'd recommended Dr. Lewiston. He was light-complected and hairless.

"What I'll be doing today," he explained to me, "is inserting something into the cervix that will slowly dilate you over the next twenty-four hours." I nodded. I was cold, so I shivered. He saw me shivering, so I stopped. On the wall was a month-by-month pictorial of fetal development until birth. Tactless. "Then, when you come in tomorrow, the procedure will prove less traumatic to the system."

I nodded again. Kept my posture straight. Couldn't look defeated by this. I stripped and spread, and he inserted something. Immediately, the familiar dull pull of menstrual cramps.

"There may be some slight cramping, but try to leave it in the full twenty-four hours." He scowled at me, so I nodded again. Lying there naked from the waist down, I was compliant, eager to please. "If you don't, it'll make it worse tomorrow." He snapped his rubber gloves off and I unhooked my heels from the icy metal stirrups. "Any questions?"

"No." I smiled, apologetic.

"Then I'll see you here tomorrow at noon." He smiled tightly and left.

The cramping had me sweating clams by the time I'd driven the two hours north to home. They intensified as I lay on the couch with Frank and watched *Mister Rogers' Neighborhood*. Jesus Jennifer, how far was this thing going to dilate me? I turned from side to side, trying to get more comfortable. My lower back was in spasms. Frank gave up and jumped to the floor. *There may be some slight cramping, but try to leave it in. . . .* I shuffled to the bathroom where I tottered onto the toilet and felt around for whatever that goddamn thing was. Finally located a string, grabbed hold, and gave a pull. I held it up; looked like a cinnamon stick that you'd find in your hot cider. Couldn't be more than a half centimeter in diameter. I'd thought it was a Cuban cigar up there.

Within minutes the cramps turned sharper and meaner, cutting through like a serrated knife. I lay in bed with an ice pack resting on top of my stomach, heating pad wedged under the small of my back. I thought once the cinnamon stick was gone, the pain would recede right away. It didn't. Dry, crackly snow tapped against the bedroom window.

I was being punished, that was it. Never once had I thought in terms of "our" child, never did I consider telling Carl that I was pregnant; we were barely dating. It was my kid from the get-go, as if there were no father at all. I was barely able to care for Frank in any responsible way, let alone a baby. I was being punished with death. The cinnamon stick had done something to me, poisoned me. I didn't want to die. I especially didn't want to die like this. Alone, with snow piling up on the windowsill and no one but Frank around, who was only a tiny kitten and would start to eat me before anyone realized I was gone.

At 2:00 A.M. I was brought back to life by the touch of something cold and wet on my stomach. I pulled the covers back, reached over to switch on the lamp next to the bed. The ice cubes had melted and the plastic bag had grown a small leak. I was shivering, still groggy from after-pain. My back was scorched where the pajamas had hiked up. I stripped out of the pj's. Clots of blood had soaked through my underwear. I went into the bathroom, needing to pee. The moment I sat down, there was a tremendous rush of fluid and a strange, small splash. What the hell? I stood up and looked down. Blood spattered the sides of the toilet bowl. It was a small, scarlet lake nestled in a valley of porcelain. I could feel rivulets of blood creeping shyly down the inside of my thigh. Tickled. Was I dying? There was something white swimming in the scarlet lake. When I realized who it was I went to the phone and called Amy.

She picked up on the fourth ring. "Hello?"

"It's me."

"What time is it?"

"I'm sick," I told her. "I need some help."

"Where are you?"

"At home. I'm sick. Can you come over?"

"I'll be there in a minute."

I didn't know what to do, so I put on clean underwear and my softest nightgown, then pushed open the front door and stepped out into the frozen dark. "After great pain, a formal feeling comes." I think that was Emily Dickinson. She knew her onions. There were ten thousand stars milling around in the sky above my head. Each one of them remained neutral, refrained from passing judgment. Northern Michigan nights are cold: chilly in July, ravenous in mid-January. That night it was clear except for a faint wedge of colorless fluff to the east. One frozen and lonely cloud in an endless field of sharp, glittering stars. Sweat froze on my forehead. Everything else was sleepy warm. I should have asked her to bring some maxipads. Maxi, mini, as if they were skirts.

I wrapped the nightgown close around my legs, leaned elbows on my knees, and chewed on my knuckle. Looked out at the sea of snow rolling across the yard. With no moon it was just a heave of gray disappearing into two or three blue spruce barely visible at the end of the driveway. The landscape was flat, two-dimensional, like someone had stuck me at the edge of a painting. A small figure with shoulders hunched, huddled beneath the stars. My kid was swimming around the toilet bowl at that moment while I gazed at a sea of snow. I imagined her climbing out, sliding across the tile floor and onto the porch. A quiet little shrimp shivering on the steps next to me.

"Better to hurt you now, like this," I'd say.

And she'd reply, "It's okay, Mom."

Me and the Shrimp would sit huddled in the corner of the flat landscape, waiting for help to arrive. And it did. A dim glow became two headlights. They turned off the street, swept across the snowy yard, and washed me all over in light. I was just a silent drift on the porch steps. Amy ran across the yard in sweats and a goose-down jacket. Without makeup her face was an indistinct smear beneath her knit cap. I stood up, leaned on the porch rail. Cold air shimmied up my legs.

"Get inside," she said as she came up the steps and grabbed my arm. "It's freezing out here."

Once in the house she hustled me into the bedroom without waiting to hear what kind of sick I was. She dropped her coat in the corner of the bedroom, pulled back the covers. Small blood-stains shouted up at her. She pushed me down into the straight-backed chair near the foot of the bed.

"What is it?" She was rummaging through the linen closet. "Bad period?"

I didn't know how to answer. I wasn't sure what happened. Do-it-yourself abortion? Like a Toni home perm? Something went wrong, but I didn't know how or why. I watched her un-fold new sheets. She was looking at me, waiting for an answer.

"I was pregnant and now I'm not."

She looked from me to the stained sheets on the floor to the half-made bed. What was she looking for, the unbent hanger? Finally she said, "Where?"

"In the bathroom. She's in the bathroom."

Amy went to look. She came right back out, pulled the goose-down quilt off the floor, and wrapped it around me where I sat. She knelt on the floor next to my chair, put her arms around me, and started to cry. I rested my head against hers and closed my eyes. It was a relief. Someone was crying over this, knew how horrible this was. She got me tucked in bed, surrounded by clean flannel sheets and my down quilt. I told her about Dr. Lewiston down in Lansing, about the cinnamon stick and Mis-ter Rogers, about dying in the snow and coming back to life.

"Why didn't you call me?" she asked.

"I didn't know. I didn't know what it was."

I gave her Dr. Lewiston's number and she went to the kitchen.

I was warm, drowsy, starving. Amy appeared by the bed out of nowhere.

"I talked to his service. Told her he'd have a malpractice suit if he doesn't call in thirty minutes."

"I'm hungry," I told her.

"I'm calling Maureen." Amy's sister, who lived down in Ann Arbor. She was a resident at the U of M Hospital.

"It's the middle of the night."

"I want to know what we're supposed to do," she said. "In case that prick doesn't call back."

Amy returned to the kitchen. I lay in bed, thinking I'd get up any minute. Amy was rattling around out there. What was she doing? I fuzzed over and cleared up, fuzzed over and cleared up, fuzzed over and stayed there. Amy loomed again.

"She says we have to check how much you're still bleeding."

"Okay."

"If it's a lot, we'll have to go to the emergency clinic up in Kalkaska."

"I can't go to any clinics around here," I told her. "You know that."

"We have to keep the discharge and bring it in to the doctor," Amy blurted, getting it out of her mouth as quickly as possible.

"Discharge?"

"Whatever's in the toilet."

"We have to scoop her out?" I didn't believe it.

"Yes."

Amy was stricken. I laughed. It had a clangy, iron sound. "With what?" I asked her.

"I don't know," she answered. "Let's wait on that until Dr. Lewiston calls."

"What do they expect us to do, use a plastic baggie?" This could not be a real conversation we were having. We could not be discussing this.

Amy rifled through the kitchen cupboards, down behind the pots and pans, and dug out a mason jar. I found a handheld tea strainer. We approached the bathroom as if it were cordoned off with police tape. There was the innocuous rim of the tub, the squeezable Charmin, the ceramic family of fish bubbling familiarly above the towel rack. I imagined a child's lullaby playing off-key and sinister in the background. I looked sideways at Amy. She was white-faced, eyes glued to the seat of the toilet. We slid closer still. I could feel Amy looking down next to me. She reached out her hand for the tea strainer.

"I'll do it," she said firmly. If I were to hand her the strainer right then, she would fish that mess out of my toilet. Amy was willing to do that for me.

"No. Just hold the jar up so I don't spill," I told her. We both knelt on the hard tile, leaning closer to the reality, the evidence, the thing. She never once averted her eyes. "Ready?" I asked.

She nodded. I made one pass with the strainer.

"You missed," Amy said quietly. I nodded. Our heads were bent close together. We were silent, concentrating. The phone rang. We both jumped. The tea strainer jumped out of my hand, landing on the tile with a wet clatter. Amy handed me the jar and went to the kitchen. I could tell by the tone of her voice that it was Dr. Lewiston. Quickly, before Amy returned, I reached into the bowl and scooped her out with my bare hand. I held her for a few seconds, letting the water run out between my fingers. Surprisingly cold. With my other hand I lowered the mason jar and let a few inches of the stained water run into it. Amy's voice faded to nothing. Peripheral vision blackened and the whole universe focused its attention on what lay in my left hand. She was small, no more than an inch long, and really shaped like a shrimp. What looked like the beginning of eyes bulged on either side, like the eyes of a fish looking in opposite directions. A tiny mass of wrinkles formed her head, as if it were already lined with worry. The thought of her worrying touched off something hot and shiny inside me.

"The worst is over," I whispered, bringing her closer. I kissed her softly, nothing more tender in this world, and slid her gently into the jar. I found the mason lid and closed it tight, washed my hands in the sink, and flushed. The light in the kitchen was soft after the emergency glare of the bathroom. Amy was cradling the phone on one shoulder and writing something on a paper towel. She continued talking, her eyes on the jar in my hand. I rummaged in the broom closet for a bag.

"As early as possible, of course." Amy was all business, clipped and tight-syllabled. I put the jar in a blue plastic bag that said, "Wally's Food Mart." Carried it over to the fridge.

"And how do we get there?" Amy asked the phone. "Yes, I'm sure she does," she said with hollow chill. "But I'd like directions myself."

I slid the bag in the fridge and closed the door. Amy was uh-huhing and writing quickly. She tore off another paper towel.

"Absolutely. Not a minute past." Amy hung up the phone with a click that echoed like a threat at the other end. "No food," she said to me.

"What?"

"No food, no drink, until he sees you."

"I'll be dead by then."

"Did you check your bleeding?" She was shoving me toward the bathroom.

"I don't want to go in there." Ever again.

I grabbed an old dish towel from the back of a drawer and went into the bedroom, closing the door behind me. Off came the nightgown, down went the underpants. Blood had soaked through, but it didn't look life-threatening. I kicked the underwear off and onto the pile of bloodied sheets. Slipped a clean pair up as far as my knees.

"How is it?" muffled the door.

"Moderate," I said. "Tapering."

"Good."

A tampon was out of the question. I formed an impromptu diaper with the doubled-up dish towel to catch any leftover bleeding. Pulled the underwear up to secure it in place. I reached for the nightgown and got a glimpse of myself in the mirror. I was ridiculous: the towel-padded underwear bunched out, legs goose pimpled and awkward, breasts shrinking from the cold, like a cruel cartoon. The hot, shiny thing came back as I looked at myself. I thought of the Shrimp. This shouldn't have happened to us.

Amy slept on the couch. Twice in the night I heard her come in to check if I was still breathing. We were both pale and bleary on the drive down to Lansing. I sat with the blue plastic bag balanced gently on my lap. When we arrived I found out what Dr. Lewiston had failed to tell Amy the night before, or maybe what Amy had failed to tell me: We had to go ahead with the procedure anyway, to get out anything that was left behind. Pregnancy tissue, uterus lining, leftovers that would turn poisonous inside me if they weren't sucked out.

Before long I was sitting on the examining table in my paper robe, hoping I wasn't bleeding on the sanitized tissue paper. Dr. Lewiston came in, visibly annoyed. Hadn't he told me not to pull that thing out? And now look what happened. My own damned fault.

"Good morning," he said.

"I want to be sedated," I answered.

"We give you Seconal to relax you," he said. "When was the last time you ate?"

I told him, hoping for a reward of general anesthesia. I was well past hungry; stomach shrunk, head light. I was taken to another room, given two small pills and a nurse's hand to clutch when it hurt more than pride. The room was overheated, but I shivered with a deep, bottomless pain. Whatever the Shrimp had left behind, it was being torn out by the roots. In another minute my uterus would collapse inside-out onto the table. The nurse's free hand was brushing damp hair off my forehead. I was cold.

"You're doing great," she lied. "We're almost there."

She had a pink scar on her chin that shimmied when she talked. I squeezed her fingers into wet clay. I thought this wasn't supposed to hurt so much. What could I have possibly done in my life to deserve this much hurt?

"Almost done," she sang softly in my ear. And then, suddenly and at last, it was over. Dr. Lewiston was all brusque efficiency, leaving the room as quickly as possible without looking at me. I tried to get up, but the nurse kept hold of my hand.

"Let's stay here another minute. Okay?"

Okay. She brought a cotton blanket and folded it over me to stop the shivering. I closed my eyes. "Don't leave," I prayed.

"I'm right here," came her voice. She was moving around the sterile, dead room. A live, warm human being was in there with me. The Seconal kicked in. There was nothing to worry about now. Now the worst was really over. Nothing to do but rest. A few hours later Amy and I were at a Burger King drive-through. She rolled down the window, letting in a clean January wind.

"I had a talk with that asshole while you were recuperating," Amy said.

"Four chicken sandwiches, please," I told her.

"Iced tea?" she asked. I nodded. She ordered into the speaker and we moved up to the window to pay.

"A talk about what?" I asked.

"You probably would have miscarried no matter what." She looked at the steering wheel. I looked at my hands.

"What does that mean?" I finally asked.

"The fetus may have been dead already," she said carefully, so as not to have to repeat it a second time. "Before you went into that office yesterday. So when he dilated you, it all just . . . happened."

"May have been?" *What are you telling me?* "Wouldn't they have checked?"

Amy sucked in her lower lip for lack of anything to say. Maybe I did not kill the Shrimp; maybe she just left me. I sat, still staring down at my hands, mouth slightly open as if to say, "Oh." Amy concentrated on counting out exact change.

"Best thing you can do is just forget it," Amy said. "It wasn't meant to be, so don't think about it."

The smell of breaded chicken filled the front seat. I took the bag from Amy and pulled out the first one.

"Get salt," I reminded her.

"It's in there," she said.

We pulled into a parking space, where I poured two packets of salt onto the hot, shredded lettuce. Was it possible that I went through weeks of agonizing doubt and guilt, all that heartache, and it was for nothing? What kind of God played a joke like that? The Shrimp had left. The thought of it kicked all the guts out of me. Two chicken sandwiches disappeared before Amy was halfway through her cheeseburger.

"Jesus God, this is good," I said. She nodded, too well brought up to talk with her mouth full, abortion or no abortion. Then my throat closed and I couldn't swallow. My chest was tight. My eyes stung.

"This didn't happen," I said. Amy nodded.

I turned away from the tiny ranch house and headed back through the darkness toward Marion's, thinking of the Shrimp, who'd gotten away long before I could do her any harm. I tossed my empty beer bottle into a nearby trash can. I couldn't go back inside, back to Amy and Carl and Peg and Jeff and good-looking Number 34. I was tired. I fired up the Mercury and drove home alone.

5

Saturday afternoon I pulled into the parking lot at the beach. The smell of dead fish filled my nose. It mingled with the hint of gasoline in the air to give me a little buzz. Dead fish and gasoline had to be the sweetest smell in the world, one that permeated the bait shop all through my growing up. I rolled up the windows on the Merc. The car was black, sleek, with gleaming chrome in sharp angles the way cars were meant to look. The Merc and I hooked up six years ago. I saw her parked in a yard down the road from the Jefferson Speedway with a FOR SALE sign sitting like an ugly sore in her front window. Now I couldn't imagine life without her. I locked her up and headed for my usual spot on the beach. Already we were into the last week of August; had to enjoy it while it lasted.

The truck that had been leaking the gasoline smell was an old Chevy idling about forty feet away. Two boys in the cab, windows down, talking to a couple of long-haired girls in bikini tops and cutoff shorts. I'd seen kids like these as a child, watching the teenagers and thinking someday . . . Saw them again when I was a flawed, tall, freak of a sixteen-year-old, forever outside that magic circle called dating. And again at the Dairy Dip when Carl and I went up there for a cone, newly married, nodding hello to some of Stacy's friends. It's a miracle I ever managed to get married. I first met Carl when he worked at the bait shop before Dad died. Didn't start dating until later when he was managing the place for Mom.

I spread my blanket out in the sand, thought about being had for the price of Culpepper's Bait & Tackle. He'd bought it from Mom six months before he sprang the divorce on me. Well, he was welcome to it. Mom rested easier knowing that it was in Carl's steady, reliable hands. All I was left with was Loretta and her grumbling; reduced to ogling teenagers at the beach.

Julianna came by loaded down with a Walkman, a small blanket, and a bottle of Sprite. Doreen and Nana had staked out their usual spot over to my right.

"I got stung by a wasp," she said. "Wanna see?" Her wrist was swollen and bloated.

"Does it hurt?"

"Itches like crazy," she said.

"Thanks for the postcard," I said.

Her face lit up and she laughed. I had received it a couple of days before. A picture of snowy wilderness with bright block letters that said, "Greetings from the Northwest Passage Historic Trail." On the back Julianna had written, "How are you? I'm having a blast here in King William Island. Sincerely, Julianna Coleros."

"I looked it up on the computer and I wrote and asked them to send me some postcards," she told me, scratching at her wrist with her free hand. "So I can keep in touch with my friends while I'm on the road. I got a bunch more too."

"Where should I send things, if I want to write back?"

She thought for minute, squinting out toward the water. "Well," she said finally, "hard telling where I'll be. You better send it to the house, then my mom can forward it to me." I nodded. She pointed to the old pines whose roots stuck out of a small disintegrating cliff at the top of the beach. "I gotta go make my fort," she said. "I'll see you tomorrow." For our Sunday morning washing and Iris DeMent.

Off she went. Sand erosion had eaten the ground out from under the trees. The giant roots were laid bare beneath, forming a sort of mini-jungle at the top of the beach. I watched her crawl back in the dark cool space behind the exposed tree roots. She laid out the blanket, meticulous with the corners. I could hear her back there, singing to herself. All it would take was some final infinitesimal erosion to take place, and that pine would come sliding down, crashing across the sand. She would be trapped underneath the tree, buried alive against the cliff. It would take forever to dig out her body.

I got up and headed for the water. Stayed in for over an hour, diving deep again and again. Enjoyed the silence of being submerged, the lack of space around me, the complete absence of the sunlit world.

When I was tired, I drifted on my back and thought idly of Number 34, my hobby, my harmless entertainment for the summer. He had been at our second tournament game two nights before. I hit a high line drive that drew whistles from the bleachers. Tore around the bases until I saw Marion behind third waving at me to slide. I sent up a cloud of dirt and confusion as my foot hooked around the bag, safe. I stood up and brushed the dirt off my ass, grinning. I was eight feet tall coming up off that slide. Still felt the pull of the bat, the power in my forearms, smacking that son of a bitch like I knew I could.

Carla Fitch hit a grounder right behind me, enough to get me home and put us on top, 7–6. The bench was yelling; I'd drink free that night. Then, because I was feeling good, because I was eight feet tall right then, I turned full around so I was facing the stands. I looked up to the top row and there he was. I wanted to run up those bleachers and maul him, straddle him, ride him until his heart stopped. That's how sweet it felt hitting that triple. I gave him what Carl used to call my Jolly Roger smile. Poor old Number 34 got the full force of it.

I had kept my ears open and learned his name was John. He was a lefty like me and played left field. Just watching the man stroll up to the plate, absently swinging the bat behind him, gave me pleasure that I once believed came only at the tail end of a cold piece of pumpkin pie. Once an old man in a pickup had yelled to Amy, "Honey, I could just toss you on a plate and sop you up with a biscuit!" That's what I felt when John strolled up to the plate. *God, thank you for making that man and setting him down near me.*

I came out of the peaceful water and flopped down on my blanket without drying off. Lay on my back and let the warm wind lick me dry. I grabbed my visor out of the Bicentennial bag and put it on to cut the sun's glare. Jen Colby appeared, painted inside my closed eyelids. Round face, pixie haircut, younger than Julianna by about five or six years. She was sitting in the school bus next to the window, in a seat by herself, wearing green baggy pants and a Little Mermaid sweatshirt. It was late fall, cool enough for a jacket. Her left gym shoe had no lace, and it flopped when she kicked her feet against the back of the seat in front of her. Then she wasn't on the bus anymore. I rubbed my eyes, blinked straight up at the sun. But there she was, curled up on an old baby blanket. Crayons. Storybooks. A toy rabbit with half its hair missing. I saw her curled up in the corner of the closet, in her nest, talking softly to herself, playing. Something millions of kids did every day. I jerked the visor off and sat up.

The sun was pressing down hard. The sand vibrated with the sound of volleyballs, boom boxes, screams of pointless laughter. I picked up the book I'd just started, *The Hobbit*. Opened it and tried to read. Julianna had left her fort; she was now busy digging a giant hole in the sand. With her was a girl I'd never seen before, maybe a year older. Their two heads were side by side, arms moving in unison, sand flying out on either side of them. I glanced farther to my left. Just a skating glance, but enough to notice a man coming up out of the water. His thick black hair was lying straight back off his forehead, waterlogged. His chest and shoulders were bare. Water ran in rivers through the hair on his legs, soaking the sand at his feet. It was the merest skim of a glance. It freeze-framed in front of my eyes as I stared at page three of *The Hobbit*. It was John, Number 34.

What was he doing here at the beach? I saw a white page with black letters marching like ants across it. "Don't look up," they seemed to say. I looked up. John stood with his feet spread slightly for balance as he toweled himself off. He must have shaken his head because the black hair had flung itself forward, nearly covering one eye. He was toweling his right shoulder, distracted. His blue eyes like sunlight were right on me. He was drying himself with the towel and smiling like he was running his hands all over me. Loretta leapt to her feet, just about to wave at him.

"Dad!" I heard Julianna's voice as John turned around toward her. She was running across the sand, holding up something silver for him to see. "Look what I found."

I dropped my eyes to the book, closed it, and tossed it aside. Dad. Suddenly I was delicate and still, like a small brown rabbit who has seen a sharp shadow veering close. In another moment the talons sank into Loretta like blades. I felt foolish sitting there for anyone to look at: the serviceable swimsuit that neither revealed nor covered enough, the cheap Keds, the coarse dark hair. Anyone's eyes could run right over me. Who did I think I was?

I kept my head down but shifted my gaze up the beach. Doreen was putting sunscreen on her legs while Nana ate an orange Push-Up. John stood off to one side with his back to me, facing the lake. The sun bore down on his wet hair; the lake glittered like diamonds in the background.

"Let's go in," Julianna hollered as she ran past him toward the water. "Come on."

John turned to Doreen. He raised his hand to shield his eyes and said, "Honey, come on and swim." She was talking to Nana and didn't hear him. "Doreen," he called to her.

She laughed and shook her head, waving him off. "You go on," she said.

I packed up my things. Within thirty seconds there was empty space where I'd set up my camp a few hours before.

Threw the towel into the Merc's backseat without shaking the sand out. Climbed behind the wheel and searched through the entire miserable Bicentennial bag before I found the goddamn keys. Tilted my head down so the visor kept my face hidden. I could hear his laughter near the shoreline as I pulled out of the parking place. The Merc crept slowly and steadily toward home.

I tried a nap, needing sleep badly. I had lain awake, helpless and paralyzed, for most of last night. I lay on the couch with the old quilt I'd bought years ago at an estate auction over in Missaukee County; old worn comfort to wrap around me on quiet afternoons. Light was creeping through the west window igniting the wood floor with a square of blazing light. Frank lay curled in the center, soaking up sunlight as if he were solar-powered. I tried to let the comfort and warmth lull Loretta into numbness. The talons of shame and anger dug deeper. I stared out the window. Far in the distance, small clouds stood out white against stark blue.

"Come here, Frank." I dropped an arm to drum my fingers on the floor. "Here Frufru. Come on, Frederico." He opened one eye, but there were no flaming squares of sunlight where I was. He closed his eye again. Unless it was a wild animal to chase, he wasn't budging.

Nag, nag, nag. Petty hurts and small, limping vanities tugged my eyelids open. John, his eyes, his smile; Mary, pathetic, ridiculous, laughable. Disgust turned my throat sour. Frank rolled onto his back. One paw came up over his eyes as if to say, "When will she stop?"

Married man, married man. The words marched in my head, bringing to life a sad little memory that I'd forgotten years ago.

It was me and Mom eating cold cereal up at the counter at the Lake Crest Café. I got my own mini-box of Frosted Flakes, which Mom opened and poured carefully into the bowl. I could hear her Rice Krispies popping while she drank black coffee and stared at the pie case behind the counter. She was young and sharp-pretty then, no more than twenty-three or twenty-four. She was pregnant with Sharon. The waitress slapped the bill down and I kept my eyes on my spoon while Mom counted change in her palm, nickels and dimes and the occasional quarter that I'd watched her dig out from the pockets of Dad's work pants. She'd also emptied her purse, scattering used tissues and old butterscotch candy wrappers across the kitchen table, scraping along the bottom for a small handful of silver. I brought out the five-dollar bill that Grandma Culpepper had sent me several months before. It came in a birthday card with a fuzzy pink kitten that said, "To the Girl Who Is Six!"

"You put that back in your music box," Mom said, not looking at me. I had a music box with a ballerina inside that twirled to the music when you opened it. I bought it for fifty cents at the Brickhams' garage sale last summer. I kept my money in it ($5.22 at the moment). It also held the friendship bracelet that Amy wove for me out of brown, white, and green telephone wire, a sinker that Dad let me bring home from the bait shop, and my blue rabbit's-foot key chain that I won at the Kassauga County Fair.

I was done with my Frosted Flakes. Tried to drink the sugary milk out of the bowl, but Mom stopped me with a hand on my arm—had to behave in a restaurant. It was winter and I was wearing my blue rubber boots with old plastic bread bags over my socks so my feet would slide in and out easier. I could feel the plastic rustling as I kicked my heels against the base of my stool. Mom went to pay the check and get our coats off the hanging hooks up front. She waddled like a duck because her stomach was getting big. Mom pulled the drawstring on my fake-fur hood and tied an absentminded bow under my chin. My mittens (knitted by Grandma Culpepper) were safety-pinned to my coat sleeves. I slipped them on, put one hand in Mom's, and out we went right past the gumball machines with the candy and toys inside. Mom didn't have any nickels left.

Outside it was white and dry. My nostrils froze, so I had to open my mouth to breathe. The snow crackled and crunched under our boots as we walked to the car. This morning I wasn't taking the bus to school. This morning Mom was driving me. We walked slowly around the front of the little Dodge Dart, careful not to slip on the frozen sheets of puddles around the car. Mom opened the door and I scootched across the seat.

"You okay?" Mom asked, wrapping her coat tight around her. "Think that'll hold you until lunch?" I nodded, looking at the frost crystals creeping across the windshield. I didn't want to bring up lunch, but she was already there. "Tell Mrs. Brandt you forgot your lunch money today. You can pay her back tomorrow."

"Okay," I said and smiled. It was the kind of smile that comes out when you know you did something wrong and now you feel guilty about it, except I hadn't done anything wrong, but that's the smile that showed up just the same. Mom shook out her keys and turned on the car. Under her breath, but loud enough so I could hear her: "Son of a bitch. Starve his own daughter to death." She turned the defrost up high and we sat there until the ice crystals disappeared one by one. I fussed with the bread bags, shoving them down so they wouldn't show at the top of my boots. Stayed busy and pretended not to notice Mom crying into her hands. My toes were roasting. She put the car in gear and dropped me off at the front doors of Abraham Lincoln Elementary.

"If they give you any trouble about being late," Mom said, "I'll write you a note for tomorrow." That was my cue to get out of the car. I walked up to the big double doors. I had a wild, vicious moment where I considered not turning around to wave. How much would it hurt her? I reached for the door handle, turned around, and raised my hand to wave good-bye. The little Dodge Dart tooted and Mom's hand fluttered in reply. I opened the door into the hot air of the front hallway, my heart losing twenty pounds of weight. What if she hadn't been there waiting? What if she'd already pulled away and there had been nothing but empty pavement when I turned around? But she had been there, and I had waved, and she had answered. She would be okay.

When I got to the classroom everyone was already at the art tables in back. Mrs. Brandt didn't yell at me for being late, just told me to take a seat at the fingerpaints. I hung my coat on the row of hooks at the side of the room, pulled my boots off easily, and lined them up carefully under my coat. My saddle shoes were under my desk. I put them on and sat down to the fingerpaints. I dug into a handful of murky blue and spread it across the paper. Drew a building in it with my index finger. Mom was driving home alone in the little Dodge Dart. Maybe she was crying again. Maybe she was crying into her hands again so she couldn't see the other cars and she'd have an accident and die. I should never have gotten out of the car. I should have stayed with her today.

I drew a bunch of windows on the building. A tear rose up over my eyelid and I blinked fast to cram it back in. It jumped out and onto my paper, making a *ping* as it landed. I filled the windows with black sky. Maybe she didn't drive home. Maybe she just kept going. Maybe she's sick of Dad and she's running away from home. And she didn't want to take me because I eat too much and besides she'd have another kid pretty soon.

"No goddamn food in the house," she had yelled earlier in the morning. "Bastard spends every cent with his whores." On and on and on and I didn't even ask for breakfast, but she kept yelling and banging cupboards. She kicked the side of the stove so hard, the little black things that sit on the burners jumped and clattered. I stayed in the living room watching *Mr. Dress-Up* on Channel Nine. I was droopy and yawning, having a hard time focusing on Casey and Finnegan on the TV screen. I hadn't gotten any sleep the night before.

"Mrs. Brandt!" came a voice from right next to me. "Mary's crying."

"I am not," I yelled at the voice. Connie Evans. Teacher's pet bossy nosy tattle-tale big mouth goddamn Connie Evans.

"Yes you are," she said, snotty and sure of herself. "Don't lie," she added.

My fist shot into her arm and down off the chair she went. Mrs. Brandt's hand came down on my shoulder. "Mary, tell Connie you're sorry."

I sat still as a stone. Inside I was thunder and lightning. And the madder I got, the more tears slid down my nose. Every other first-grade head was turned toward me. I looked back at them and thought of the worst word I could say.

"Bastards." Twenty-five pairs of eyes widened in thrilled horror. I turned to Connie on the floor. "Whore."

Mrs. Brandt led me out of the room. She talked and I stared at my saddle shoes. One lace was coming loose. I bent down to retie it. Mrs. Brandt asked me was I listening to her so I nodded and stayed still as a stone again.

"Where did you hear those words?" she wanted to know. This was back in the seventies, when kids didn't toss around words like *whore* and *bastard*. No one was going to accuse my mom of bad language.

"Do you know what a whore is?" she asked me. I nodded. I could see out of the corner of my eye that she was surprised. "Tell me what it is, then."

"A lady who kisses a man when his wife and his kids can see."

Mom and I walked into that place last night when I was still groggy from being dragged out of bed and there was Dad and there was the lady and Mom jerked my arm so that I stumbled forward.

"See that?" she yelled. "See that whore?" The music was too loud. I could hardly focus my eyes.

"That's who your father loves more than you." Mom shouted it so that everyone could hear her over the music.

"What did you call me?" asked the lady.

Then the whore was yelling and Dad was yelling and he and Mom were hollering in each other's faces. Finally Mom told him don't come home, ever.

"Say good-bye to your son-of-a-bitch father," she said to me.

I couldn't look at him. I heard his voice saying, "Annette, Annette, stop it." He didn't say anything to me and I didn't say anything to him and then Mom and I left. All the way home she talked.

"Don't you ever trust a man," she said over and over. "Men are selfish sons of bitches." Then after a few minutes, "And women are worse. You scratch the surface on any one of 'em and you get a whore."

I curled into a ball in the seat beside her as she drove. I could feel her big stomach move as she talked. I pressed my ear to it and heard her voice rumbling like a bear. A chorus of *bitch, slut, whore* rising and falling until I fell asleep.

Dad had plenty of other girlfriends after that. Mom would drag me out of bed, take me with her to confront him in bars, motels, even the women's homes. After Sharon, then Stacy were born she left them seat-belted in the back of the Dodge Dart while she and I went indoors and found him. Eventually she left us at home.

I was a junior in high school when Dad died. Four of his old girlfriends were at the funeral. Mom had stopped caring years before; not enough love left to even hold them a grudge. I kept my eyes lowered when they came near, when they touched my arm, wiped their eyes, said things to me.

"Bitch," I'd murmur under my breath, just loud enough for the woman to hear.

"What, honey?" she'd ask, confused. "What'd you say?"

"Slut." It was softly spoken, but they heard it clearly all right. I never looked up at their faces, so I don't know what effect it had on them. Not one of them answered me back. Not one of them slapped me or cried out or responded at all. They just let go of my arm, my hand, my shoulder.

"Whore," I whispered to their backs as they turned away.

I pulled the old quilt tighter around me. The bitterness of that funeral was fresh as ever. *Scratch the surface on any one of 'em and you get a whore.* And I had nearly handed the bitterness down to Julianna. I lay there while a fragile wall of relief held back the thought of John's smile.

It was a little shocking to remember how young Mom had been that day in the diner. Seventeen when she had me, only twenty-four when Sharon came along. She was a widow with three kids by the time she was my age now. I had heard her telling Harold Tucker once that living with Dad was like having four kids instead of three. I wondered how old Patricia Colby had been when her husband went away, leaving her with two young children and a new baby.

6

That night, Saturday night, Mom called. I was in the middle of cutting my hair, clipping the wings that were sprouting over my ears and driving me up a wall. Amy and I used to cut each other's hair all through school. Now it made her crazy that I wouldn't pay money to have a professional do it.

"You have all those thick curls to play with, and you chop it up like someone took a lawn mower to your head."

"You color your hair at home," I said.

"Yes, but it doesn't *look* like I do."

She drove me to the House of Style up on Main Street one morning and personally supervised a cut and a color rinse. "Just a dash of auburn, for highlights in all that black," she'd told them. They cut and moussed and blew me dry. Then we went for lunch in Cadillac. All afternoon I was startled by glimpses of myself in store windows. I looked like someone on

TV. It took too much time to fuss with it the next day, so I trimmed it back to normal. Each birthday Amy gave me jewelry or another skirt and sweater set that hung at the back of my closet. One year she got me a gift certificate to a health spa in Traverse City: massage, facial, total beauty makeover. I gave it to Stacy.

When the phone rang I brushed the loose hairs from my face and neck, and shooed Frank off the bathroom sink, where he'd been watching my progress.

"Are you coming for dinner tomorrow night?" Mom asked.

"Yeah." No matter how long I'd been coming to eat on Sunday night, she still had to ask, as if to reassure me that I was still welcome.

"Do me a favor if you have time, bring a couple loaves of zucchini bread, will you?"

"Okay."

"Not frozen. Bake some fresh, okay?"

This time of year everyone with a garden had zucchini coming out of their eyeballs. I spent several weeks each summer baking enough bread to freeze for the rest of the year. Mom kept me on the phone telling me about the latest baby equipment that Stacy had stockpiled, making me care through the force of her will. I should've been happy to be an aunt. I couldn't muster more than an angry impatience.

That night I hardly slept. I woke at every creak, every thud in the dark, afraid the Night Visitor had returned. At dawn I got out of bed and took down all the curtains to wash, shaking out the film of dust along the hems. Scrubbed the windows with ammonia and newspaper. I was in the backyard hanging clothes on the line when Amy drove up. She helped me hang up the sheets and curtains, then we went inside and cooked a late breakfast of scrambled eggs and hash.

"I'm heading over to McBain later this afternoon," Amy said, pouring coffee for us. "For my reading group. You want to go with me?" Amy belonged to every club, group, or organization in Kassauga County.

"I got a lot to do around here," I told her.

"We can stop off at JoAnn Fabrics," she added. "They have notions on sale fifty percent off this weekend."

"Pick me up some pinking shears. I broke mine." Using them as pliers to pull out rusty nails. After we were done eating, she reached in the cupboard for the old pickle jar lid that I kept as her ashtray.

"Want one?" she asked, lighting up.

"No thanks." I had cleared the dishes off the table. "Stick around and grate some zucchini for me." I mixed up the bread batter, offered her the wooden spoon. "That guy you saw in Marion's the other night? The one you asked me about?"

"Yeah." She licked one side of the spoon clean and handed the rest back to me. "What about him?"

"What'd you think?"

Bits of zucchini covered her hands as they flew up and down the grater. To look at her perfectly manicured fingers you'd never guess how good she was in the kitchen; my knuckles would've been sliced to pieces by now. "He's bad news," she said.

"You know him?"

She laughed and shook her head. "You know a man that good-looking has to be a son of a bitch."

After she left I washed the dishes and mopped the floor. I was waiting to wash the Merc until Julianna showed up; she was late. It was noon already, too hot to work in the house. I started up the push mower and cut the grass. Always wore my sturdy steel-toed shoes since I watched Jeff Richardson lose half his big toe when he was thirteen. Stopped and poured myself a giant glass of iced tea. Set a jug with new tea bags out on the back stoop to brew in the sun.

I came around to the front porch with my glass tinkling dark and cool. Threw myself into the big lawn chair and there I sat. Cars were going by on Tomford Road full of teenage kids on their way to the lake, windows down, radios serenading the road. It was a busy day at the beach, but I was busy at home. I let my head fall back on the chair and closed my eyes. It was midafternoon and a breeze whipped lightly around the corner of the cottage, ruffling the sleeves on my T-shirt like a tap on the arm saying, "Hey, hey you."

All day I had been good. I was proud, content to be myself. No going to the beach. The sun pressed its thumbs on my eyelids, keeping them closed. This was a good tired, the best tired. Inside the shadowy dark of the kitchen my countertops gleamed, floors lay crumbless, and three loaves of bread cooled on the counter. There was a light meow from the window behind my head. Frank reclined on the sill, chewing on Sock Buddy and soaking up the breeze as it moved past him into the cottage.

"That's right, Frank," I murmured to him. Lifted my hand to tap on the screen in greeting. He pushed his forehead against my hand. Just as Loretta began to stir, thinking of Julianna's father, I opened my eyes and noticed that the shutters were badly peeled. I got my paint scraper out of the shed and set to work.

There were two gallons of yellow paint I'd been saving. I'd get the front windows scraped, sanded down smooth, and painted before I ran out of daylight.

A few hours later I was up on a stepladder, spreading a smooth, cheerful yellow. Between the scraping, sanding, and endless paint-stirring my arms would feel like swollen logs tomorrow. I stopped for a minute and took a long pull from the now-warm tea on the porch. I hadn't had a productive weekend like this since last winter. No more staying up all night. No more flirting with married men. And after this Friday no more Mad Dog Mahoney and her endless goddamn questions. My entire body hummed happily with sore muscles and fatigue, the way you were supposed to feel late on a Sunday afternoon. I wondered what had happened to Julianna.

The cars were going in the other direction now, heading back into town from the lake; driving slower, radios softer, laughter quiet and tender. The birds that sang loudly in the woods next door had quieted down. A fine spray of yellow had grown up from knuckles to wrists to forearms. I had the peculiar, dry-all-over feeling that came from scraping and painting for hours. I was already thinking ahead to an early return from Mom's house that night, a quiet evening watching the Nature Channel. A clean, quiet, warm and well-lit evening alone.

Tires slowed down on the road and turned into the two-track gravel driveway. I lowered the brush and turned to see who it was. Sharon? Amy? It was not Sharon or Amy. It was a dark green Cutlass, coming to a stop thirty feet away from where I stood on the stepladder. The car was identical to Doreen's and for a moment I thought it was Julianna and her mother come to accuse me. I rested the brush carefully against the paint tray and climbed down to the grass. Both front doors opened and two impossibilities climbed out, first Julianna and then her dad. I stayed next to the ladder and didn't move; Loretta broke into a tight red sweat. He was looking right at me as he and Julianna walked across the grass toward the porch.

"You forgot your book," she said, as if it were obvious. She held *The Hobbit* out to me. My face caught fire as I remembered the last time I saw it: yesterday, the sight of John, the scramble to get away. I kept my eyes on the book. The creased cover was unfamiliar, alien. Was that my book? I wiped my hands on my shorts and took it from her.

"Thank you," I said.

"You left it on the beach yesterday." John's voice came drifting over like a moth. "We thought you'd be back today, but you didn't show up." Another killing blush started at my shoulders. John shifted his eyes to the newly painted shutters and talked to them while I turned the shade of an eggplant. "So we thought we'd drop it by."

"Thank you," I said again to Julianna. "That was nice of you to go out of your way." Was that me sounding cool as cucumbers?

"What's a hobbit?" she wanted to know.

"It's a short person like a dwarf, with fur on the top of his feet and leather on the bottom."

She nodded. "This is my dad," she said.

So I met him as if I'd never seen him before, as if this were a neutral situation, as if he were nobody at all. "Hi," I said with the fakest smile imaginable.

"Hi. John Coleros." We shook hands.

"John. Hi. I'm Mary."

He said, "I've heard a lot about you."

I yanked my hand away and shoved it in the pocket of my shorts. Now was the moment when we would all lapse into a profound and excruciating silence. I had seen it coming and I was ready.

"Would you like something to drink?" I asked the empty space between father and daughter.

Julianna asked, "What have you got?"

"Stroh's, water, iced tea."

She looked at her dad for permission.

"Iced tea would be great," he said to me with a smile so paralyzing that I had to look away. A fire had ignited in my gut, below my stomach.

"Come on in." I opened the screen door on the porch. His face was there in the doorway, there in the cupboard where I reached for the glasses, there in the tea jug that I brought in off the back stoop.

"This is fresh brewed," I told them for no reason. "Have a seat."

"Does your cat bite?" John asked.

"Not really," I answered.

"What's his name?"

"Frank," said Julianna.

More conversation happened while I poured the tea and carried it across to the couch where they were both seated. Frank leapt from the windowsill onto John's lap. Was that my cat? My Frank on his lap? He was trying to stick his head in John's glass. John held it out of reach with one hand, and stroked Frank's neck softly with the other. This man was sitting in my living

room and running his hands all over my cat. The fire below my
stomach burned warmer. I wanted to laugh out loud.

"You can push him off onto the floor if he's bothering you," I
said.

"No, he's fine," John replied. Julianna held her glass so that
Frank could drink out of it, which he did with telltale ease.

"Juju, maybe Mary doesn't want you sharing your germs with
Frank," John said.

"It doesn't bother me if it doesn't bother you," I told her.

Julianna and Frank shared a drink while I wondered what I
was going to say next. My eyes were still adjusting to the dark
interior after hours in the overexposed sunlight. Was that my
ragged quilt on the couch behind him? Was that my old braided
rug under his feet?

"Do you teach or something?" he asked, looking at the stack
of *National Geographic*s on the coffee table.

"No. I look at the pictures." Like a moron, like I didn't know
how to read.

"What do you do?" he asked.

My jaw opened, then closed. A breath stopped halfway in. I
used to drive the school bus. I don't now. I don't know if I ever
will again. "Psycho leave," as Sharon called it with her usual
tiny cruelty. And what would happen at the end of the summer?

"I told you," said Julianna. "She's the bus lady."

"Where is the rest of the family today?" I countered. This betrayed the fact that I'd noticed there was a rest of the family, but
the subject had to be changed. John couldn't answer. He was
taking a long pull from his glass, his complexion darkening suddenly. Julianna told me that Doreen and Nana had gone to an

estate auction in Manton to buy a bunch of old junk, so she and her father had come to the beach early today, which is why she didn't come to wash Eleanor Prudhomme because he almost never has weekends off and they had brought *The Hobbit* with them thinking I would be at the beach later because "you're always there, but you weren't, so we dropped it off to you instead and now we're here." Julianna looked up at me with her yellow cat eyes and smiled. For an instant, her presence took up the whole room.

"How is Eleanor?" I asked.

"She's great. We're in Spence Bay right now." She was twirling her fishing hat on one finger, seeing how fast it would go before it flew off.

"How is it up there?"

"Gets colder the farther north you go," she said with authority.

"I bet her dinner at McDonald's she won't make it before Halloween," John added. Oh, yes, of course he was still sitting there, complexion back to normal.

"I'm so far ahead of schedule it's not even funny," Julianna said, with a look to her dad. "I'm gonna be the youngest person ever to walk on the North Pole."

"How old are you, exactly?" I'd never asked her before.

"Exactly . . ." She stopped and counted in her head. I could see John out of the corner of my eye. He was looking around the cottage, seeing me. "Twelve years, seven months. How old are you?"

"Thirty-four."

She bit her tongue, but her eyebrows lifted enough to say, "Old!"

"Me too," John said.

"Same as your jersey number," I said before my brain caught up and closed my mouth with a snap.

He smiled and said, "Yeah. I never thought about it." He lifted his tea toward me. "Here's to being thirty-four." We clinked glasses. My fingers felt the heat from his hand. "And to being twelve and a half," he continued. Julianna clinked with us and we drank. It couldn't have been more easy and comfortable, three old chums on a Sunday afternoon drinking to good times.

The phone rang. John jumped so hard his ice cubes danced, and Loretta sobbed with longing like the drama queen that she was. I excused myself as if nothing were wrong. The walk into the kitchen was stretching ten feet for every step I took. The phone gave off an ugly, hysterical shriek. I considered not answering, letting it scream until it wore itself out like an exhausted two-year-old.

"What," I said quietly into the grimy mouthpiece.

"Mary?" It was Mom. When was the last time I'd cleaned this phone?

"I can't talk now." Funny how you didn't see the dirt in your house until someone else came over.

"I'm at the hospital," Mom said. "In Traverse City."

"What happened?"

"We think the baby's coming."

"I'll be there." I hung up and turned back to the living room.

"Anything wrong?" He was standing up now. He was exactly my height.

"My sister's having a baby," I told him.

"Now?"

"Yes. It's not due for another month." I was moving in and out of the living room as I talked, grabbing things along the way to throw into my Bicentennial bag. "They're at the hospital, in Traverse City."

"Wow," Julianna said, taking her empty glass into the kitchen. "She's having a baby right this second?"

"Yes," I answered.

"Can we give you a ride over there?" John asked.

Why was I packing my Bicentennial bag? I looked at the man standing in front of me. Wanted to ask him why he was here in my house, why he was so goddamn beautiful, why he was looking at me with those magical blue beams that scrambled my brain waves.

"My car's out back," I said, looking directly at him. It was like being thrown off a horse and there you were on your back with the wind knocked out of you, staring up at a blue sky that never ended.

"I thought maybe, if you didn't want to drive . . ." and he stopped because he didn't know how to finish the sentence, and I stopped because I didn't know how to answer him.

"Let us drive you," Julianna said, heading for the door. "Come on, I know how to get to Traverse City."

"Won't they be expecting you at home?" I asked.

"Not especially," he answered, with a smile that could have meant anything.

I wrapped up the fresh zucchini bread for Mom and shoved it in my bag while they started up the car. I was a mess, yellow-dabbled and sweat-smudged from going like hell all day. Julianna was in the backseat of the Cutlass. I climbed in the front. I set my bag between my feet on the floor. The radio was playing a song by Fleetwood Mac, "Hypnotized." Must've been one of those classic rock stations. The car was suffocating even with the windows rolled down. Sun-baked vinyl radiated heat against my bare legs, which were three or four feet away from him. He could be staring at my thighs right that minute and I wouldn't know it. I looked down. They were my legs, all right: grass-stained from the mower, a big scar above the right knee where I fell out of the elm tree in the backyard at age seven—a broken branch went in clear to the bone. I looked away from my naked legs, which were strong and sturdy, and to hell with him if he didn't like them. There was the hand lever for the emergency brake between our seats. I wanted to yank it up as far as it would go. *Stop!*

"It hurts when you have a baby, doesn't it?" Julianna asked behind me. She was sitting upside-down so that her head hung off the seat, her feet pressed against the rear window. She had her flip-flops off, leaving sweaty footprints in a neat line across the glass.

"I've heard it does," I said.

"And the baby comes out all bloody and gross, right?" she asked.

"Pretty much," I said. "I've never seen one in person." I shoved aside a thought of the Shrimp. Didn't exactly count.

John was staying quiet, letting her talk. I'd noticed that about both him and Doreen; they let Julianna talk and weren't shushing her all the time.

"Was I slimy and gross?" She directed this at her dad.

"Yes."

"Was Donna?"

"I don't know," he answered. "I wasn't there."

"My cousin," Julianna reminded me. "She's fourteen. She has her period."

We were quiet in the car, thinking about Cousin Donna and her period. We were already on Route 108, heading north into Kalkaska. The sun was angling in the car window, shining across John's bare arms, lighting up a few dark hairs that curled near his wrist. My eye meandered up the line of his forearm as far as the elbow. Tanned but not too dark, muscular yet lean. It was the most exquisite forearm I'd ever seen. I looked out the open window on my right. We were passing a semitrailer hauling cattle. I kept my eyes on the disjointed legs, tails, furry ears, and inhaled the rich scent of cow shit. Thought of Stacy and her bovine complacency. Imagined her lowing frantically as they loaded her into the car for the trip to the hospital. Serves her right, having a baby as if it was no big deal, as if people did it every day.

"I hope your sister's all right."

I jumped, afraid he'd read my thoughts. "Thank you."

I sent a smile in his direction. It stopped halfway across the seat and scuttled back to me, overcome. This was too intimate, too private, driving in a car like this, even with Julianna doing tap routines across the back windshield.

"She'll be fine," I said to the road in front of me. "She'll have a beautiful child and be perfectly fine." He looked over at me for a moment. I kept my eyes on the road.

"We could keep driving," he said lightly. "Skip the hospital and drive until we hit the bridge, scoot up into Canada."

Julianna twirled upright in the backseat. "Yeah! Then you could catch up with me in Spence Bay and we could all go camping!"

I laughed. Risked a small glance in his direction.

"What d'you say? You like camping?" he asked, eyes in the rearview mirror as he eased in front of the cattle truck.

"No." Amy loved camping. Just hours ago Amy had called him a son of a bitch. Amy was someone I didn't know at all in that moment.

"Don't like camping?" Julianna's voice was a mix of disbelief and disgust.

"We could change your mind," he said. "Couldn't we, Juju?"

He looked over his shoulder at her as she agreed they could change my mind. Turning back to the road again, his eyes stopped for a moment on me. It wasn't just a look. It was a *look*. I got a ridiculous image in my head of the two of us in green waders, casting for trout at the edge of a sky-filled lake. The fresh air was filled with the smell of live bait and sex. I swear to God he was thinking the same thing right that moment. The hair on the back of my neck wiggled.

"Can Mom come? And Nana?" Julianna asked. "Can they go camping with us?"

"Sure," said John. This time there was no deeper color at the mention of his wife. He seemed perfectly at ease, like a guiltless husband and father, like a good man, which is what he was.

"What do you say? Hospital or Canada?" He was slowing down for the turn onto 72, waiting for an answer. "Can't talk you into running away, huh?"

At those words the world stopped. He was giving me the same smile that I'd seen at the bar. I shook my head no and turned to look out the window. Blinked hard, four five six times.

"Can we at least see the baby?" Julianna was striking a bargain after the lost camping trip. I don't know what was said

after that. Words were spoken, answers were given, my mouth
moved, but something had ripped inside. It was gaping open in
my chest. Loretta had fallen into a big black pit of something I
didn't even have a name for. I blinked again. I just wanted to get
the hell out of the car, away from both of them. We pulled up in
front of the main entrance to Munson Medical Center. I'd already searched out the door handle so there wouldn't be any
gross last-minute fumbling. I thanked Julianna for returning
my book, thanked John for the ride. I was out of the car without hearing what either of them said in return. Heard tires
rolling away and turned to look as Julianna waved out the back
window. I waved back, just the slightest flutter of my hand.

7

I stood still for a moment outside Munson Medical Center, milking the opportunity for quiet, for a chance to glue myself back together before heading to the maternity ward. The clouds above were low and flat on the bottom, as if sitting on a glass-topped coffee table. They stretched out across the entire length of the horizon, catching the rays of the sun and throwing them back again. I saw the line of his nose with the slight bump along the bridge, and the eyelids that were slightly hooded, giving him a sleepy look like Robert Mitchum. Mom would call them bed-room eyes. I hated the thought of it, of other women reacting to him, women like Doreen, for instance; Doreen to whom he was married. I stopped at the information desk and asked for Stacy Baumann.

"She's having a baby," I told the nurse.

"Right now?" he asked.

What was the matter with people? Of course right now. "I believe so. Yes."

He typed mysterious things into a keyboard, stared at the computer screen.

"She's right here," he gestured to the left. "In maternity."

Maybe the labor was all over and I wouldn't have to hang around, just see Stacy, see the baby, go home. I walked into the waiting room. Ruther's mom was crying. An electric shock radiated out of my chest, an adrenaline rush telling every molecule that something was wrong. Where was Sharon? Mom? Over in the corner near the bathroom and pay phone. Mom saw me and stood up.

"What—"

"She's going to be all right," Mom interrupted me. "We have to keep saying that."

"What happened?" I asked Sharon.

"They've got her in the emergency room," she told me. "No one's allowed, not even Ruther."

A woman came to the door. Couldn't tell if she was a doctor or nurse or someone in between. She asked for Mr. Baumann. Ruther looked around for a hole to crawl in, his face whitish green. He joined the woman out in the hall. Mom and the Baumanns followed, closing the door behind them. All thoughts of the married, pregnant pain-in-the-ass disappeared. Stacy used to eat spoonfuls right out of the sugar bowl. She made me read *We Like Kindergarten* out loud sixty thousand times when she was barely walking. She had the longest eyelashes of anyone I knew.

Sharon said, "You're chewing your knuckle."

"Sorry."

I wanted to go in the bathroom and scrub this layer of sunshine off me, but I didn't want to miss whatever news Mom might have. I sat down, sticking close to Sharon, and looked around the room. Ruther's sister, Lori, was sitting in a chair swinging one crossed leg back and forth. She had her genuine leather pump half off. It balanced on her toe, up and down, up and down. Lori worked as a sales associate at Lehmann's, a swank department store there in Traverse City. She was always turned out to a tee. I reminded myself that she was just a salesgirl, but my eyes strayed to the professional manicure on her smooth, flawless hands. I looked down at my own hands, at the paint spatters and the deep gouges along the right thumbnail where I slipped with the scraper earlier. Lori and Stacy got along like a house afire.

"You're doing it again," Sharon said beside me. "It's making me sick."

"Sorry." I dropped my knuckle to my lap, then shoved it in the back pocket of my cutoffs.

"Do you have anything to eat?" I asked her.

"Bag of Combos. I ate 'em all," she told me. "There's a vending machine on the way to the cafeteria." Of course she would know that. She spent a lot of time here last winter when I'd been admitted to Munson Medical for minor injuries and psychiatric observation. The LaLa Ward. Was Sharon thinking how the waiting room up on that floor had looked exactly like this one?

The door opened and Mom came in. Mr. and Mrs. Baumann went straight to Lori and the three of them bent their heads. I hated them. Look what they did to Stacy with their rotten son and his murderous dick.

"They got the baby out," Mom told us. "It's on a respirator."

Me: "How's Stacy?"

Sharon: "What about Stacy?"

"They're stabilizing her."

"Is she okay?" I asked.

"I'm sure she is. We just have to wait." She added, "It's a boy."

"I wish she'd never had the damn thing," Sharon said.

"I wish she'd never married that asshole," I added quietly.

"She's fine," Mom said. "Just relax."

"Look at them," Sharon whispered, indicating the Baumanns across the room. "Close as three fleas on a Chihuahua's ass."

"Ssh, now stop." Mom had that tone, so we stopped.

I slipped into the bathroom at the far end of the waiting room. Turned the water on full blast and pumped the little soap pump until I had a handful of stinking pink foam. I had to scrub with my fingernails to get the paint off. It felt good, though. Up my arms, clear to the sleeves of my T-shirt. Scrub, scrub, scrape, scrape. I leaned low over the sink to get the whole arm rinsed, careful not to bang my elbow on the hard porcelain. Looked into the mirror. Yellow specks mixed with the occasional gray hair. Why were my eyes so tired? Where did I get such a funny chin? I dried my hands, noticed they were shaking badly. Stacy was fine. Stacy had had the baby, and she was fine. Still, the small bathroom was shrinking, the tile floor tilting. I didn't want to be anywhere near this. I yanked the door open and walked until I was out of the waiting room.

The cafeteria looked like a Holiday Inn conference room, all brass and hanging plants. I concentrated on the grilled cheese sandwich that I'd thought I was dying for. Melted Velveeta had pooled and hardened on the edges of the bread. The air-conditioning had me chilly in my shorts and T-shirt. I was still wearing my sturdy, steel-toed shoes, looking ridiculous. I poked at my bowl of red Jell-O, small blocks of soft rubber trembling together in a heap. I used to poke at those blocks with my fork while Sharon sat across from me in this same room last winter. Asking me why, and what was wrong, and did I even know? I just tormented the red cubes and lifted my eyes to give her an "I'm sorry" smile. Words hadn't come back yet, just that substitute smile.

It had been late February, and we were back to a brutal, carnivorous winter. The false spring of two weeks before had been a typical Michigan dirty trick. It was my first day back on the bus since finding Jen in that closet two weeks before. Two weeks of lying in my bed, sleeping or staring at the wall, my mind an empty bag of nonthoughts, keeping what had happened far away from me. Now I was back to work and there were all my kids, all my responsibilities. I deposited the load of them to Lincoln Elementary as I had every morning for over ten years. Then I drove the empty bus all through Kassauga County, driving farther and farther from the Colby house until I hit Manistee, where Lake Michigan blocked my path. The newspaper articles had said that Brian Colby, Jen's father, lived in Manistee. He had taken custody of the other two kids. I was haunted by the entire goddamn Colby family. I had two and a half beers in Manistee and drove back to Riverton, back to Lincoln Elementary to pick up my little responsibilities. By the time the last kid climbed down the little stairwell and out into the snow— goddamn false spring, goddamn lie, cruel snow killing every hopeful blossom—by the time the last responsibility stepped off the bus, my left knuckle was throbbing from the relentless chewing. And it was the next morning that Rebecca Whitehurst called from the school, called Mom, worried because I hadn't shown up for work, hadn't even called, which was not like me. There was no answer out to my house.

Sharon pulled into my driveway around 9:15 A.M. I was admitted to Munson Medical by 10:00 A.M. She didn't bother with an ambulance, just loaded me into the bucket seat of her little blue Bug and drove like hell. Sang "Home on the Range" over and over. It was the only song she could think of, trying to keep me quiet. She didn't have to worry; there was nothing left but quiet by then. That and a broken collarbone, mild concussion, multiple contusions.

This is what Sharon saw when she walked in my front door: kitchen cabinet half torn from the wall and the fridge tipped over. An explosion of wet, dark grounds where the Mr. Coffee sailed into the wall. The kitchen table lying on its side against the stove. Two weeks' worth of dirty dishes lay in pieces all over the floor. Sharon looked in the living room, searching for my dead body. Curtains with broken rods lay under the overturned couch. Books and magazines vomited themselves across the floor. Good old Sharon went back to the kitchen and grabbed my bread knife out of a skewed drawer, working up the nerve to face the bedroom. That's when she heard the noise out back. And God bless her, she came flying onto the porch with the bread knife raised, ready to sink it into my assailant.

It was just me there on the cement stoop. Every glass left in the house was stacked on the top step: coffee mugs, juice glasses, the set of lead crystal wineglasses from Grandma Culpepper. And I was sitting with knees spread, dropping them one at a time onto the cement between my feet. I was barefoot;

shards of broken glass had torn up my ankles. Blood was nestling warm and soft between my toes.

I wished for some memory of this. Awful as it must have been, I'd have given anything for the sight of Sharon standing over me with a knife raised like Boris Karloff. I only remembered what came before, the Night Visitor appearing for the first time through the bedroom window, the pursuit through the house.

While I sat mute and surprised at the hospital Sharon and Ruther cleaned up the mess I'd made. Mom wanted to help, but they wouldn't let her near the cottage, didn't want her to see it. Stacy bought new curtains and dishes. One of my punishments would be living with her taste. They had it looking like new by the time I was released. I walked into a stage, a setting for a play, accurate but not real. Pillows were in the wrong place, pictures were arranged oddly on the bookshelves. A light film of shame had settled over every surface. After a week, I noticed the tiny seam along the arm of the wooden rocker where Ruther had glued it back together, the shelf paper with yellow tulips where before it had been red roosters. And with each new discovery came the small shock of remembering: Someone else had been here, not Ruther or Stacy or Sharon, but someone else whom I did not know.

"What happened?" they asked. "What were you thinking?" And from Ruther: "How did you knock over the refrigerator?"

Granite was all I remembered. The gray shape of him coming after me no matter how I fought, no matter what I threw. And the images he brought with him, pictures I'd been busy erasing for two weeks. I didn't remember if he caught me, didn't remember if I chased him away. Just his relentless pursuit, then the hospital and red cubes of Jell-O in white plastic bowls.

And now I was back. I pushed away my grilled cheese, no longer hungry. Sharon came in, plopped down in the opposite chair, and helped herself to half the sandwich. I grabbed a paper napkin off the small stack next to me and handed it to her.

"Thanks," she said, chewing.

"Any news?"

"Nah."

I crumbled a handful of saltines and dropped them into my tomato soup. Followed that with salt and pepper. Sharon watched me, disgusted.

"Think you got enough salt in there?" she asked me.

I gave it a few more shakes for emphasis and stirred. We ate in silence for a while. "What are they naming it?" I asked.

"Rutherford, probably. He'll be the fourth."

"Jesus." I shook my head. "If anyone had told me that some-day I'd have to call my nephew Ruther."

"I know." Sharon rolled her eyes. "Maybe we could call him Stinky."

"Hmm." I slurped my soup, thinking. "Rudy?"

She shook her head and took another bite. "Pin Head," she said after a hard swallow.

"Too common," I answered.

"We'll call him Turd Ball," she decided.

"Turd Ball."

"It works on two levels."

"T.B. in front of Stace."

Sharon considered, nodded, reached for the other half of my sandwich. "It's weird to be here again," she said.

"Hmm."

She looked at me cautiously. "How is it now?"

"Better."

"I thought it was a delayed reaction to Carl, maybe." I looked at her. She hurried on. "But that wasn't it. Then I thought maybe it was because of that girl that died, but you said no—"

"Well, that wasn't it either," I said.

"I just said that, didn't I? I just said that wasn't it." She was irritated. I forked one cube, then another, into my mouth. Placed them in my cheek and then squeezed them through my teeth onto my tongue. It made a squelchy noise.

"So what was it?" she finally asked. "You never said."

I took my time swallowing. My throat had closed up. "It was a lot of things." I thought for a moment before I went on. Trying to think up something plausible. "Been coming for a long time."

"Obviously," Sharon agreed.

I dropped my spoon into the bowl and asked, "What do you mean, 'obviously'?"

"Well Jesus," she said all innocent. "I mean the force of it when it hit."

Oh. Obviously. I shot a sideways look at her. She was licking crumbs off the butt of her palm. "What?" she asked when I caught her eye.

"C'mon," I said. "Let's go see if they killed her yet."

Sharon popped the last greasy crust into her mouth and took the tray up to the counter. We headed back through the hallways to the maternity ward while I wracked my brain for something to top Turd Ball. When we walked in the waiting room Lori smiled and buried her gaze in an issue of *Mademoiselle*. We checked in with Mom, who was sitting quietly with her head resting on the back of her chair. They were having trouble stopping Stacy's bleeding, but it would be okay. Sharon sat down beside Mom and reached in her bag. Out came *Moby Dick.*

"How is it?" I asked her.

"I'm on page 498 and the fish hasn't shown up yet."

"You blew through it fast enough."

"I skimmed a little."

I looked across the room to see what the others were up to. Mrs. Baumann was on the pay phone with her back to the room. Mr. Baumann was either in the bathroom or he'd gone back to work. Ruther must be with Stacy. I wandered back to my previous seat. Sat down and closed my eyes.

Can't talk you into running away, huh? I saw his face, the look he gave me. I reached out my hand and touched the glass-brick wall. Not here, not in this cold, sterile place with all of these people around me. Come back to me when I'm alone, when I can wallow and pine and hate myself in private.

Ninety minutes slumped by and nothing. Sharon had finished *Moby Dick.* The fish had showed up on page 505. "It was worth the wait," she said with a dark look. Now she was looking up and down the halls for a doctor or nurse to tell us what was going on. Lori had plowed through all the ways *Mademoiselle* could make her hate herself, so she started on *Glamour.* Mom and Mrs. Baumann were talking quietly on the couch. Ruther came in the door and motioned to me. I unfolded myself from the chair. Mom started up, but Ruther shook his head.

"Just Mary," he said. When I was at the door he said quietly, "She's okay. She wants to see you." He pointed down the hall. "Third on the left."

It was then, walking down the cluttered hallway and counting doors, that my hands began to shake again. The first bed was empty. Smooth, crisp, and heartless. Behind the half-drawn divider curtain I saw feet under a light gray blanket. She had an I.V. stuck rudely in her arm. She looked half-pregnant still.

"Stace?"

No answer, the drugs had knocked her out. Her skin was hot, flushed, with a damp strand of blond hair clinging across her forehead. I lifted it with one finger and set it back on the pillow. Her mouth was open. She looked like a kid. Hot summer afternoons, she and Sharon would lie down for their nap, sweat-filmed and salty smelling, on the daybed on the back porch.

Now I wondered what she wanted to see me for. Why ask for me? Why not Mom or Sharon? *Stacy, what did you want me for?* I decided to wait, so that when she woke up she'd know I was there. I stepped toward the only chair as a doctor poked her head in the door. I braced myself for a shooing, a scolding, a fight. She came to the edge of the curtain and looked at Stacy. "They say we forget how much it hurts," she whispered. "But I never did."

Stacy had a baby. There was no going back now. Instead of joy, I was swamped with a sense of hopelessness. "Let's let her dream as long as she likes," the doctor said, so gently that I followed her out of the dark room. I never knew what Stacy wanted. I never tried to find out.

We stayed at the hospital until 9:00 P.M. It turned out they'd had to give Stacy twelve stitches and pump her full of vitamin K to make the blood clot. We took a quick peek at the baby. Rutherford Stanton Baumann the Fourth looked like a frog that had met with a truck on a lonely curve of road. Red and scaly, he had an ugly bruise on his face from the forceps. He lay spread-eagle inside the respirator. I had envisioned an accordion-like machine, pumping and fanning its gills as it breathed for the baby. Respirator. But it was a benign fixture of Plexiglas and efficiency that didn't move at all. We stood staring through the window.

"Hello, Turd Ball," Sharon whispered so only I could hear.

We saw him for less than a minute before we were herded out. Mom was giggling and crying simultaneously. Ruther looked distracted and surprised. Stacy was out for the night. It wasn't until we'd said our good-byes to the Baumanns and were walking out the main entrance that I quietly asked Sharon to give me a ride home.

"Where's your car?"

"Never mind," I told her. "Give me a ride home and don't make a big deal about it."

"How'd you get here?"

"I'll tell you in the car." I steered her out of Mom's hearing. "Just shut up."

We walked into a mild summer night. The chanting crickets escorted us to the parking lot. It had been easy in the dry, inhuman vacuum of hospital corridors, easy to encase poor old Loretta in cellophane, clench the jaws tight, and tend to the business at hand. Now she was coming alive, sniffing the petaled scent of a clear night sky. I needed to be home, alone and quiet. Sharon and I headed for her Volkswagen.

"What's up?" Sharon wanted to know as soon as we were strapped in. I told her as little as possible: I got a ride over there with an acquaintance from softball, no big deal, returned a lost book, had his daughter with him. Sharon could tell I didn't want to talk about it, so she needled me with questions. Was he good-looking? I guess. What was his wife like? She's nice. How long had I known him? Not long.

"Looks like the old mule's got some kick left in her," she said, lighting a cigarette. She was definitely not the serious smoker I used to be. This was her first since 5:00 P.M. I would have been inhaling hard before the doors had closed behind me, gulping it down in convulsive snorts. I rested my head back on the vibrating seat and looked out the open window beside me. Star light, star bright. I closed my eyes and imagined that the cool rush of air was creeping in my bedroom window and down across my pillow, Frank curled at my feet. The next moment, we were in my driveway. The moment after that, I was in the house.

8

I pulled off the paint-speckled T-shirt, stepped out of my cutoffs, let my bra drop wherever it would. I was too tired to take a shower, too filthy not to. The water made tiny bruises where the drops hit my skin. I stepped out, ran a towel once over quickly, and fell into bed in just a clean T-shirt. Frank landed on my feet as I pulled the covers up under my chin. My body was a 160-pound slab of lead. Thoughts slid sideways, then jumped in random, nonsensical spurts.

I couldn't sleep. The Night Visitor would show up the moment I drifted off. Jesus, how could I be that tired and still so wide awake? A baby. A kid running around. She'd be asking me to baby-sit the damn thing. Jaw clenched, shoulders bunched up around my neck. Tried to relax everything. I ran a hand along my stomach. I saw wide shoulders tapering down to a strong waist, the number 34, and the dark wavy tilt of a head.

My breasts woke up, nipples tightening at the thought of brushing a hand through those warm dark waves of hair, across his shoulder, down his chest.

My hand moved softly back and forth across my stomach, under my T-shirt. A soft, familiar hand. If it were a stranger's hand, a man's hard, tender touch . . . I lifted the T-shirt higher, closed my eyes to see him more clearly. The breeze crept to the window, saw me lying there, and swooped in to kiss me on the neck. His mouth would be that sweet, that playful. My hand moved in slow circles around a breast that welcomed the company, the rare attention. My other hand moved downward, saying hello to the inside of my thigh. Fingers moved toward the tickling hum between my legs. Wet and swollen, my vulva practically cried out at my touch. Lightly, delicately, I ran my finger across a grateful clitoris. It purred, burning softly.

The phone rang. Every inch of me jumped in a shock of embarrassment. The breeze died. Second ring. I yanked the T-shirt down viciously and rolled out of bed.

"What," I said acidly.

"What's the matter?"

"Hey, Amy."

"What are you doing?" she wanted to know.

"Masturbating."

She laughed. Oh yeah, it was funny.

"I had an idea," she said. "And don't say no until you've heard it all."

And she told me how great it would be if I went with her and Carl on their trip to New Orleans. They traveled somewhere new every autumn: the Grand Canyon, Las Vegas, Hawaii. This year it was New Orleans. And this year, suddenly, I was invited along. They'd discussed it, had decided that I could use the vacation, get away for a while, change of venue, etc.

"We'll help with the money," she concluded. "If that's a problem."

"Why do I want to go to New Orleans?" I asked stupidly.

"With us. It's not like you're going off alone," she reminded me. "Wouldn't it be fun?"

She dressed it up as a cure from the incident last winter, claimed that she and Carl were worried about me. "What's going on?" I asked.

"I just thought you might like to get away for a while."

"I want to be home." When I said it, I realized how true it was.

"Remember how we used to have great trips together?" I did remember. Me and Carl, Amy and her old boyfriend Rick, weekends at Mackinac Island, the summer art fair in Ann Arbor, a weeklong stay in D.C. "You know we'd have a blast."

"It's different now," I said. An electric silence greeted this statement. "We're older," I added.

"You're closing yourself off from life."

"Amy, you're a good friend. Good night."

Back in the bedroom the breeze hung sullenly behind the curtains. Frank jumped onto the bed and flopped across my shins. I pulled the sheet up over me and realized that I'd forgotten to tell Amy about the baby.

Amy. Married to Carl for the last seven years, two years longer than I had been. We had lived out on Tupper Road. He ran the bait shop and I drove the school bus. I was considerate, stopping to pick up Coke and Fig Newtons so Carl would have them next to his recliner when he came in from work; five or six o'clock in the winter, as late as ten in the summer. I brought warm washcloths to put over his eyes when he got one of his sick headaches. He built a wooden cabinet to hold my collection of teacups and saucers. It fell from the wall and every piece of china shattered except one cup. It was from Grandma Culpepper, its delicate rosebud design mysteriously intact amid the wreckage.

In the winter I refinished the furniture and painted the spare bedrooms. In the summer I froze vegetables and cut giant bouquets of peonies for the living room. Each fall Carl shot a deer and hauled it home in the back of his pickup to string up headfirst from the old maple out back. I'd take a snapshot of him with the dead thing: smiling next to it one year, arm slung around it another year, its forelegs around Carl's shoulder the next. One autumn he nailed a sixteen-point buck with a twenty-one-inch spread, big enough to get him an appearance on *Michigan Outdoors' Big Buck Night.*

No one took snapshots of the deer several hours later, after Carl cut it open and dug out all the guts, saving the heart for the neighbor's dog. Left it there overnight for the blood to drain out, dripping slowly down the inside of its leg, leaping from a hind hoof to the ground. The venison sausage was delicious, though. We had enough to freeze all year and still give some away for Christmas. I've received venison sausage from Carl for the last seven years, religiously.

One summer evening I was cooking Swedish meatballs for dinner. I'd baked some potatoes that were dug up from the garden that afternoon. Green beans just picked and snapped were steaming in a colander on the stove. Carl's truck pulled up past the house and around back to the garage. I poured out the water from the cooked beans into the sink. Turned my face away from the steam and looked out the window. There was Carl coming up the back walk; tall, quiet, looking down at his boots as he came toward the house.

He stooped in the back door and kicked his boots off. "I still can't believe I get to come home to you." He kissed the back of my neck and said, "What's for dinner?" When I told him, he snorted, "Ah hell, I can do that."

One thing about Carl, he was a good cook when he set himself to it. I lounged with my feet up on the table while he finished cooking dinner and told me all about the bait shop that day. After dinner we left the dirty dishes there on the table, went upstairs and made love. Fell asleep after he farted loud and held the covers over my head. Carl and I had a lot of fun.

Then one night he said he wanted a divorce and he told me why: my best friend, Amy Richardson. Amy with her endless groups and committees, her exquisite eyebrow that lifted sardonically, her fierce loyalty. He broke it to me during dinner up to Marion's, the Tuesday before Christmas. We sat in a booth near the front, under the railroad clock and a mounted deer head wearing a Santa hat.

"You're wonderful, Mary," he said, tossing out table scraps of affection. "You know I think you're wonderful." It was only two days to Christmas, for God's sake. Couldn't he have waited?

"But you're like macaroni and cheese," he continued, finishing his second gin gimlet since we sat down. He went on. "Delicious and filling, but you know exactly what you're getting." He broke off and let out a little huff of breath. "I'm not saying this very well."

"I get it," I said.

"Well, a steady diet of macaroni and cheese wears on a man's spirit."

I wondered if a worm had eaten Carl's brain and this was an imposter calling me delicious and filling, as if I were a frozen pot pie. And drinking gin gimlets instead of the usual beer. When did that start? He took my silence as some kind of assent.

"Now, Amy . . ." Hearing him say her name at that moment was difficult. I glanced at my bottle of Stroh's, imagined the glass shattered, the jagged edge imbedded in my eye. Then Marion brought our dinner, stayed to chat a bit, wished us a Merry Christmas as if everything were okay. ". . . Amy is more like spicy Hungarian goulash."

I ate my dinner in small bites so I could swallow them, wondering whom in our acquaintance he would call a bacon cheeseburger.

"When did it start?" I asked, although suddenly I knew exactly when it had started.

"About a year ago," he said. And even though I knew, still a jolt went through me as though I'd been punched in the chest. It was last year's New Year's Eve party at our house. We had a lot of friends then. Amy came over early to help with the food. Jeff had gone with Carl to get the keg, and now they were out on the back porch trying to get the tap to work. Amy pulled a tray of chocolate chip cookies out of the oven and set them on the counter to cool. I was washing up the dishes, trying to keep the chaos to a minimum.

"Mary, come here a second," Carl yelled. My hands were wet and soapy. I reached for a dish towel, but Amy said, "I'll go."

He needed someone to hold the keg steady while he and Jeff dumped bags of ice into the washtub. They were out there laughing and screwing around, the three of them. I finished the dishes and turned around to see Carl come in the door and reach for a cookie. Amy appeared behind him and slapped his hand.

"No!" she said severely.

"Oh baby," he said. "Slap me again."

"Pig," she said, and gave him a cookie. I dried my hands on the dish towel, smiled at their horsing around, and carried a half dozen clean ashtrays out to the living room. A few months later I remember being surprised when Carl asked me if anything were wrong; said I'd been a little distant.

"I can't put my finger on it," he said. "You're here, but you're not."

"Where on earth would I be?" I asked.

"I don't know," he answered. "I wish you'd come back."

And suddenly, sitting there in Marion's, it was so clear. Amy had been around a lot, with her direct eye contact, her merriment, her relentless charm. She was full of scoldings for Carl, advice on how to treat his sick headaches. She was the same as ever toward me. One night she gave him a shoulder rub while he lay on the couch and I sat in the chair five feet away, chatting along like usual. Our Saturday euchre nights had always included Amy; now those nights lasted later and later. I would call it quits at one or two in the morning and go to bed, only to lie awake and hear the laughter wafting up from the kitchen at four, five, six o'clock. They were tireless at euchre. Every silent look, every unexplained absence, how could I not have seen it? How could I have been that blind?

I sat across from Carl that Tuesday before Christmas and looked him in the eye, listening. Yes, I understood. I appreciated his honesty. No, of course I didn't hate him, couldn't hate her. When he and I left the bar that night Marion and the regulars said so long, thinking we were still married. That night I made up a bed for him on the couch.

"Tell her she can call me," I said. "Tell her it's okay."

"Mary . . ."

"Hmm?" My eyebrows shot up, all affability. *Yes? Yes, Carl?*

"I didn't want this to happen." In the little pause, there on our couch in our living room, he waited for me to say something.

"Best not to think about it, then." And I headed up the stairs alone.

I was in a little state of shock the next day when Amy came to our house. Carl was at work, she and I were alone. She sat down at my kitchen table where the two of them had spent so much time in the past year, trumping one another's aces and carving me out of their lives. I was wounded and off balance, like a barn owl I'd seen once that had been shot in the wing. I wanted to spare Amy the sight of me flapping around in futile distress. I sat still, feathers spread over the wound. As long as I didn't move she would never know I'd been hit.

"God, you can't imagine how much better I feel now that you know," Amy said. She had her two tapered hands wrapped around one of my coffee cups, the one that said, "Friends are Forever," a gift from her. She hadn't blinked when I set it on the table in front of her. Now I couldn't tear my eyes away from that cup; "iends are rever" peeped out at me from between her coral-colored nails.

"Yes, I'm glad it's out in the open," I agreed.

She let out a little laugh. "Do you have any idea how awful it was, not having you to talk to about it?"

"It must have been." It hadn't shown. She'd seemed the same as ever.

"I mean, I'm not used to keeping things from you." She was gallingly honest, now. Her hand rested for a moment on my arm. "And I want you to know," she said, "that I'm here to listen whenever you need me."

"Thank you," I answered, sipping coffee out of Grandma Culpepper's old teacup, the cup that had survived Carl's plunging china cabinet.

"You must be hurt and angry," she said, looking me straight in the eye. "You can say whatever you want to me. That hasn't changed, right?"

"Of course not."

Amy leaned back in her chair, smiling at me. "I was afraid you'd never forgive me," she said, running a hand through her hair as if to shake off the fear.

"Really?"

"Well, it *was* a shitty thing to do." She laughed again with the sheer relief of the restored honesty between us. "To tell you the truth, I thought you'd hate me forever."

And you went ahead anyway. I didn't say it out loud. I wiped the thought right out of my mind. When she stood up to leave an hour later, my tongue lay numb and useless against my teeth. Logic told me I should be angry. But she gave me a hug as I walked her out to the car and said, "The best thing about this, I think it's making you and me closer."

The sight of them together at the bait shop, or perhaps driving through the green light out in front of Federal Savings, it wasn't real, as if someone were just out of camera range, about to yell, "Cut!" I moved out of the house on Tupper Road and rented the cottage near the lake. Amy helped me hang curtains, buy rugs, make the place a home. Carl lived alone for three months. I wondered if he picked up his own Fig Newtons and Coke now, or if he did without. We avoided each other. I discovered there were lilacs out back of my new cottage, and what promised to be wild roses in the summer. There was enough land to plant a vegetable garden in the spring. All that was missing was Carl. After those three months, Amy asked me to be a bridesmaid.

"You know people are having a field day, talking about this," she said.

"Probably," I agreed.

"We can't have the whole town hating my guts," she said. "What better way to . . ." She faltered for a moment, at a loss. "You know," she went on. "Let everyone know it's okay."

"Wouldn't it be a little tacky?"

"It would if you were the maid of honor," she replied. "But I would never do that to you."

We wore the palest green taffeta and carried sprigs of silk apple blossoms in our arms. Taffeta doesn't suit me, but Sharon worked with grim skill to give me some dignity that day. She looked at the dress Amy had picked out and started the alterations after muttering "bitch" for the hundredth time under her breath. Less flounce at the shoulder, more snugness in the bodice, a smoother line all up and down. The morning of the wedding, Stacy started in on my hair and makeup.

"How about if we skip it?" I didn't like her fingers brushing my face, making me someone new.

"You have to stand out from the rest," she said in a tone that withered any argument. "And it can't look like you tried."

Sharon insisted on four-inch heels.

"I can't walk on these. I'm cramping."

"Too bad," she replied. "Maybe you don't have any pride, but I do. Bend your head."

We were practicing a specific tilt of the head that allowed you to look down on someone graciously, yet still look down on them. I went along with all of this only because I needed something to hold me in tight all day and all evening. I was so busy comporting myself according to Sharon and Stacy's instructions, the day passed in a blur. In the wedding pictures I looked like the last of the Romanovs surrounded by Ziegfeld girls. On that blue, new-washed day in early June, Amy was resplendent. It was a huge outdoor wedding with over five hundred guests. Even I couldn't believe Amy knew that many people. She wrote the vows herself. And instead of a receiving line the guests and wedding party alike performed a Sufi dance that Amy had read about in one of her travel books. It involved the touching of one another's hands and the looking into of one another's eyes, except we all stared at one another's foreheads.

After the ceremony Carl gripped my elbow tightly and for a moment I thought he would fall to the grass if he let go. But he did let go, and stood there smiling shamefacedly at his guests as he had all day long. As the reception wore on I drank more than I should have. Jeff Richardson had escorted me down the aisle during the service. At that time he'd been just eighteen years old. In his gray tuxedo he looked younger. The bridal couple left around 1:00 A.M., and Jeff and I began trading tequila shots at the open bar. He was a kid, Amy's baby brother. Growing up, we'd always tormented him when we weren't ignoring him. Now he laid a hand on my bare arm.

"What are you trying to do, kill me?" He was breathing hard through his fourth shot.

"Trying to make a man out of you, Jeff."

His body leaned close to mine. "I wish you would," he grinned, half joking, leaving me free to laugh and push him away. He'd taken off his tuxedo jacket; the white starched shirt was untucked and hanging limp with sweat. From the neck down, he looked like a man.

I said, "Come on then."

I didn't let him stay the whole night. Didn't get up to show him out. I listened to his tires on the gravel driveway and climbed out of the bed that was suddenly the last place I wanted to be. Threw on my bathrobe and shuffled out to the backyard. I laid beneath the pear trees and looked up at stars that seemed to fade with embarrassment.

"To hell with you," I said out loud to the sky. "To hell with it."

I was awakened by my own sweat, the afternoon sun beating me to death. I rolled over to bury my scratchy eyes in one arm. My skull followed in bits and pieces. I began rolling slowly toward the porch. I could hear Frank terrorizing something smaller than him near the woodpile.

My brain had shrunk to a peanut. The sun ate the hair off the top of my head. I scootched the few feet across the porch and in the open door to the kitchen. The clock on the stove said 1:00

P.M. I made it to the sink, took big gulps of water, paused for breath. The phone rang, my head cleaved. I gripped the edge of the kitchen sink and threw the water right back up again, along with wedding cake and random bits of strawberries. Where did strawberries come from? Rinsed out my mouth, rinsed out the sink. Tiny sips.

I took one of the kitchen chairs into the bathroom—slowly, slowly—and set it in the tub. Sat carefully on the chair and turned on the shower. I was precise, careful not to drop the soap out of reach. Everything got washed in due time. Sat there for a long time with the water patting my head, rubbing my back, telling me it was going to be okay. Dried myself still seated in the chair.

By 3:00 P.M. I was curled up on the couch, propped up with pillows and my quilt wrapped around me. A tray with plain toast and tea sat on the coffee table, and the television was on low: a Bette Davis double feature. I dozed on and off. The phone rang several more times and went unanswered. I was out of the normal orbit of things, in a parallel universe now, the world of the hangover. I concentrated on keeping down the toast and tea.

Toward the end of *Now, Voyager* Loretta slipped out from underneath my rib cage and skulked across the floor. I saw movement out of the corner of my eye and turned in time to see her slip, red and worn, around the corner. After a few minutes I heard muffled sobs. I climbed out from under the quilt and went to find her. In the bedroom I saw Frank sitting guard before the closet, looking grave. Sniffles and moans emanated.

"Come on out." Not unkind, but firm.

"Shut the door," she sulked from the deepest, darkest corner.

"What's wrong?" All I heard was her muttering in the shadows. "What?"

"You're going to forgive them," she answered.

I sighed heavily and sat on the bare floor, my back against the doorjamb. "There's nothing to forgive."

"Bullshit," she hissed, and I heard a shoe overturn somewhere in the depths of the closet. "You've been burying me, covering me over, just so you can keep your lousy friends."

"They're your friends too."

"Not anymore."

I fished a pack of cigarettes out of the pocket of my bathrobe. Grabbed an ashtray off the dresser and resumed my seat on the floor. I could hear her behind the door, beating with sorrow and indignation.

"Come out where I can see you," I said.

"Why?"

"Please."

Frank leapt onto the bed and lay with his chin resting on one paw. I heard soft thuds, then she came slowly out. She stood there looking at me, covered with dust bunnies and bits of cat hair.

"Say it's not my fault."

I told her, "It's not your fault."

"Say I don't have to forgive them," she demanded.

"Suit yourself."

She climbed up onto my lap and rested there, beating weakly. I finished my cigarette, then took her into the bathroom, where I rinsed her in the sink. Carried her out to the living room, where we curled up together on the couch to watch the end of the movie. During a commercial break she slipped under my rib cage and settled back in.

"Let's quit smoking," she said quietly. So I stopped cold. A show of good faith after the beating I'd given myself. Carl and I had always promised we'd quit together someday.

I avoided Jeff Richardson until he figured out I wasn't interested. I kept to myself until two years into my singlehood. Carl appeared at my door late on a Friday night. Been drinking, but he was mostly sober by then. Sat at my kitchen table telling me about the twelve-point buck he'd missed that morning, how Amy slept in sweats because her poor circulation made her cold at night. After three or four long silences, I asked him if he was happy.

"It's like someone else's dream," he said. "I keep expecting to wake up next to you."

Like a movie, waiting to hear, "Cut!"

"How did I get to this?" he said. He looked like a little boy who couldn't find his mom.

The next day he would forget what was said and so would I. But that night, in a new bed under a strange ceiling, there was the dear old weight of his thighs, the circle of his arms bracing me against each thrust, the damp smell of his neck. When it was over I got up and made coffee that we drank sitting up in the bed. Two hours later he left for good.

■　　　■　　　■

The Sunday night after Stacy's baby was born, I woke up to the smell of charred wood. It was coming in the open window, someone's campfire out in the woods. I didn't turn my head to see the clock. I knew it was around 3:30, could tell by the weight on my chest. Tonight he smelled the charred wood as well. His head was cocked to one side, sniffing toward the window. The gray stone was colder than usual tonight, as if he'd aged an extra thousand years or so, absorbing the chill of as many winters. He scratched absently at his left shoulder as if I weren't there.

That first night he appeared at my window I fought with everything I had. All it got me was a two-week's stay at Munson Medical, and my family treating me like something out of *The Snake Pit*. The first night after I was released he was there again. Even with my new dishes and mended furniture, there he was coming in over the sill. That time I didn't fight, didn't budge. I preferred the impassive bulk of him to the careful looks from Mom, the syrup-brained feeling from the hospital drugs. What was a little terror compared to straps holding you down at the wrists and knees?

The sheets were tucked in too tight, curling my toes as his weight stretched the smooth cotton. The Night Visitor brought a mindlessness that was close to death itself. Then came the picture of the room, the door, and behind it: dark circles like blue petals under her eyes; dried snot crusted around a pinched nostril; an elbow that looked swollen in a thin six-year-old arm; the dark stain in her hair.

Outside in the woods there must've been people sleeping near that still-smoldering campfire. Maybe there were shapes in sleeping bags, spray cans of OFF!, empty gym shoes lying nearby. In the dark ink of 3:30 A.M., a cricket or spider could make its way over the laces, down beneath the gaping tongue, into the fragrant warmth of the shoe. Lots of sleeping things. Everyone asleep but me, and the creature that rested on top of me like a gravestone. Is this what I would become, turning to granite from the inside out? When the pictures faded, his impossible weight shifted, then rose up and disappeared. Shivering in my damp sheets, I finally slept until morning.

9

The day after Turd Ball was born, Monday, a gray veil of rain fell steadily as I made the drive to Traverse City. Stacy was diminished. Those twelve stitches had taken the wind out of her.

"How long are they going to keep you?" I asked her.

"Four days." She was propped up on pillows, the hospital bed raised almost to a sitting position. She balanced a plastic cup on her chest, holding it steady with two fingers, taking tiny sips now and then from the flexistraw. "They want me to get out of bed and walk this afternoon."

"Have to get that muscle strength back quick as you can." I was parroting what Mom had said to me out in the waiting room minutes before. Stacy didn't answer, sipped at her flexistraw without swallowing. I considered opening her blinds. There was nothing out there but rain.

"Where's Ruther?" I asked her.

"He went home to get some things for me," she said. "Tooth-brush. Slippers."

"Why didn't you call? I could've brought it."

"No." Sip. "He needed to get out of here. Slept on a cot over there last night." She looked toward the end of the bed. "Had to shower and change, get out of here." Sip. "You know."

I nodded. She was on painkillers. That would explain the pearly glass of her skin, the see-through quality in her voice.

"You look tired," she said to me.

"You too."

"Have you seen him?" she asked, staring at the bump that her knees made under the blanket.

"No, that's why I asked."

"No. I mean the baby," she said quietly.

"Yes."

"When?" Still staring at her bumpy knee.

"Last night and just now."

"How's he look?" she asked. I didn't answer. She said, "They're keeping us separated for our own good, I guess." She stared and gave a laugh like string unraveling. "How's he look?" she asked again.

"He's small. Red. Scaly, but that'll wear off." I was watching the water slide part way up her clear Flexistraw and come down again, over and over. She was watching it too. "Look, Stace. All newborns look gross, especially if it's hard labor."

"Hard labor," and Stacy laughed again. "Like a prison term. Twenty years hard labor."

"I'll bet it felt like twenty years yesterday."

"Longer." She dragged her eyes away from the blanket and

gave me a small, embarrassed smile. "Thanks," she said. Tears were falling all over her face.

"What for?"

"Telling me the truth. Mom and Ruther kept saying how beautiful he was," she said. "So I thought, you know, he was dead."

"He's not dead."

"Or deformed."

"He's ugly."

"Is that all?"

"Well, really ugly," I continued. "No bigger than a cow pie."

She was giggling now. "They were so evasive every time I asked how he was, I thought they were waiting until I was stronger before telling me," she said. "You know, that he died."

"Nope," I told her. "He's just down the hall."

"Why can't I see him?" The forgotten cup tilted on her chest. She was trying to sit up straighter in the slanted bed.

"I don't know."

"Go ask. Go get a nurse and ask her for a wheelchair."

I had a conference at the nurse's station. Charts were checked and doctors consulted. Finally Sharon and the nurse loaded Stacy into the wheelchair, and I pushed her out to the hall. Mom followed alongside with the I.V. cart, asking, "Shouldn't we wait for Ruther?"

"No," I replied.

I watched Stacy looking at the little lump of flesh and bone that lay sleeping in the respirator. She didn't look scared. How could anyone be that oblivious to the reality staring her in the face? She looked like there was nothing ahead for the kid but sunshine and goddamn daisies. I left as soon as I could, ignoring the hurt on her face when I slid away.

■ ■ ■

Monday afternoon, home from visiting Stacy, and the silver fur of rain continued outside. I was ironing the kitchen curtains I'd washed the day before, and listening to Gillian Welch on the stereo. Starched sleeveless blouses and cotton shorts lay neatly folded and wrinkle-free. Soon as I was done ironing I would head over to Marion's house to continue the six-month-long cribbage tournament we'd started when I was in the hospital last winter. But for now the smell of wet grass drifted in the open windows, and Gillian's voice rang hard as a frozen pipe. Loretta leaned on the bars of her rib cage, gazing out at the rain.

The phone rang. I felt so good there alone in the rain, I ignored it. Earlier when I'd picked up the phone it was Mad Dog Mahoney reminding me of the trial date four days away.

"I may not call you the first day," she'd said. "But you need to be available." As if I would forget, not show up. The thought of getting on the witness stand made my stomach lurch with stage fright. Mahoney had gone on to say again how helpful it would be to "put this woman away" if I could scrape up just one single previous injury.

"Anything," she said. "Didn't you ever see a Band-Aid on the damn kid?"

I told her for the hundredth time she was barking up the wrong tree. Hell, I'd spent half of my childhood in Band-Aids. And I'd had about the most normal childhood you could imagine. Like Ozzie and Harriet, for Christ's sake. The phone continued to ring. It might be something wrong at the hospital.

"What."

"Mary?"

A fuzzy knob sprouted at the back of my throat. Yes yes yes. "Yes," I said.

"This is John Coleros."

"I know." I said it like I was congratulating him. There was a brief, bottomless pause in my ear. In the background I heard men's voices, truck doors slamming. A bell dinged like an air pump at a gas station. Then he remembered what he'd planned to say.

"I was calling to see how your sister made out with the baby." It came out rehearsed. My blood shot the rapids.

"She's okay. The baby'll have to stay for a while. In the hospital." La di da, chatting away. I stared at my stove, not recognizing it. "Thank you for driving me all that way." Why did you? Why did I let you? Why are you calling me?

"My pleasure." Then he stopped short as if he'd said too much. A rumble came from his end like a garage door closing.

"What's all the noise?" I asked.

"I'm at work. Sorry."

"Where's work?" Keep him on the phone.

"Sizemor Septic," he said. "They've got the backhoe in here, working on it. Making a lot of noise."

I pictured him in a sweat-stained work shirt, sleeves rolled up to his elbows revealing those goddamn beautiful forearms. Saw him in the midst of all that noise and confusion. I looked out at the rain falling in a sweet curtain all around me, a private canopy of quiet. Like a bird in a magic cage, I could say anything. I could say the truth. I could say, "I'm glad you called."

Another pause while he absorbed the shock of the truth coming at him. Then he rebounded. "So am I."

The hand that held the phone to my ear was strong enough to crush metal. I could yank him right through that phone line and onto my lap. Suddenly Loretta said, "Do you want to get something to eat sometime?"

And his voice answered, "Yes."

Holy shit. I sat down, bruising my hip on the corner of the kitchen table before skidding into the chair with a small grunt.

"I have to hang up now," I said.

"I'll call you later, then."

"Okay."

I hung up the phone, careful not to rip it out of the wall. Floated into the living room with my head just inches from the ceiling, and unplugged the iron. Back in the kitchen, Frank lay belly-up on the linoleum near the kitchen table. All four legs were splayed, relaxed. I floated down next to him, flat on my back, hands folded loosely across my stomach. So this is what Frank saw all day. There was a small brown spot on the ceiling above the stove. Last winter I'd been cooking a mess of liver and onions. I poked a piece of liver with a fork and it exploded in the skillet. Made a loud popping noise and sent grease spattering onto my neck and arms. The hunk of liver flew in a hundred pieces that embedded themselves into the ceiling like shrapnel. God, those were good liver and onions, though. Couple of pounds of fresh liver, a half bag of white onions thinly sliced, two sticks of butter, and a lot of patience. Heaven on earth.

I sat up. On the kitchen counter, waiting to go out in the mailbox, sat a postcard that I had written earlier. It was a shot of Lake Kassauga at sunset. On the back it said, "Dear Julianna. How are you? It is raining here in Riverton and I am thinking about you. I hope you and Eleanor Prudhomme are having a great trip. Love, Mary." I could not connect Julianna with the man who had just called me. The two existed in separate worlds. I grabbed my keys and visor off the counter and headed out the door. Put the postcard in the mailbox and flipped up the red flag. Maybe he wouldn't call back. Maybe he would return to the old anonymous Number 34 and I could return to myself.

Marion's houseboat was on the east dock flanked by motorboats and pontoons. It was shaped like a cracker box, like a house built of bright red Legos. Marion's dead husband had a bullet head with close-cropped hair. He used to finish Marion's sentences for her. She always wore dresses and skirts, and kept her hair back in a puffy bun. Nobody heard a curse word out of her mouth until the day he was killed in an accident at the feed mill. Marion cut her hair, wore pants, and bought the bar with his insurance money. A year later she moved into the houseboat. She had a round moonface with a short gray pageboy. I thought she looked like the little Dutch boy. Amy said she looked like the man from the Monopoly game.

Marion was outside in the back. She was changing a propane tank and didn't see me. When I stepped onto the deck, the whole thing shifted under my weight and she looked up. "I'm in the middle of cooking some goddamn dinner," she said from under her rain slicker. "You want some?"

"What is it?" I asked, leaning against the wall for balance. The deck was wet and slippery.

"Goulash," she said, heaving the full propane tank into place. "I was cooking goddamn goulash and ran out of fuel."

"Yeah, I'll have goulash," I said, brushing aside the inevitable thought of Carl. I looked out over the marina while she connected hoses. Rain plucked at the water's surface all around me, the marina coming to a low boil. The veil that was silver outside my cottage had turned dull and gray. The familiar pontoons and motorboats hunched under the colorless gloom, blue skies a forgotten dream. Marion swore quietly beside me. Maybe that phone never really rang. Maybe I'd imagined the whole conversation. But my hip was still sore where I'd whacked it on the corner of the table. That was real.

"Go on inside," Marion said. "I'll be there in a minute."

I stepped carefully around the narrow deck, ducked my head, and stepped through the little door. Inside everything was scaled to Marion-size, who was five feet flat. I took off my visor and set it on top of the fridge, which came to my chin. A skillet sat on the two-burner stove, hamburger half cooked and soaking up its own grease. The colander in the little sink was filled with elbow macaroni cooked and drained. Curtains covered all the windows. They were attached to rods at the top and bottom for maximum privacy at close range. Dozens of little black Scottie dogs marched in and out across the pleats. It was dark in there, like a rabbit hole.

"Try the burner," Marion shouted in through the closed window. I turned the black knob. A hiss, a series of clicks, but no flame. I flipped the knob back to OFF. Shoved the Scottie dogs aside and shook my head no at her. I could hear a couple of muffled "hells" and "shits," then the room tilted and her weight moved along the side deck. The door burst open and Marion said, "Goddamn pilot light's out."

There was only room for one body at a time in the kitchen. I retreated to the living room area: plywood paneling and a hard-cushioned couch that folded back to make a bed. Magazines sat on a wooden side table next to a replica hurricane lamp. *Michigan Outdoors, McCall's, Reader's Digest.* I pictured Marion here alone in the evenings, reading magazines in the lamplight. It was spotless but the smell of mildew was inevitable, like mushrooms growing in a cave. Marion's head was inside the oven. She had a pack of matches in her hand. I pictured the two of us blown to pieces, pontoons rocking in a panic, arms and legs stacked like kindling along the dock. I kept my mouth shut, not wanting to distract her. Even seated, my head was too close to the ceiling. Christ, didn't she ever let any air in here?

"Are you really hungry or a little bit?" Her voice was swallowed by the oven.

"Medium." I wasn't hungry at all. I had no stomach. Just a pair of lungs working harder by the minute to get a goddamn breath. "Mind if I let a little air in?" I was on my feet and shoving open those awful curtains. Turned the little knob that cranked open the window. Six inches was as far as it budged. My cottage had all the windows wide open on all sides, breezes crisscrossing through each room. Why wasn't I there now? The knuckle of my index finger had deep teeth marks all over it. I shoved the hand in my back pocket.

"When's the last time you were on a date?" I asked Marion.

The answer was a rush and whoosh from the oven. She lurched back and landed on her ass on the tile floor.

"Got it," she said, standing up. "I didn't hear you."

"You like living alone?"

Without answering, she opened a mason jar of stewed tomatoes, drained them, chopped them up, then added them to the cooking hamburger. She stabbed the skillet hard a few times with the spatula and sighed out a slow, reflective string of curses.

"I got peace of mind, for Christ's sake," she said at the end. "I'll tell you what I miss though," she said, draining grease off the skillet. "Having someone to laugh with." Marion was smiling to herself. "Shit, he was funny."

We each had a Stroh's with dinner. I set up a couple of TV trays and there we sat on the couch. The goulash was smothered in Parmesan cheese, with bread and butter on the side. I'd managed to crank open a couple more windows. Once in a while a damp breeze would gust across my forehead.

We watched *Jeopardy!* and played cribbage. She had a Marion-size TV that I had to squint at to read the clues.

"Who is Morley Safer?" she said.

"Who is Hugh Downs?" I countered.

I beat her by $1,400. She double-skunked me in cribbage, which put her up by three games. On the way home I played with the buttons on the Merc's AM radio. Talk, static, jingle, static, more talk. I got thirty seconds of Elton John's "Elderberry Wine" before it faded to an ad for Michigan Lotto. I parked the Merc out back and let myself in the kitchen door. Needed to stay busy, stay busy, do something productive. I headed toward the living room to grab the curtains that needed rehanging.

Stopped dead about six feet short of the couch and put my hand to my chest. I couldn't take another step. I sucked in a long breath and closed my eyes. Let the air out slowly, enjoying the power of my lungs, the simple animal joy of breathing. The pores of my skin sighed under the tender brush of air as I raised my arms over my head. I could hear the drip drip drip of the eaves outside the window.

"He'll call soon," I said out loud. The absolute surety of it made me run a hand slowly through my hair. He crowded everything else out of my head. No Night Visitor, no Jen Colby. Even Julianna was small and far away. The tilt of my neck was precious, the power in my hips invincible, every inch of me was exaggerated. When the phone rang, I wasn't startled.

"What are you doing?" he asked.

"Standing in the middle of my living room thinking about you."

"How's your sister?"

"Still the same," I told him, while in the background Loretta whispered, "What sister?"

"I'm over at Marion's," he said. At first I thought he meant the houseboat, which caught me off guard. Then the hot buzz of neon reached me through the phone. He was at the bar. Something in me sent a spark and hum in reply. There was a pause. "I'm hungry," he finally added.

I laughed. It was my Jolly Roger laugh. "There's a truck stop by the old Edison plant past Houghton Lake," I said. "You know it?"

"I'll find it," he answered.

"Uncle Eddie's." I didn't trust the magic of the moment to guide him there. "On Morton Road."

"I'm leaving right now," he said. I expected him to hang up, but his voice broke in again, past the clamor of the neon, the voices, the jukebox. "Mary?"

"Yes?"

"Look, I don't know. I'll tell you when I see you. I mean, it's just a bite to eat. Forget it." Then he coughed to shut himself up.

"Okay." I hung up. "Bye."

10

I walked through the door to Uncle Eddie's in jeans and a gray tank top. Brushed the bangs off my forehead with a quick hand as I came across the parking lot. Truckers lined the counter, drinking coffee and eating pie. Electronic laughter barked out of a video game in the back. John was at a booth by the front window, looking out at the half dozen semitrucks parked outside. He was wearing a bluish-green golf shirt unbuttoned at the neck. Two things struck me when he turned his head toward me: the open neck revealed dark hairs where his collarbones met, and the color of the shirt made his blue eyes reach out and grab you by the throat. I could not believe that the man sitting there was waiting for me. Then he was standing up, and I was taking a wide berth around some tables so as not to bump into one of them and then have to kill myself.

"Hi," he said. For an instant I saw him as he must have been at age seven, all lit up with excitement. That's how he looked.

"Hey," I answered.

We slid into our seats. Two plastic menus sat on the table. They seemed so intimate lying one on top of the other I couldn't bring myself to touch them. I looked away and there he was, a few feet across from me.

"I'm glad you came," he said.

"Were you afraid I wouldn't?"

"I'm afraid of you, period." He grinned, and something shot across the table between us, a blue lightning bolt. Loretta broke into lilac blossoms and fluttered down around my feet. I looked up at the specials board. It hung on the wall next to a *Field & Stream* calendar showing a rainbow trout twisting in the air above the water. Biscuits and gravy with two eggs for $2.49. Having made a decision, I took a deep breath and relaxed one iota.

"What do you want?" I asked him.

"That's what I want to talk about."

"To eat."

He picked up a menu and opened it, shut it again, tossed it down, and looked at me, frowning. "What am I doing?"

Somehow food was ordered. I drank iced tea; he had black coffee. The waitress was young with blue eye shadow and two deep dimples on the right side of her smile, which she directed mostly at me. When she looked at John, a dark flush spread across her face, chest, and arms. That's how good-looking he was. When she left he was still there across from me.

"So, you're married," I said.

His head turned to look out the window. Maybe searching for the right answer out there among the semis. Once he found it, he turned back to me and said, "It's complicated."

"No it's not."

"Yeah." He was rolling and unrolling the corner of his paper place mat. "I'm married."

I waited, hoping for a ". . . but we're separated," or even ". . . but she's crazy." All he did was open up his palms in a there-you-have-it gesture. Above his head was a piece of polished bark laminated with a photograph of a white-tail buck. I imagined tearing it off the wall and bashing him over the head with it. I stacked his unused Half 'n Halfs into a small tower on the table, then knocked them down. He took a pack of Winstons out of the front pocket of his jeans, lit a match and dropped it in the ash-tray where it kept burning.

"Your hand's shaking," I said with a slice of meanness.

"Yeah," he said, and held it out, palm down and fingers straight. The Winston vibrated. "My stomach's in a knot, and my mouth is all dry too."

"Why?"

"Because you're sitting there."

I don't know what I said after that. Dimples brought out a turkey club for John, blushing scarlet when he smiled a friendly thank you. She set my plate in front of me and scrammed fast.

"Do you want me to put it out?" John gave the Winston a slight wave.

"No." I dug into my food. Nothing stood between me and bis-cuits and gravy, not a gut full of goulash or Prince Charming himself.

"How is it?" he asked, not touching his turkey club.

"Great," I told him between bites. "You always get good bis-cuits and gravy at a truck stop."

"Doreen never eats gravy or—"

I cut him off. "She seems like a nice person."

"She is," he said. I hated him.

He stubbed out the cigarette and went for his sandwich. I re-membered Doreen as I'd seen her at the beach, in her red one-piece swimsuit with a brightly colored parrot down the front. She had Julianna's foot balanced on top of her knee, Kleenex wedged between the small toes. She dipped the nail brush, drained off the excess polish, and dabbed color onto the wig-gling toenails with a casual sort of concentration. The two of them were talking like a couple of girlfriends, like two old women, as if they liked each other despite being mother and daughter. Julianna said something that made Doreen throw her head back and laugh out loud. Bottle of polish in one hand, tiny brush in the other, she used her wrist to brush the bangs from her forehead as she said, "Oh, you got that right, kiddo."

It was a small moment, a nothing moment. I don't know what they were talking about. The sun shone down, and the breeze carried her laughter over to me. That was all.

"Her mother lives with us," he said after a while. "Doreen works evenings at the supermarket in Lake City. Nana takes care of Juju." I kept quiet and let him talk. He made some head-way into his sandwich. "We don't see each other much," he went on.

I looked out the window at the Merc. She was right where I'd parked her under a light pole, chrome sparkling like Lake Kas-sauga on a sunny day. How many different kinds of lonely were there in the world? From the kitchen some kid was shouting, "Marcia! Marcia! Gimme a kiss, will ya?" every few minutes while another voice laughed. Dimples called into the kitchen through the service window, "Shut your hole, why don't you?"

A trucker at the counter was giving himself a work over with a toothpick. His upper lip was hitched up to his nose, eyebrows lifted in concentration. He gestured to the kitchen with his free hand and said to Dimples, "He's got it bad, honey."

"Got his head up his ass, more like it," she answered.

John leaned back, stretching his legs out under the table. He was taking his time now with the fries. He dipped them slowly, one at a time, into the ketchup and popped them into his mouth. Then he wiped his thumb and forefinger on his napkin before reaching for the next one.

"Leave her if you're lonely," I said, black and white and over-simplified.

"I didn't know I was lonely," he replied. "Until I saw you standing with a bat in your hands, waiting for the pitcher to warm up, swinging like you were going to knock someone's head off."

"That's what did it for you, huh?"

"I like the idea that you could kick my ass if you were mad enough." He held my eyes for as long as either of us could stand it. "Besides, you got a triple."

"Have you ever done this before?" I asked with some perverse urge to hurt myself.

"Done what?"

"This."

He sat and thought about lying to me. He said, "Yeah. Once. It was a mistake."

"So's this."

"I know," he said with a lazy smile, his eyes raking me up and down. Oh, he *was* a son of a bitch. The conversation went from softball to school sports to Julianna's junior high cheerleader tryouts a few months before.

"She drove us up the wall with her splits and her cartwheels and jumping all over the place," he said over his third cup of coffee. "Two weeks, her and Donna doing the same songs, the same routines, over and over."

I remembered when Sharon, then Stacy, went through those tryouts each spring. In the end, Stacy was a cheerleader for life and Sharon had been spared.

"On the big day I got home from work and, for one thing, it's quiet."

"Uh-oh," I said.

"She's up in the tree house, not a sound."

"Did Donna make it?"

"Neither of them," he told me. "And all she said, when I asked her how it went, she tells me she'd never have tried to be a cheerleader if she'd known how goddamn mean they were."

I was telling him about the time Dad hosed down the electrical station east of town and shorted out half the county, when Dimples brought the check. "No rush," she said. "You can sit here all night if you want."

Trucks had pulled in, trucks had pulled out. Three men sat a few booths away talking about whether or not the Wolverine Truck Stop on I-94 charged two dollars for the shower itself or if it was just the deposit on the towel.

"It's two dollars to get a towel, but you don't get no money back when you return it," said one in a Schnieder Trucking cap.

"Okay, but say you got your own towel, then the showers are free," said another, pushing the Jim's Heating and Cooling cap farther back on his forehead.

"Ain't nobody gonna bother returning the towel if you don't get no money back," argued the third.

"Maybe it's a three-dollar deposit and a buck back," said Jim's Heating and Cooling.

"Then it's the same as I said," interrupted Schnieder Trucking. "Two dollars for the damned towel."

It sounded like every conversation I'd ever heard when I was young and Dad would take me to the Shoreline Pub with him. I half expected to see him rise up out of their booth. Tiny hairs prickled on my arm. John and I split the bill and headed for the door. He gave Dimples a smile as she headed over to clear our table. He didn't have the slightest idea what he'd done to her. We came to the door and John dug in his pocket for a quarter. He dropped it in a gumball machine against the wall, beneath the Jerry Lewis Muscular Dystrophy Telethon poster. Turned the crank and out came a plastic bubble. He palmed it neatly and opened the door. We stepped out into the buzz of the parking lot lights. The rain had stopped. The Merc sparkled like a jubilee. I closed my eyes and took in a big breath of clean wet air. When I opened them, John was opening up the plastic bubble. He took out a child's ring and held it out to me with a half smile. I slipped it on. The ring had a round plastic jewel glued to the expandable band. A deep, gaudy pink gazed up at me from my little finger.

"Thanks," I said. I held my hand out for him to admire it.

"Suits you," he said, which struck me funny. We walked slowly across the wet pavement. The night held its breath. When we reached the Merc he leaned against her with his elbow on the roof, head resting on the butt of his palm, and looked at me.

"Not many women could pull off a car like this." He knew the way to win a girl. "I have to go home," he added. "Otherwise I'd ask you for a ride in it."

"Next time," I said, crushed and relieved.

"Promise?"

I nodded again. Out on U.S. 27 red lights were flashing a half mile away. Flares dotted the highway around a wreck. I tried to imagine someone hurt, someone's life changed forever in an instant of broken glass and folded metal. The idea was foreign, unthinkable while we stood there close together. They were nothing but lights in the distance. He traced a finger lightly along the line of my jaw, then withdrew his hand. There wasn't anything to say, so we tilted our heads back as the moon tore through the old gray lace of clouds and shone its face down on us. My skin felt raw where his finger had been. Tomorrow there would be a telltale mark. Everyone who saw me would gasp and say, "Mary! Someone touched you." I got in the car and rolled the window down. He leaned in, arms crossed on the door. The dark hair on his forearms brushed my shoulder, setting it on fire.

"I'll see you tomorrow. At the ballpark," he said.

"Yes." I stared at his wrist.

"Are you going to be up to Marion's after?"

"Yes." I could brush my lips against the bones in that wrist.

"Will you have a beer with me? If I promise not to make goo-goo eyes at you?"

"Well." I started the car up. "Not so anyone can see, anyway."

He laid his hand on the top of my head and ran it gently down my hair to the back of my neck.

"I'm not going to sleep much tonight," he told me. Then he stood away from the car.

"Me either," I answered. "See you tomorrow."

He was small in the rearview mirror walking toward his car, hands in the pockets of his jeans. I took the back roads, avoiding the wreck on U.S. 27. Stopped at a Shell station a few miles out of Riverton. I stood at the back of the Merc, filling her up under an island of bright, garish fluorescence. All around me cricket-song rose up from the dripping dark. A single cashier stood inside the glass walls of the Shell station. He was leaning forward on the counter reading who knows what. The light inside the station was brilliant, the night outside deadly dark. The only movement was the flipping of numbers on the pump. I'd stumbled into a painting by Edward Hopper, as alone as it gets. The hose jerked and went dry. I topped off the tank and went in to pay.

"Pack of Kools," I said, putting a six-pack of Stroh's on the counter.

He reached above his head and pulled down the cigarettes. Tossed a book of matches on top of them.

"Nice night," I didn't say.

"Rain finally stopped," he never answered.

The pack was a bar of gold in my hand. I climbed into the Merc and peeled open the cellophane, knocking the pack against my wrist a few times to settle the tobacco tight. Tore open the foil, tapped one out and put it to my lips, each movement old and familiar and magic.

I started the Merc and pulled out. Once on the road I pushed in the silver knob of the lighter. Punched the radio until I found some old Motown station. I pulled the lighter free and held it to the cigarette, inhaling deep. First smoke in seven years. Jesus, that first drag went through my lungs like a beautiful sword. I came to the turnoff toward Riverton, but I couldn't go home yet. The cigarette snuggled happily between my fingers resting on the wheel. In my other hand was an open bottle. Another drag, another stab of joy. After seven years of clean living, there was still no comfort like it; people who couldn't stop smoking were people who had failed to find any other consolation. My brain began to fizz and tingle. Hands were swollen and heavy, legs filled with lead. Inconsolable people, and I was one of them. He was married. He had a wife, and he had Julianna. I could see her there in front of me as I drove. Her hand was up to shade her yellow eyes and she was looking at me. She had a look on her face.

I kept driving, drinking my beer, through "Let's Stay To-gether," through "Under My Thumb." The road hissed wet in the darkness. The red dot of the cigarette burned like a beacon above the wheel. I drove straight, braked, turned, drove straight again, my brain a blank. Nothing mattered so long as I kept driving and smoking like this. No consequences, no regrets. The world was an easy place inside the Merc, with the low static of music humming in my ears, with my right arm slung loosely across the back of the seat and the wind coming in the open window. The moon had dropped her shyness, hung unafraid outside the window on my left. Her light shone down on the jagged tips of the pines that ridged the north horizon.

When I was a kid Dad and I would go ice fishing. On the way home we stopped at the Shoreline Pub, where all the other ice fishers were warming up with Wild Turkey or Maker's Mark. I climbed up on a bar stool with the others, frozen blue but happy to be with Dad. Behind the bar, Fran put on her perfect dead-pan and said, "What'll you have, kid?"

"Rum and Coke," I shot back.

She responded with the briefest of nods. Anyone else would have said I was just an eight-year-old kid, but she knew that we were two no-nonsense broads in a tough backwoods dive. Someday I would grow up, dye my hair, and tend bar just like Fran.

"Jameson's, Frannie." Dad shook his coat off by the door, adding to a puddle of melting snow on the floor. He heaved a leg over the bar stool next to mine. Fran brought a double shot of whiskey for him, and a Coke for me with three drops of rum in it. Dad was the only one I ever heard call her Frannie.

I sat leaning one elbow on the bar, the other arm reaching for the bowl of pretzels Fran brought me. I knew how to act in the Shoreline. I didn't fidget, didn't kick the heels of my boots against the bar stool, didn't nag Dad for quarters for the peanut machine. I kept my mouth shut, drank my drink, and listened to the men talk.

"Colder than a bitch on the rag out there." General agreement all around. I didn't know what rag he meant. I nodded just the same.

"How'd Mary do?"

"Ah Christ, I like to've died," Dad said, slapping his hand flat on the bar. "Don't you know she stepped right into an old fishing hole." Several heads shook in unison. I chewed my pretzel, keeping my eyes on the yellow plastic bowl. "I had her backing up with a bite on the cane pole. Heard a crack and damned if her whole leg wasn't down in the ice." Now they're all looking at me with interest. "I shit you not, she's sitting there with one leg straight in front of her, one disappeared altogether, and I'll be goddamned if she isn't still hanging onto that pole. I like to've died, I'm telling you."

Harold Tucker put a hand on Fran's arm. "I'm buying that girl a drink," he said.

"Catch anything?" asked a man in a red-and-black-plaid flannel shirt.

"Caught the limit," I replied.

Which got a big laugh all around and Dad's proud, heavy hand coming down on my shoulder. Fran placed another rum and Coke in front of me and pointed a thumb at Harold Tucker, who gave me a nod. I nodded back, face stern and back straight.

"Jesus Christ, don't tell your mother you got stuck in a hole in the ice," Dad said laughing. "She'd throw my ass out of the house."

Don't tell your mother where we stopped on the way home, that you been drinking rum and Cokes, that you heard that joke from me, that I had Frannie sitting on my lap, that you're my best girlfriend. Don't tell your mother; as if I would in a million years. We played pool, me and Harold against Dad and the guy in the red-and-black-plaid flannel. I nudged in the eight ball for the game and Mr. Plaid put his hand on the small of my back.

"If you was a little taller, I'd take you home with me."

His breath was whiskey hot and smoky, just like Dad's. I

smiled and tried to step away without hurting his feelings. Dad's arm came sliding around my shoulder.

"Hands off, Joe." He steered me easily out of reach. "Gotta find your own girlfriend."

"Any more like her at home?" Joe asked, chalking his pool cue and grinning down at me.

"Sure, if you like 'em in diapers."

Someone broke, sending the balls racing in all directions, slamming into one another in their panic. The men were laughing. I had a knot in my stomach. I wanted to go home, wanted to stay. I climbed on a nearby stool and sat the next game out. Fran hit a few shots with a blue-and-gold aluminum stick that she kept behind the bar. There was a cocktail napkin on the table near my elbow. It had a cartoon of two men in suits talking to a woman who was naked. She had huge round naked tits and a huge round naked butt to match. The two men were grinning. I put my glass over it without reading the caption. My face burned hot. I looked down at the knobby knees in my corduroy pants. My Detroit Tigers sweatshirt hung flat against my eight-year-old chest.

"Mary!" Dad was looking over at me, fishing in his pocket. Had he caught me looking at the dirty cartoon? My face burned in the dim light.

"Put something on, will you?" He flipped me a couple of quarters. I clumped over to the jukebox in my boots, punched in three of his favorite songs, and clumped back to the table, where a fresh bowl of pretzels waited for me.

"You want a burger or something?" Fran said over her shoulder while she lined up a shot. I shook my head no; the knot in my stomach took up too much room. As the first strains of music rained down on the pool table, Dad looked up and grinned at me through his cigarette smoke.

"She picks out Merle Haggard," he said. "Did a man ever have a better girlfriend?"

He patted Fran on the ass, ruining her shot. She smacked him on the hand, then planted a loud kiss right on his mouth. I used a thumbnail to pick the salt off my pretzel. I'd swallow a fish hook before I'd cry at the Shoreline Pub. When he finished the pool game Dad lifted me off the bar stool and we danced a jazzed up fox-trot. Maybe I didn't have big round tits and a big round butt, but I could dance. And everyone there knew it.

Don't tell your mother. One peep out of me and these afternoons with Dad would end forever. Always on the drive home, the same routine: Dad drifting onto the shoulder and jerking the truck back onto the road. Me talking nonstop, asking lots of questions to keep him awake and alert. A mile or so from the house, he'd open the glove box and tell me to fish around for the sticks of Juicy Fruit that he'd pop in his mouth and order me to do the same.

"No reason to get your mother all pissed off 'cause we been drinking again," he said. I'd chew that gum to hide the three or six or nine drops of rum I'd had. Dad's drinking buddy, the best girlfriend a man ever had, and God didn't we have a lot of fun together. By the time I hit fifteen I was the one driving even though I was underage. Mom had given up caring where he was, and only sent me out to bring him home when she needed money. He wouldn't leave until I agreed to sit down and have last call with him "like old times."

"Your mother doesn't understand one goddamn thing . . ."

the conversation would start. Either that or "Your mother and the girls . . ." meaning Sharon and Stacy. And he'd tell me all about the latest woman, how she took care of him and didn't bitch or carp or get pregnant. "She understands things, like you do."

"Dad, you're a drunk old skirt-chasing asshole."

"Drunk old asshole," he'd confirm for everyone's benefit. "You're still my best girlfriend." And then we'd dance to Patsy Cline or Ray Price, and I'd get him out the door and home.

Two years later, after his lungs and liver ate him alive, Fran was one of the old girlfriends at the funeral. I stood next to Mom, and Fran kept her distance, though of course she'd seen me. When she went out in the hallway for a cigarette I followed her. I was seventeen years old now, taller than her.

"Did he love you?" I asked, keeping my eyes on the picture of Jesus hanging behind her.

"He was a good man," she said vaguely.

"Did you love him?" *Tell me something. Tell me something that makes sense.*

Finally she gave a small, embarrassed shrug. "You're too young to understand."

"Slut," I had answered, staring at Jesus' blond beard.

She didn't ask me to repeat what I'd said; she'd heard it all right. I looked up then and met her eyes, hating myself but hating her more.

The moon had disappeared, taking its pale glow with it. I drove all over two counties with the meager beams of the headlights clinging close to the car. Impenetrable walls of pine rose on either side of me. If anything was moving out there in the dark, it was up to no good.

I'm not going to sleep much tonight. John's head on a pillow, wide awake. John's head on a pillow next to me. I wondered if Julianna was awake. Was she wondering where her dad was right now?

The headlights picked up a black shadow on the shoulder of the road. Several dark shapes, too small for deer. Two heads lifted, dark bulks with eyes reflecting red in the Merc's stare. Blood gleamed on the edge of the pavement. The tableau came and went quickly on my right. Then I was looking at nothing but a sandy dirt shoulder rolling by. Too large for fox, too dark for coyote, and wolves had been killed off from this part of the state years ago. It was the abandoned dogs that roamed all over the woods, hunting or eating fresh roadkill when they found it. The Millers down the road had lost a couple lambs to them last spring.

The night turned blacker and colder. I switched off the radio. I had a home to go to. I had locks on my doors. But just outside were dark hungry shapes that had once had names like Hero or Jack. Muzzles that used to nudge someone's hand for a pat now sniffed the air for prey. People walked away from the things they were responsible for, like those things weren't going to come back in the middle of the night and tear your throat open. I rolled up the window against the chill. Lit another cigarette with my head pounding like a kettle drum. The Merc rolled toward home.

11

The next day after Uncle Eddie's was a Tuesday. I had a tournament game that night and John would be there at the ballpark. Mom called early from the hospital, yanking me from a fitful, exhausting sleep. She'd gone to check on Stacy, who was doing okay. Turd Ball was taking his time pulling through, but he'd make it. No, they didn't need anything up there, but could I meet her and Sharon later on in the morning? I drove to the Kassauga County Fairgrounds around 10:30. The parking lot was full of pickup trucks, livestock trucks, minivans, anything people found handy to tote the goods. I walked past the small-livestock building all in chaos. Flop-eared bunnies jumped in nervous circles in their cages. Exotic chickens shook the gold and red feathers erupting off their necks.

"All domestic poultry in Section C," shouted a woman in a yellow plastic vest.

"Daniel! Daniel! You're sloshing the water pan, take it easy."

"Ducks, geese, chickens, Section C please."

"Set it down gentle, honey. That's not a football in there."

I remembered last year, Jen Colby had entered a guinea pig or something and took a red ribbon in the Peewee Division. She carried it in her pocket all through September, protected in a Ziploc sandwich bag. She was like every other kid there, like the kids in front of me now. I watched the small bodies that swirled all around. You simply could not tell to look at any of them.

He was small in the rearview mirror, walking toward his car with his hands in the pockets of his jeans. Silver sparks flew out of my head. My knees jellied. Felt like flying, like crashing head-first into a house made of glass.

I made my way across the muddy midway to the tent that held the baked goods and preserves entered for ribbons. Judging wasn't until noon but already the volume of pies, breads, cakes, and jellies was oppressive. Somewhere some kid wasn't having breakfast, an old man couldn't get a goddamn cup of coffee, but pride and vanity had worked together to heap up this obscene mountain of homemade crap. A mason jar with a clever gingham skirt over the lid claimed to be mulberry ginger jam. Name me one person who could tell good mulberry ginger jam from bad. Dad always told me that mulberries were poisonous. Was that just another story to keep me and Amy out of the Brickhams' yard? Their mulberries were no more poisonous than their cocker spaniel had bitten off Mr. Brickham's fingers.

"Stuart, stop that right now," Mom had said. "That dog doesn't even have its teeth."

Oh God, the nightmares he gave us about the Brickhams. Even now, a quarter century later, I still could barely bring myself to speak to them at the bank, or if they were coming out for the mail as I pulled into Mom's driveway. They never had any kids, which made them suspect from the start as far as Amy and I were concerned. Mrs. Brickham still wore a jet-black Elizabeth Taylor beehive. Dad told me once he saw a mama mouse and four babies dart out the back of her hair and run right down her neck.

Cranberry sauce, sour cherry crumble, mincemeat applesauce. And there, finally, "Mrs. Annette Culpepper. Bread & Butter Pickles. Judging at 12:30 P.M." So they'd finished in here. I'd have to catch up with them over at the crafts shed. It was the biggest building at the fair, usually the most competitive except for the fruit, vegetable, and flower building, which housed sunflowers big around as footstools, and green peppers the size of Turd Ball.

I was nearly out the door when a card caught my eye. "Miss Mary Culpepper. Zucchini Bread. Judging at 1:00 P.M." My name, my bread, there for everyone to judge. The bread I'd made for Mom on Sunday morning.

I finally found Sharon waiting to register for the hand-sewn children's clothes. Mom was looking at an embroidered baptismal gown across the aisle. Sharon held the stack of rompers we'd made for Stacy's shower last month.

"About time," she said when I walked up. "We're almost done."

"Stacy let you enter those?" I asked, nodding toward the rompers.

"She doesn't know," Sharon replied.

"I told you not to," Mom said. "She doesn't need any aggravation right now."

"How's she going to know?" countered Sharon. "Unless you tell her?"

The rompers were neatly folded to show off the baby animals I'd embroidered. "You went over there and helped yourself?" I asked.

"I have a key," she answered, as if I'd accused her of robbery. I could see her walking quietly into the nursery where the $900 crib gleamed like a rocket ship. Pilfering through the Peter Rabbit dresser until she found what she came for, while Stacy and Turd Ball lay helpless in the hospital. "They were in the *bottom* drawer," Sharon added.

"Next to my zucchini bread?"

"Girls, stop it." Mom's lips were tight. We shut up. Sharon turned to the entry table and handed over her card. Her left hand held the stack of rompers while her right smoothed nonexistent wrinkles from the pleats and cuffs. A fat, fluffy bear cub rolled on his back, clutching his toes and laughing up at Sharon's face. He thought he'd been made for love. Now someone's critical fingers would count his stitches per inch, inspect his underside for unmoored backthreads.

"They'll judge your group at one o'clock," Suzanne O'Dell told Sharon from behind the entry table. She smiled. "Hi, Mary."

I smiled back. Busy woman, Suzanne O'Dell. Manning the crafts shed, organizing the Beer Tent, hitting three-run homers. She was getting to be as bad as Amy. Not that it was any of my business.

"Don't stand there like a bump on a pickle." Mom was at the door, waiting for me. "We're going to get some lunch."

"Why was I supposed to meet you here?" I asked.

"I'm sorry," Mom said, which meant her feelings were hurt. "Did you have something else to do today?"

"Yes," I said. I said it, and then I did have something else to do that day. A tiny idea had sprouted in my brain. Small and tentative, it grew tendrils that clung to my frontal lobes like ivy. "I was going to see Stacy."

"We need to talk about that," Sharon said.

"About what?"

"Stacy. She's coming home on Friday."

We walked toward the picnic tables, past wagons selling hot dogs, kielbasa, elephant ears. A clump of teenage girls milled in front of the sloppy joe wagon. Sleek honey-colored pony-tails, blue jeans tucked into gleaming boots, straight noses and teeth. The horse barn girls. A splash of laughter erupted as we passed. I flinched on instinct although I was twenty years older than they were, and they could no longer hurt me.

"What time is it?" I asked the air.

"Eleven," said Mom. "Are we keeping you?"

I didn't answer, got myself some chili fries and a cup of coffee and picked out a table in the shade. Mom followed with a hamburger and Coke. Sharon waited in line for cheese pizza. I ate, watching a kid in overalls fill up the metal water trough next to the livestock barn. The air was full of the sound of steers snorting whooshes of wet air out of their noses and assholes at the same time. Nice place to set the picnic tables.

"You look tired," said Mom.

"What else is new?" I blew on my coffee.

"I just thought it would be nice to arrange a housekeeping schedule for Stacy," she said.

Sharon joined us. "You're not working," she said. "We figure you can take on the bulk of it."

"Ho ho," I mumbled through a french fry.

"What's up your ass this morning?" Sharon asked. "It was a joke."

"And I said, 'Ho ho.' "

"Didn't you sleep again last night?" Mom asked.

"I'm not going to sleep much tonight."

"Me either."

I looked at my mother. I looked at my sister. I pushed the chili fries toward Sharon. Pulled out a cigarette and lit it. Mom looked away and literally bit her tongue. The effort pushed her cheeks out, made her look like Marlon Brando. Sharon stared at me, chewing on her pizza crust.

"Whose idea was it to enter my zucchini bread without asking me?" I exhaled smoke away from the two of them.

"You see?" said Sharon. "I told you she'd blow a nut."

"I have some shopping I need to do this afternoon," I said. "I can't wait around long."

"Fine," said Mom, looking in the opposite direction. On the seat next to me were carved the words *suck me*. God, you just couldn't win.

"Where'd you get the ring?" asked Sharon.

"Gumball machine," I answered, keeping my eyes on the table. I hadn't taken it off except to shower that morning. The sentimental stupidity of it gazed up at me from the liquid surface of my coffee.

"Thought maybe it was from your boyfriend," she said lightly. This was a constant theme with Sharon, my imaginary boyfriend. I put my hand in my lap.

"I'm sorry about the zucchini bread," said Sharon.

"Don't be sorry," snapped Mom. "You didn't do it. I did it." She turned to me. "You have so much creativity and you never let anyone see it. I thought it would give you confidence." She sat there glaring at me and my creativity. "You could sell that bread," she went on. "You could sell your embroidery in that little shop in Grayling. People pay a lot of money for that stuff. You're so good, and you don't want anyone to see it. It just makes me sick to watch you." She poked at her hamburger, demonstrating how I'd ruined her lunch. "Are you going to drive a school bus your whole life?"

"There's worse things I could do than get those kids to school and home safely." I stopped short. Sharon was staring at Mom to shut her up.

Mom stopped poking her hamburger and let her hand drop like a dead limb onto the picnic table. A real I-give-up gesture. Sharon looked ashamed of both of them. She said, "I gotta work tonight but maybe I'll stop at Marion's when the shift's over."

The last thing I wanted was Sharon spying on me. "What are we going to do with Stacy?" I asked.

"This is what we were thinking—" Sharon started.

"Just an idea, nothing carved in stone," Mom interrupted.

"I'll go over in the morning," Sharon continued. "And Mom'll pop over at night to fix supper or whatever." I waited to see where I fit in. "And maybe you could cover weekends," she finished.

"Just for a couple of weeks," Mom added. "Okay?" The two of them watched me like I was sulfuric acid about to spatter on them.

"That's fine," I said. There was a pause while they put away the arguments they'd prepared.

"Okay?" asked Mom again.

"That's what family's for, right?" I answered. "You all took care of me when I was sick, we all take care of Stacy now." I stood up and tossed the coffee cup into the trash can. "Anything else?"

"You can't even stay for the pickles at 12:30?" Mom asked.

"Gotta go. Sorry."

"We'll call you if you get a ribbon," Sharon said.

"Won't be home," I said, walking away.

"We'll call anyway," she yelled after me.

"Go right ahead," I called back, drowned out by the anxious snorting of pigs in wooden pens. I finished the pack of Kools on the drive to Traverse City, almost nodding off a couple of times. I'd slept four hours the night before. If this kept up, I'd be dead before the trial started on Friday and all the wrangling with Mad Dog Mahoney would be for nothing. I sat with Stacy through her lunch, finished the Jell-O she barely touched. Turd Ball was out of danger and Ruther was back to work at the dealership. Stacy was regaining her stride, showing off her breast pump and explaining how it worked.

"And look at this," she giggled. "Look at this!" She crossed her arms in front of her, forcing cleavage up through the neckline of her yellow cotton nightgown.

"You're huge, Stace," I conceded.

I left the hospital and drove downtown. This was the new idea I'd had at the fairgrounds, the tender green shoot of an idea: I would go on a little shopping spree, the first one in my life. The simplest choice would have been Lehmann's department store, but I couldn't run the risk of seeing Lori Baumann. I parked the Merc and put money in the meter. Got half a block away and went back to put in another quarter to keep the Merc safe.

First stop was The Candle Shoppe. A bell tinkled above the door and three heads swiveled in my direction. I furrowed my brow and looked intently at the bayberry sticks, a serious shopper too busy for chitchat. Row after row of candles assaulted my nose. There were long, thin tapers and round balls with wicks like fruity bombs. On the bottom shelf was a basket labeled "50 percent off." It was filled with little candles, all of them a mottled white. "Wildflowers," said one. Another, "After the Rain." I held each one to my nose, barely smelled anything. Up close I could see tiny forget-me-nots encased in the wax. I bought two of each, dumping them into the impromptu pouch I made by holding out the bottom of my T-shirt. Hesitated over "Starry Night" before adding it to the stash. I paid with my credit card, still too busy to chitchat.

Mercifully, no tinkly bell announced my entrance to Lorelei's Closet. The place smelled faint and warm, like roasted lemons. Cream carpet matched the raw silk drapes hanging in thick folds around the front window. No noise from the street penetrated. Classical piano music trickled across the ceiling, soft and melodious. A woman stood folding silk scarves at a small round table. She smiled. "I'm Carol, if you have any questions."

I'd forgotten how much I liked this place. Amy and I had come here to buy a gift for Stacy's bridal shower. There were chemises, tap pants, half slips and full slips in long, short, fitted, or full. Bras with underwire, full support or demi-cups in spandex, lace, cotton, Lycra, and every imaginable combination. Usually I couldn't get out of a lingerie section fast enough. But here the nightgowns shimmered loosely on padded hangers in peach, ivory, seashell pink. They folded and draped, whispering, "Touch me, touch me, touch me."

I ran my fingertips along the satiny necklines, let the silk sleeves feather across my palm. Picked out a honey-colored wrap and draped the fabric on my arm. Two other women entered by the time I'd selected two chemises cut high around the thigh, four bra and panty sets, and three nightgowns (two short, one long and sliiiiiinky). Carol led me to the women's lounge. It was as large as the shop area out front, with the same pliant carpeting, and cushioned divans in chocolate and honey cream. Warm lighting hummed. Kind, gentle mirrors hung here or there, not everywhere.

"It's all yours," she said. "One customer at a time in the lounge."

As I hung the wispy waspy nothings on the hooks along the far wall, Carol returned with a discreet knock. She carried a tray to one of the tables. It held a glass, a pitcher of lemonade, and a large cloth napkin.

"If you need me to bring other sizes, punch this button right here." She pointed to a small knob near the door. "Enjoy," she added, closing the door softly behind her. I felt like both the bride and the groom on my wedding night.

But this was where the fun ended. This was where the fantasy crashed and burned. I kicked off my Keds, unbuttoned my shorts. Peeled, stretched, wiggled, and kicked everything off until I stood naked in the center of the room. The mirrors were easy to avoid if you wished; there if you wanted them. I took a breath and looked at myself. Maybe it was the lighting, diffuse and warm like peering through gauze. Maybe I'd been seduced into a kind of drunkenness. I looked great. All five feet ten inches and 160 pounds of me. There wasn't a sharp edge or a hard line in sight. All was golden slopes and curves. When I flexed my arms and shoulders, well-defined muscle emerged. I was a goddamn Venus standing there. I tried the clothes on slowly, enjoying every butterfly kiss of silk. I drank the lemonade, dabbed my mouth with the cloth napkin, never once disturbed by Carol or anyone else. There wasn't an item that didn't look like a million bucks on me, so I had to get them all. When I emerged from the women's lounge Carol took everything up to the counter. I wandered through the bath section while she took another woman back with an armful of delight.

I picked out some wildflower bath salts to go with the candles and a clean, grassy-smelling after-bath lotion. A pumice stone, loofah sponge, and the absolute topper: a round pink container of scentless body powder with a satin-lined powder puff. It was fun having a body after all. By the time I stood at the cash register with credit card in hand, I was a sexual dynamo. I could've seduced anything: man, woman, or beast.

"You have lovely taste," said Carol, tucking satin straps delicately into tissue paper.

"Thank you," I said, no longer too busy for chitchat. A faint perfume rose from her hands as she sealed the tissue paper with a gold sticker embossed with "LC." Her name tag said "Carole." Carol with a senseless "E" on the end. I loved her. She filled two big bags with my loot, each one a pink and gold advertisement for Lorelei's Closet. She handed them over the counter to me. My hands, rough and sandpapery, accidentally brushed her fingers. She smiled. I pushed open the door and stepped into the sun's glare. Took two steps toward the Merc and ran smack into Carl. Caught with two bags from Lorelei's, I couldn't have been more horrified if we'd still been married. My face went red, white, and back to red again in the time it took for him to ask me what I was doing in Traverse City.

"Stacy," I said. My nose itched suddenly, but my hands were loaded down with the evidence of my rampant sexuality. "I visited Stacy I bought her some presents these are presents for Stacy because she's depressed you know she had to have twelve stitches and she's afraid she'll have to take hormones so she doesn't grow a mustache so I bought some presents to make her feel like a woman again." Oh God, what was I saying?

"Mary, this is Ann," he said. He turned to a woman standing next to him. "Ann, this is Mary. My former wife."

I shifted my packages to shake the hand that she held out to me, then immediately scratched my itching nose.

"I'm glad to meet you," she said. Short curly blond hair, pale pink lipstick, extremely good teeth. "I've heard a lot about you." This statement hung in the air between the three of us like a truly awful fart. I pulled myself together.

"And you," I said, "are a complete surprise." I looked directly into her eyes. Dark hazel. She didn't look away. In one more minute, I was going to lean over and kiss her hard on the mouth, just to see her run. She took a small step back and glanced at Carl, who'd been distracted, thinking of what to say.

"Ann works for the DNR," he offered.

"Hmm," I said.

"So Stacy had the baby," he tried again.

"Sunday."

"Yeah. Your mom called me." Meaning, You didn't. I waited, letting him dangle. "I'm sorry she had such a tough time," he continued.

Had I really said she might grow a mustache? I kept quiet, smiling first at him, then at Ann.

"Is this your first nephew?" she asked.

"Yes."

"You must be thrilled," she said.

"Hmm."

"Well, Ann needs to get back," Carl said. This was the cue for all of us to escape.

"What are *you* doing in Traverse City?" I asked, fingering John's pink plastic ring and turning the high beam on Carl. He looked at me the way he used to when I stole the deal in euchre.

"Work."

"Are you playing tonight?" I asked him.

"No. You?"

"Yeah," I said. "The Watering Hole."

"Battle of the bars, huh?" he said. Unlike Marion's, you didn't take your kids to The Watering Hole for a burger. "Good luck," he added, turning to leave.

"Thanks." I turned my attention to Ann but didn't say anything.

"Nice to have met you, Mary." She smiled sincerely.

"Thanks." I stepped back, swinging my bags back and forth, daring them to peek inside. "So long," I said.

I stayed like that for a while, watching them walk away. How many blocks would it take before either of them spoke? It occurred to me that if he hadn't left me for Amy, it would have been someone else eventually. It was a new thought, an unwelcome one. Finally I headed for the Merc. The sun was beating me over the head like a baseball bat. Heat bounced off the sidewalk. I unlocked the trunk, set the bags in gently. Checked my watch and put two more quarters in the meter. What the hell, I was on a roll now. I crossed the street, looked to see if there was anyone else I knew, and ducked into a nail salon a half block down. A girl in a black pageboy glanced up from her magazine and smiled.

"Hi," she said.

"I don't have an appointment," I answered.

"Aw, that's no problem," she beamed. "What can we do for you today?"

"Manicure."

"French, full, tips, or acrylic?" My mouth opened slightly, at a loss. The only thing that kept me in the shop was the column of smoke rising from an unseen ashtray on her left. I was fresh out.

"I don't know," I said boldly. "I've never had one before."

"Well, come on in, for God's sake." She turned toward the back. "Sandy," called the girl. "You free?"

"Can I have one of those?" I pointed to the Merits at her side.

"Oh sure." She handed me the flip-top box. "Gotta smoke it up here, though."

Sandy came out from behind a curtained area in back. Beckoned me over to her station with a minimal nod of her head. I obeyed, tucking the unlit smoke behind my ear. Sat down across from Sandy and repeated my situation. She was a cooler customer than the black-haired girl. Barely a flicker on her face when she suggested a basic manicure for my first time: condition, massage, clean, cuticle trim, shape, buff, and polish for fifteen dollars.

"Sounds good," I said, planting my hands on the table between us. There were two women having things done to them at other tables. I avoided looking at them, wondering if there was some unspoken protocol like in a men's urinal. Sandy reached for my left hand, picked it up, and stopped. She examined each nail as if it were contagious.

"Oh man," she said. "What'd you do to them?"

The gumball ring winked happily up at us. I had forgotten to take it off.

"Cheryl," said Sandy loudly, still gripping my hand. "Come look at this." No one spoke while the black-haired girl came back to have a look.

"Wow," said Cheryl. "I better get Elizabeth." She whispered to someone behind a curtain in back. Sandy and I continued to inspect the gashes and snaggles that made up my cuticles. Bits of yellow paint were still in evidence from Sunday, refusing to scrub off. Voices came at me from the curtain.

"I need Elizabeth."

"She's in the john."

"Tell her to come out quick, I got someone for her."

"I'm not dragging her off the toilet. She's on break."

"She'll be out in a second," Cheryl said breezily. "You're lucky you came to us." She joined in gazing at my hand as if it were a dead animal. I remembered Carole's scented fingertips brushing against mine. I would not apologize to these people. I would not back out. I was getting a manicure if I had to drag Elizabeth off the toilet myself.

A half hour later Elizabeth and I had formed a silent alliance. She didn't sigh or exclaim or ask for explanations. I didn't cry out or flinch in pain as she dug in with surgical tools. Her hands were strong and dry, no nonsense. I let go of the tension in my arms and let her bend and twist my fingers into whatever position she wished. The mini-massage had me heavy-lidded and syrupy. I liked a person who could give you a manicure, a haircut, or a Pap smear without yacking your head off.

"That's fifteen dollars," she said abruptly.

"Can I get some polish on them?" I asked.

"After you pay," she said with thin patience. I paid. "What color you want?"

I looked behind her to the racks of nail polish. Panic crept up my arms as I squinted at corals, frosts, and wines. "What do you suggest?" I countered.

"Clear," she answered, reaching back for the bottle.

When she was done my hands looked like someone else's. Maybe not slender and pearly, but great nonetheless. She finished the top coat and led me up front where the little heaters hummed busily. I sat where she told me and held my hands like she demonstrated, palms down under the blower.

"There you go," she said, and walked away. I immediately asked Cheryl for a light. There I sat, one hand under the heater and the other holding a cigarette. I crossed my legs and leaned back, alternating hands every few minutes.

"Look at that," Cheryl said, her smooth black helmet of hair bending over the table to admire the work. "Don't you feel amazing?" she asked.

"Yes."

"Just fifteen bucks, but it makes a new woman of you."

12

I spent the rest of the afternoon in the tub, playing with my new girlie toys and blowing bubbles for Frank to chase across the bathroom floor. A can of Stroh's sat on the toilet seat within easy reach. Amy's old pickle jar lid sat beside it. Every few minutes I'd admire how nice my nails looked as I struck a match or took the pumice to my elbow. The pink gumball ring glistened on my finger, right at home in the iridescent foam. Soaking, sipping, smoking, and singing to myself, why had I never done this before? This was Tuesday. I had four days before that damned trial started, before I had to talk in front of all those people. Four days that stretched out luxuriously, endlessly. Friday was a million years away. Friday was nothing I had to think about.

"Your hand's shaking."

"My stomach's in a knot and my mouth is all dry too."

The thought of him no longer caused sparks to ignite, rather a languid melting of my intestines. The phone rang twice. I ignored it. Figured the first call was Sharon about my blue ribbon, and the second Carl to say God knows what. John would be up at Everett Park that night; I didn't want anything or anyone to intrude into the space between now and then. "Wildflowers" burned evenly on the corner of the sink, the little flame making the forget-me-nots dance. When I got out of the tub, the beer and cigarettes had given me a sweet little buzz, just enough to form an optimistic outlook. I patted myself dry with a thick guest towel, a housewarming gift from Carl's mother when I'd moved into the cottage. These were huge, wastefully sumptuous towels that I never used for myself, let alone nonexistent guests. I opened the seal on the lotion and tested a bit on my hands to see how strong it was. Wet grass hinted around my nose. I spread it on my arms, shoulders, breasts, and neck. The coolness penetrated my pores, made every inch of my skin breathe deeply. I squeezed out another palmful and dabbed delicious bits onto my stomach, thighs, hips, and legs. Smoothed it in gently as if it were a service I was performing for someone I loved. I sat on the edge of the tub and slathered my feet. If they'd had tear ducts, they would have wept in gratitude.

I lit another smoke, grabbed another beer, and carried it into the bedroom. Before I got dressed I dusted myself here and there with the scentless powder, again taking a precautionary sniff beforehand. Pouf-poufing away and humming "I Enjoy Being a Girl." It had been our theme song when Amy and I formed the Girliest Girl Club our freshman year. For one week we wore dresses and makeup and combed our hair religiously. We giggled and bent our heads down in order to look up through our lashes at the boys who, for that one week, fell all over us. We'd come home each day and compare notes in her bedroom, laughing, scornful at how they opened doors for us and blushed purple when we leaned our heads toward them. Ted Hearling offered to carry Amy's books.

"Are you kidding?" I snorted. "He carried your *books* for you?"

At the end of the week we went back to painter pants, baseball shirts, and anonymity, the experiment over. But the following fall she pretended to need help lifting a full garbage bag when our class was building the homecoming float. Jimmy Heath, the guy I was secretly going wild over, came to her rescue. Before the night was over she was his date for the homecoming dance. After a while it was only when we were alone that Amy was her old self, laughing at eyelash curlers and lip gloss, racing to see who could run around Everett Park the fastest, collecting rocks out of the Kassauga River. When I told her to knock off the glamour she said, "I'm not like you. You never care if anyone asks you out." I was about to argue, but the note of admiration in her voice kept me quiet.

Now I had to laugh at how proud she'd be of me, the Girliest Girl of them all. I finished with the powder and carefully closed the lid. Frank sat on the corner of the dresser, fascinated. By now my skin had lost a layer of armor and was vulnerable to every stray touch. Just opening the tissue paper on the lingerie was an intense kind of foreplay. At that point John had nearly become superfluous. I slipped on a pair of cotton panties and matching bra in watered lilac. When it came to underwear, sexy or not, anything other than cotton made me sweat and itch. I looked in the mirror over the dresser, afraid that what had looked good in Lorelei's Closet would lose all its magic in my bedroom. I looked terrific. I pulled on my socks, also one hundred percent cotton. Then stretch pants and my Marion's Bar & Grill T-shirt. Walked out to the kitchen and back again a few times, feeling the thrill of the new under the familiar of the old, the two selves sliding against one another, not quite in sync. I tidied up the place, changed the sheets and the cat litter. Loaded up the Bicentennial bag with a bottle of tap water, my mitt, wallet, and visor. Checked for my Carmex, put some on for good measure. I was as ready for romance as a woman in cotton panties could be. Grabbed my Kools, kissed Frank between the ears and headed for the ballpark and John.

The game was a rout, the Watering Hole going down easily. I hit a two-run homer in the sixth to quiet any questions as to whether or not I still had the goods. All the way around the bases I thought about a pair of bottomless blue eyes at the top of the bleachers, following me from base to base. He'd arrived in the bottom of the third inning. My thighs were so warm by the time I crossed home plate, I wondered how I'd make it through the rest of the game. Sizemor Septic wasn't playing that night, which meant no Carl and no Amy, a little breathing space once we got to Marion's. It also meant John had come for no other reason than to see me. After the game I gave him an offhand wave on my way to the Merc. "See you up there," I said, as if he were Sharon, or Peg Monroe.

The jukebox sang about sex, sex, and nothing but sex from the moment I walked in the bar. When John arrived a few minutes after me I fled into the bathroom. I stood in there for a long time, surrounded by plywood paneling and Glade air freshener. I looked in the mirror at the coarse wavy hair, at the strong neck, the funny chin. I met my eyes. Loretta paced up and down, her arms wrapped around herself. Out in the bar the jukebox launched into "Prove It All Night." Hadn't thought about that song in years. Amy and I had paid a scalper $200 for tickets when Springsteen came to Detroit in our junior year. Told our moms we were staying over at the other one's house. Drove Amy's Pinto wagon all the way to Detroit, listening to Springsteen cassettes the entire five-hour trip. Back then I was suffocating in Riverton with no dates and a body on fire. Back then I wouldn't have hidden in the bathroom when trouble walked in the door; I'd have jumped to my feet and bought trouble a beer. I left the bathroom. Spotted John standing at the end of the bar talking with someone I didn't know. I came up behind him, rested one arm carelessly around his shoulders (Touching him! Touching him!) and said, "What're you having, John?"

"Whiskey and water," he answered, turning from his buddy with a smile that would have sent me through the back wall. But Loretta slapped a twenty on the bar without missing a beat and told Marion what I wanted. We put them away until my twenty, and then his, was gone. I don't remember a word of what was said. Then we carried our drinks back to the pool table. The place was half empty, most folks still watching the men's league. I only recognized a few faces. When did a pool table grow to look so much like a bed? Since when was chalking the stick so full of friction? He racked the balls like a pro while I watched, leaning against the wall. When he broke, it was hard and quick. The warmth in my thighs kindled again as balls flew in all directions. We were evenly matched. I was stronger on the long straight shots, but he could bank anything into a pocket. Each time we passed near one another, flames burst in midair that no one could see but us. The stick was sliding smoothly in my hand, the jukebox kept playing Springsteen, the balls dropped in like I was guiding them with a magnet. I felt his eyes on me, felt the Johnny Walker running through my veins and the cigarette smoldering at the corner of my mouth. He leaned over for a shot. My eyes ate up his bare forearms, the exquisite shoulders working under his T-shirt. He was lining up the eight ball, concentration giving his face a hard, unapproachable look. I leaned over the table, close up next to him. With our backs to everyone else in the bar, I placed one hand over his on the pool stick.

"Hey," I whispered. "Let's go."

The eight ball stayed where it was, the pool stick beside it, as we crossed the parking lot. "Let's take your car," he said.

I unlocked the passenger door like it was Pandora's box. We drove through the hot August night with nothing but disbelieving smiles for company. He lit us a couple of cigarettes. I hit the gas pedal harder. Tomford Road fell beneath the Merc like a lover. I pulled deep into the driveway, back around the side of the cottage. We sat in the silence, no one around but him and me and a couple of gray moths waltzing outside the windshield. His hand moved for the door handle. I reached for him, caught a handful of his T-shirt. My knuckles brushed the warm skin of his neck. The feel of him knocked apart something inside me. Here was another human being beside me, getting too close. I wanted to push him away, punish him, tear him to pieces. I couldn't have stopped what came next if a fleet of cops had hit the Merc with floodlights.

I slid toward him from behind the wheel. My mouth was on his, easing it open. My tongue tasted the warm wetness of his. My fist yanked and tore until his T-shirt gave with a loud rip.

Then my hands were all over his bare chest, the hard stomach that disappeared into his jeans. I tugged and fumbled at those as well, until they opened as sweetly as his mouth had. His dick leaned insistently into my hand, warm and welcoming. My fingers closed around it tightly as my teeth closed on his shoulder. He tasted hot and salty and sweet. I was over him now, pushing him down on his back, his legs sliding across the front seat. I pulled his jeans down to his knees, too impatient to bother with them further. His fingers were all over me. I plowed one hand into his hair and bent his head back as I tasted his neck, his ears, his chest, each goddamn beautiful shoulder. It took six lifetimes to get one leg of my stretch pants all the way off. He was nearly naked beneath me. The blood under his skin gave off an animal heat, an animal smell. I got the Marion's Bar & Grill T-shirt over my head. He pulled the bra off as if it were tissue paper. Then I pinned his wrists over his head and plunged my tongue deep, bruising his mouth. I eased myself slowly onto him, guiding his dick carefully at first with my free hand, then lowering myself hard when I felt his hips jut up toward me. Once my cunt closed around the length of him, all the emptiness that had lived there for years engulfed me. My throat thickened with loneliness. Goddamn him for making me feel this. I thrust myself onto him, vicious, my pubic bone bruising his. I hated him for not showing up sooner.

"I'm going to fuck you until you're blind," I hissed at him in the dark. There was no answer but the movement of his hips heaving up underneath me. The fullness was too sweet, I couldn't contain it. I let go of his wrists and sent a punch into the tender part of his shoulder. Another blow landed on the side of his head. Still we bucked and jerked as he grew harder inside me. He grabbed my breast and squeezed until his fingernails broke the skin. His other hand reached up and found my throat. My back arched, my clitoris burned. I gripped his wrists hard enough to crack the bone. He stayed with me while every molecule turned inward. I heard his voice, then my cunt swelled and pulsed, and a wave of icy heat turned me inside out.

"You're coming," he whispered. I nodded, grinding myself into him. His hand closed around my throat as he moved me up and down faster. The air grew thick and tingly. I couldn't breathe. Oh yes, oblivion. He shouted and pulled me down toward him as he came, the last few strokes splitting me clear to the top of my head. We lay like that until we got our breath back. My left leg was falling asleep, wedged under the dash. I shifted one arm and smacked my elbow on the metal edge of a seat-belt buckle. "Ow," I said softly.

We unfolded ourselves from the Merc, leaving half our clothes inside, and headed straight for the bedroom. The hair on his legs was surprisingly soft and silky as it ran up to his stomach and chest. His pubic hair wasn't springy and coarse, but curled shyly around my fingers in warm, feathery swirls. Before long the emptiness inside rose around me once more, choking me with loneliness, and we tore into each other again with the same raw ferocity. The clock by the bed claimed that it wasn't yet midnight, but years had been redeemed. Sweat-slick and turned inside out, we took a shower together. He tenderly dried me off with the guest towel. In the bedroom we stretched across the bed and pouf-poufed each other with the scentless powder puff. We lay there quietly, kissing the bruises we'd given each other. Finally we slid together into a dozy silence. His fingers stroked the hair off my forehead, over and over, until he fell asleep.

I lay there in the moonshadowy light. An empty beer can stood where I'd left it on the dresser earlier that afternoon. The bookshelves across the room blinked gold-embossed titles from their spines. I imagined my watered-lilac bra and panties strewn somewhere in the Merc. Joy ran like a small wild thing through my veins. A dim light still glowed from the kitchen. The radio was on low in the living room. In the liquid stillness, not a cricket whispering, I could make out the song "Black Coffee in Bed." The music was tiny, far away. Tonight there would be no visions of Jen Colby lying motionless in a makeshift nest, no Night Visitor to crush me. Tonight was never going to end.

Time sat down on her haunches and I stayed awake to enjoy the elastic moment. Just me and that old song, rolling along in a standing-still universe. John was beside me, plunged deep in sleep where too much pleasure will send you. I was as far away from him in this time bubble as I'd been close just minutes before. Gravity drained out of me. I rose up off the sheets, still flat on my back. Drifted over John on the bed, past Frank curled up in a gold ball near the dresser, and floated out the window. The night breeze lifted me up and I hung suspended and porous. There I was, cut loose from the string of time and free to swing sideways as wide as I liked. One last look at John—the slight knobbiness where his spine ran like a serpent beneath the skin—and I let the wind nudge me up and away from the cottage. The blanket of pines rolled wild and black beneath me. I wasn't more than fifty feet above their ragged tips, yet the moon and the mountainous clouds felt just an arm's length away. I could see the security lights outside the Millers' house up the road, the headlights of a single logging truck flying down Route 108. The light from the moon had an X-ray clarity. Beneath the surface of the trees, star-nosed moles and possums curled, dreaming of the leaves soon to descend. Beneath the ground, grubs and nightcrawlers hummed an untroubled tune all down the length of their bodies. I drifted farther up. I had escaped. I was air. I was nothing but a wish fulfilled.

▪   ▪   ▪

When I opened my eyes the next morning, I was in my bed and John was still there. In the cold white light of day he looked very married. His face revealed all the details that a wife would have memorized years ago. The shadow of a beard broke through the skin. Small, tender wrinkles ventured out from the corner of his eye. A tiny L-shaped scar sat at the bridge of his nose. I lay still. Once he awoke I would have to contend with him. What we did last night, all that energy, all that sex, it didn't seem to have any-thing to do with the face lying beside me now. Now he looked like Julianna's father. If he wanted to make love again right away, there would be trouble. Or maybe he'd wake up with a strained smile, minimal eye contact, a quick retreat. Except there would be no graceful flight; his car was still parked behind Marion's Bar. He was naked in my house with no way to escape. Don't let him wake up.

Outside the open window the mourning doves were sounding doom across the day. With all the noise I could no longer make out the radio in the living room. The daylight was unusually bright and colorless. Someone had replaced the sun with a big fluorescent bulb. Frank jumped on the bed and walked across the back of John's legs. He stirred. Panicking, I considered faking sleep. Give him a chance to dress, sneak out the back door, and walk into town. He opened the eye that wasn't smashed into my pillow and used it to look at me for a moment. He took in the bruises that had risen on my shoulders and breasts. He looked at me looking back at him.

"You're still here," he said.

His eyes filled. I reached up to touch him as they spilled over. In another moment I had both arms around him, holding on while he cried into my neck. I stroked his back, his arm, his hair, without saying a word. That quickly, that simply, the John of last night and the man beside me were one and the same. He made me French toast for breakfast while I sat at the table with a cup of coffee and a cigarette. In one of the shorter satin nightgowns from Lorelei's, I felt like Bonnie Parker. He'd slipped on his jeans, but that was all. Every time I looked up and saw his bare back at the stove, Friday's witness stand slid farther and farther away.

"You like 'em soft or crispy?" he asked.

"Soft."

He looked over his shoulder at me, as if to make sure I hadn't disappeared. Frank twined between his bare feet, rubbing and purring. I sympathized.

"My favorite color is blue," he told me, sliding half the French toast onto a plate. "What's yours?"

"Green," I answered. Actually it was pink, but I was too embarrassed to admit it. "Pink."

He turned around again and smiled at me, at the gumball ring I still wore, and said, "See, that's why you're wonderful." He brought my plate to me. "Soft," he said.

I put out the cigarette and refilled our coffee cups while he overcooked his toast. I thought about last Sunday when I'd asked him if they weren't expecting him at home and the odd look on his face when he said, "Not especially." What sort of breakfast were Julianna and her mother having right now?

"What are your plans today?" he asked.

"Mope around and think about you," I said.

He brought his plate over and joined me. Frank jumped onto the table and positioned himself as the third point of the triangle. He sat up straight with his ears forward, tail curled politely around his front legs, just there for the conversation.

"What are you doing today?" I asked.

"Thought I'd sit around here and watch you mope."

"Don't you have a job to go to?"

"Wednesday's my day off. I work weekends." He stopped chewing and looked embarrassed. "Unless you have something else to do."

"No," I said. "Nothing."

I took two small chunks of toast from my plate and slid them over toward Frank who sniffed twice, twitched his tail, and ate. John added a piece from his own plate.

"Do you like fishing?" he asked.

When breakfast was over, we loaded the Merc with my tackle box and two poles. Drove into town so he could pick up his car and meet me at the marina. Marion let me use her boat with the little 9.9 horsepower motor whenever I wanted, so long as I called ahead. I stopped at the bait shop on the way to pick up some fresh nightcrawlers and a carton of crickets. The black cowbell clonged once as the screen door slapped shut behind me. Carl was busy arguing with some guy about issuing

another bear-permit application. I nodded hello, helped myself
to an empty carton, and headed for the cricket tank behind the
counter. I remembered running into Carl yesterday in Traverse
City; it seemed like a long time ago. I grabbed the cricket net
and set to work filling the carton, both arms reaching deep behind the wire mesh. Nothing made a bluegill hungrier than a little brown cricket trying to kick his way off a hook.

"Look, it's gone. I don't know where it is," the guy up front
said. "That's why I need you to reissue it."

"You're six weeks past the deadline," Carl said. "I can't do it."

"I've been getting my applications here since Stu Culpepper
opened the place," the man said, shaking his head. He looked
around the walls of the shop and sighed morosely. His gaze
traveled to the dusty trophy trout mounted, frowning wildly,
above the door. "It's a shame," he murmured.

I glanced up front at Carl, who was smiling. "Well, I feel for
you, Jerry," he said. "I really do."

"Yeah," Jerry responded absently. He continued to look
around the shop, eyebrows furrowed pathetically as if each rod
and reel, every minnow bucket, brought a fresh pang of melan-
choly. "Stu never stood on ceremony."

"Nope," Carl agreed. "He sure didn't."

I used to go with Dad to open the shop in the early morning.
He'd pull the truck around back behind the minnow tanks. I'd
plunge my arm in, trying to catch one. I was barely tall enough
to stand on tiptoe and reach my arm in to the elbow, sweater
sleeve pulled up, fingers spread wide, moving my hand back
and forth. I could feel the minnows! I could see their silvery
backs darting left, right, left in the dark water.

"C'mon," Dad said. "Git your arm out of there."

I pulled it out. Cold air hit the wet skin. I yanked my sweater sleeve down.

"Hold this," he said, handing over the bag from Howard's Bakery and unlocking the back door. "Lucky those aren't piranhas in there. Strip all the meat off your bones in ten seconds."

"What's a piranha?" Sugar smell rose from the bakery bag in my hand.

"Man-eating fish, only this big." He held up his thumb. "Big jaws with long teeth like needles. Go out in a canoe in the jungle, a guy lets his hand dangle in the river, all of a sudden the water looks like it's boiling where his arm is."

He was turning on lights as he talked, opening window shades, unlocking the front door with the black cowbell attached at the top.

"Bubbling and foaming from the feeding frenzy," he continued. "Never felt a thing, it happened so fast. He pulls out his hand, but there's nothing there. Just a bloody, ragged stump of an arm. Died of shock and loss of blood. Happens all the time." He punched the button on the old cash register to cap off the story. The drawer popped open. He pulled the blue plastic money pouch out of his jacket and laid bills carefully in the drawer. Singles, fives, tens, a couple of twenties.

"One of these days," he told me, "they'll accidentally ship a piranha in with a batch of minnows, and then we'll be calling you Stumpy."

"That can't happen," I said, biting into a jelly doughnut.

"Happens all the time."

These are things he told me: If you turn off the lights, look in the mirror, and count backward from ten, you'll see the ghost of George Washington. Amy and I never made it past four-three-two. If you shit in the woods, a squirrel will run up your leg and wipe your ass with its tail. If you put your tongue on a frozen metal fence, it'll stick there. (That one turned out to be true.) One day ice fishing he told me that the only way to thaw out frozen waxworms was to put them in your mouth for a few minutes before you stuck them on the hook. So I did, which had the crowd up to the Shoreline Pub falling off their bar stools when they heard. A waxworm is a glorified maggot.

I folded down the lid of the cricket carton and set it on the counter by the ancient cash register.

"You got any nightcrawlers today?" I asked Carl. He and Jerry both turned toward me, intent on their stalemate.

"What?"

"Nightcrawlers," I repeated.

"You going out today?" He had a proprietary tone, as if I were sixteen years old and running wild all over town. There followed a suspenseful moment in which Carl looked at Jerry.

"Don't mind me," Jerry said with his hands in his pockets. "I'm not going anywhere." He poked through a rack of orange vests, looking for a new angle. Carl and I went back to the coolers, where he took out a large plastic bucket. I wanted to get back to John. I felt bereft without him, exposed to the real world and its real perils.

Jerry's voice traveled from the front of the shop. "You got to be kidding, $18.99!" he said. "They got these at Kmart for $14.50, you know that, Carl?"

"Maybe they got an extra bear license too," Carl yelled back. Jerry laughed. Carl reached into the bucket and loaded a few handfuls of wriggling dirt into a cup.

"Don't mention Ann to Amy," he said, looking into the cooler as if one of the two were lurking within. John was three doors down at the Gas 'n Go, pulling a package of Slim Jims off the rack or balancing an eight-pack of Pepsi under one arm. I missed him with a queasy longing, like homesickness. Carl said, "You won't, will you?"

"What's going on?" I asked. He wouldn't look at me. Familiar flakes of dandruff nestled around his ear. Without thinking, I reached up and lightly brushed them off.

"Nothing," he said to the cooler door. "Just that Amy over-reacts to stuff. You know."

"Only lately."

Carl handed me my worms. We walked back up to the front counter where Jerry was tossing a 59¢ bobber in one hand. "Cracked," he said, flipping it to Carl.

I paid and went out the back way, running my hand through the minnow tank. A delicious terror ran from my fingertips up the length of my arm. It could be happening right that second, and I wouldn't know because you don't feel a thing. I kept my arm in as long as I could stand it. Pulled out a whitish-blue hand aching from the cold water, full of relief and triumph. I heard Jerry through the door—". . . hate to take my business over to McBain . . ."—and Carl's faint laughter. The soggy clouds drooped so low they reflected on the glossy hood of the Merc. A perfect day to fish. Seeing him when I pulled into the marina was like sighting land after a year at sea. I pulled along-side his Cutlass and got out. He leaned against the car with his arms crossed.

"I thought for a minute that you'd changed your mind," he said.

"Decided to mope around at home after all?"

"That, and everything else. I thought you'd never get here."

I caught seven bluegill and John reeled in a walleye so big we thought at first he'd snagged on some weeds under water. A drizzle had set in. John was wearing his jeans, an old T-shirt of mine, and a yellow rain poncho, also mine. I had the hood up on my pullover, over my visor. The two of us were huddled side by side with legs touching, poles arching over either side of the boat. Our voices were muffled by a velvety fog that hid the shore in all directions. The water lay flat and mud-colored around the boat. Somewhere a fish jumped with a lonely swoosh and plop.

We fished away the rest of the morning, eating Little Debbies and Fritos, washing them down with Pepsi. John hooked a few perch. Soon it would be time to go back. Already the spell was fading. Questions popped to the surface of the water, small air bubbles of anxiety. When would I see him again? I swatted a mosquito hard enough to make a small explosion of blood across my knee. I rubbed at it furiously, as if it held all the neediness that was roiling up inside me. No fair being offered a few hours of sweet oblivion, then having to go back to a dead six-year-old haunting me as if I were the one who had killed her. What was wrong with me? When would I see him again? I reached for a cricket and jammed it, kicking frantically, onto my hook. That line of thinking led to a whole lot of misery. I cast the rod in a smooth arc, let out some more line, settled in to wait for one more bite.

"What's wrong?" he asked.

"You still married?"

He looked down at his feet as if checking to see whether he was or not. "Yeah."

"You going to stay married?"

"Yeah."

"Why don't you wear a ring?"

"The equipment I work with," he answered. "It could get caught, rip my finger off."

For lunch, I fried up the bluegills while John and Frank rolled a little ball of tinfoil across the kitchen floor. We ate until we were dazed, then made love again. After he was gone, I looked at myself in the mirror over the dresser. Bruises covered my chest and shoulders, crying out with silent alarm. When my mouth and hands had turned vicious, he'd welcomed it, answered with more. Maybe he was fighting off a ghost of his own. There was no harm in this. I wasn't hurting anyone except myself. In the shower, darts of guilt stung me with each drop of water. I dressed as quickly as I could, and got out of there.

13

Stacy's room at Munson Medical was full of visitors. Turd Ball was off the ventilator and looking sturdier by the hour, so folks weren't afraid to come visit. Stacy sat propped up in bed like Marie Antoinette.

"How're you holding up?" I asked Ruther, having forgiven him and his killer dick.

"I'm great," he said. He looked like hell, like maybe he needed a hospital bed of his own. "It's just great, isn't it? I mean, it's just so great."

During a lull in the visitors, when Ruther was walking some friends out to their car, Stacy said, "What's with you today?"

"Why?"

"I don't know. You're all glowy."

"Glowy?"

"Yeah," she said. I twisted the plastic ring on my pinky

and got glowier. Stacy's eyes narrowed. "You've had sex," she announced.

I was too surprised to deny it. "How do you know?"

"I can always tell. It's a thing I have."

"No shit?"

"Ruther better never cheat on me."

"He looks like hell," I told her.

"Don't change the subject," she said. I fell silent. "Who is it?"

"No one."

"Oh come on, give me a break. Who is it?" She was scootching up against the pillow, her fatigue forgotten.

"No one. And don't go blabbing to Mom or Sharon either."

She looked offended. "Do I tell you every time Sharon has sex?"

"Okay, when's the last time?"

"Monday," Stacy stated with conviction.

"Monday?" I said. "This past Monday? Two days ago?"

"She was here yesterday afternoon, after you left."

"I saw her in the morning. She didn't look any different."

"Not to you, maybe," Stacy said primly. Sharon, yesterday morning up at the fairgrounds cool as could be, grilling me about my ring and my imaginary boyfriend. Jesus, that girl was something else.

"I didn't know she was seeing anyone," I said lamely.

Stacy erupted in laughter. "Seeing anyone?" she said. "God, you sound like Mom."

I sat there unable to discern what was so goddamn funny. Wished Ruther would return. "What?"

"She's not *seeing anyone*. Please. She had sex, that's all. God, you are too much."

This was not a generational thing. There was only seven years difference between us. The truth is, I was mortified at the thought of Sharon sleeping with just any guy. My little glow became a burning scourge.

"You're such a prig, you know that?" Her laughter was meant to take the edge off her words. It didn't.

"Who are these from?" I asked, suddenly admiring a bouquet of chrysanthemums on the windowsill. Stacy remained silent for a moment, agonizing whether to continue torturing me or brag about her many admirers.

"They're from you and Mom and Sharon," she said. "And the baby's much better, thanks for asking."

"Okay," I said. "I'm an asshole. Sorry."

"I guess you're just preoccupied, having all that sex," she shot at me.

"You're jealous because you've been a disgusting pregnant cow all summer that Ruther wouldn't fuck if you paid him."

Silence pooled around us. Oh, where did that come from? Stacy's mouth opened slightly. No words came out.

"I'm sorry," I said. "I didn't mean it."

"I think you did," she replied. "It's been written all over your face for months."

"Don't give me that. I threw you a damned baby shower, didn't I?" Stop now. Shut up.

"You need to pull your head out of your ass and see that there are some things that are a *really big deal.*"

"I don't happen to think sanctimonious motherhood is one of them." Jesus, why was I doing this?

"You have no idea what you're talking about," Stacy said, near tears. "You've never been pregnant. You've never—"

"Yes," I interrupted her. "I have."

I kept my eyes on my thumbnail. There was already a tiny chip in the clear polish. How did we get here? Where had this come from?

"I'm sorry," Stacy said simply.

"Forget it," I replied. "It was a long time ago." Fifteen years. The Shrimp would be three years older than Julianna.

"Was it— Did you— God, I'm sorry." Stacy was stricken. How could I have dumped this load of shit on her?

"Mom and Sharon don't know."

"Why?" she asked.

"Why what?" I answered stupidly.

"Why didn't you have it?"

"What kind of horrible mother would I make?"

"Just because Mom and Dad did such a crappy job, doesn't mean you would." Stacy was suddenly angry. "You can bet Ruther and I are gonna do a hell of a better job than that."

"What are you talking about?" I frowned. "What was wrong with Mom and Dad?"

"You're kidding, right?" Stacy was laughing again. It was ugly.

"We were a great family," I said. "Mom and Dad were great."

"Mary, all they did was fight."

"So?" I was talking too loudly. "Every family fights."

"Dad was a drunk. He was never home."

"That doesn't mean he wasn't a great dad." The words sounded ludicrous, even to me. "You're making it sound—"

"Mom was always gone—"

"—like there was something wrong—"

"—out looking for him. Hell, you raised us."

"I did *not*." I wanted to punch her.

"Ask Sharon." Stacy was looking at me oddly. "Where've you been, living in a cave all these years?"

I stood up. This was unfair, and I wasn't going to listen to any more of it.

"Look, Stace . . ." I didn't know what to say. "I'm sorry about the pregnant cow crack. It was a shitty thing to say."

"Am I sanctimonious?" she asked, forehead puckered.

"Yes," I said lightly, heading for the door.

"If you see Ruther out there, send him in."

At the door I looked back. I wanted to shake her, demand that she take back everything she'd said. Her eyes were closed, resting. *Why didn't you have it?* No answer came, just a blank space where my thoughts had been.

I stopped to buy a *Riverton Gazette* on the way home. Picked up a twelve-pack while I was at it, thinking maybe I'd call Amy and see if she felt like company. There was no answer at their place, so I kicked back in my armchair and checked on the tournament standings. The *Gazette* came out each Wednesday. Big coverage that week of the Kassauga County Fair, the Labor Day Festival, the softball finals. All summer long the town geared itself up for the grand three-day weekend over Labor Day. Other towns could boast "The Greatest Fourth in the North," but everyone came to Riverton at summer's end. Afterward, it returned to a ghost town until the following June.

An editorial snagged my eye. Usually it was just carping and bitching about the zoning laws or the Water Treatment Commission. But the headline said, DO-GOODERS MAKE OUTRAGE OUT OF TRAGEDY. The piece went on to claim that Patricia Colby was being martyred to assuage public outrage over several spectacular cases of child abuse that had come out of Detroit in the past year.

"This is not an inner-city welfare mother with drug-crazed boyfriends parading in and out of her apartment. This is a respectable woman being fed to the sharks to help the career of a militant liberal lawyer." It was unsigned. It could have come from anyone: Peg Monroe, Harold Tucker, Marion. My stomach tilted inside me.

"Hey," said a voice from the front porch. "Who do you gotta blow to get some iced tea around here?"

I tucked the paper away and went to the door. Julianna sat on Eleanor Prudhomme, scowling and breathing hard.

"I suppose you heard that from Uncle Ted too."

She nodded. Sweat dampened her tank top. Her fishing hat was jammed in the pocket of her shorts. She sat with both feet on the pedals, balancing herself with one hand on the porch railing.

"Where you headed?" I asked.

"I got six more miles to hit the Gulf of Bothia," she said, wiping away the sweat around her eyes and looking at the odometer. "Then I can quit for the day."

"Come on, I'll get you a drink."

She parked Eleanor carefully along the side of the cottage, and a half hour later we were playing Yahtzee at the kitchen table. Frank meowed to go out. I opened the back door and he raced across the back porch toward the woodpile, chasing God knows what. Soon it would be time to start supper, but the humidity had me lazy. Julianna was distracted, quiet. Usually she was full of trash talk during Yahtzee, a sore loser and an insufferable winner. Now she got a large straight on her first roll with no comment.

"What's up?"

"I'm thinking I might stay in Canada," she said, pulling her hat out of her pocket and jamming it low on her head.

"Not come back at all?" I asked, shaking the dice onto the table with a clatter. Two sixes.

"I don't like it here," she scowled. "This town sucks."

It didn't sound like Julianna. A small shadow crept over the table. There were a million things that could be bothering her, but I didn't ask. I rolled again. Full house.

"Goofy ring," she said, nodding at my pinky finger. "Where'd you get it?"

"Gumball machine."

A low animal noise came through the back door. What was Frank into? He'd killed two baby possum this summer. Or he was chasing a garter snake through the grass. It was a low warning growl that prickled my skin, coming from near the woodpile. I stood up from the table. The growl exploded into shrieks and hisses. Through the door I saw a flash of gold and brown, Frank. And there was something bigger and darker. I shouted, but the dog was too big to get scared off by noise. The goddamn miserable beast had Frank's shoulders in its jaws, whipping its head back and forth. I ran into the bedroom, fell on my knees, and reached under the bed for the Remington. Julianna stood in the doorway behind me.

"Stay in here," I told her as I yanked the gun toward me. I was up on my feet and running through the kitchen, smacking my leg on the corner of the table as I went. A chair scraped across the floor; the screen door flew open. I undid the safety with one hand and pumped the barrel with the other. Came off the steps and shot once in the air to scare him. He dropped Frank and ran toward the woods. I pumped again, aimed a little ahead of him, and pulled the trigger. A wooden fist slammed into my shoulder. His hindquarters sank. He staggered a few more steps, then fell. I ran toward him.

I could hear Dad now, *Never run with a gun in your hand.* I stopped a few feet from the dog. It was a German shepherd–Lab mix, half-starved and lying there full of buckshot, but still alive. I stepped back, pumped again, and fired at his head. Then I went to find Frank.

"Mary?" Julianna's voice came from the back porch.

"Stay there," I yelled over my shoulder.

Frank lay in the grass not moving. I carefully touched his front paw. He hissed and spat but didn't move. His neck was opened up from his ear to his chest.

"Frank, Frank, it's okay. Mama's here." I kept my voice light, playful, my "time for supper" voice. Julianna appeared beside me as I knelt over him. I hadn't heard her approach. She looked at Frank bleeding on the ground.

"Go in the bathroom and bring me some towels, quick."

She ran across the yard, her hat flying off onto the grass. I waited until she was in the house before I reached out a hand slowly and rested my fingers on the side of his face. He growled and lay still. I stroked him, murmuring softly, but he was in a world of his own.

"Here Frank." Voice light and sweet. "That's my Mister Frufru. Mama's right here."

How bad was it? Could I get him to a vet, or would it be more merciful to use another shell right now? I imagined what the buckshot would do to him. I would sooner ram the barrel into my own mouth. The screen door slammed. I flicked the safety back on the Remington and leaned it carefully against the trunk of the pear tree, talking quietly to Frank all the while. Met Julianna halfway across the yard and took the towels from her.

"Is he dead?" she asked.

"No," I told her. "Go on back in the house." I didn't want her to see what was left of the dog.

"I don't want to be in there by myself," Julianna said. She looked at me with her yellow eyes wide. Behind her, the cottage became someplace where I wouldn't want to be alone either.

"Sit with him and talk to him," I told her. "But don't touch him."

I hurried to the shed to grab my gardening gloves and an empty burlap feed sack. He used one leg to claw and fight as I wrapped the towels carefully around him, scratching me through the gloves until I had the feed sack wrapped around the towels. Julianna knelt next to me on the grass. Her voice was shaky but she kept up a steady refrain of "Hey Frank, hey Frank," to calm him.

"Quick." I lifted the bundle and held it tight to my chest. "Run and get my wallet and my keys off the counter."

Stacy had given Frank to me as a going-away present when I first moved into the place on Second Street. She'd been only twelve years old, and bought him from a couple of kids selling a box full of kittens in front of Kmart. She thought I'd get lonely in a house all by myself. Frank came with me when I married Carl, came with me when I left there to settle in at the cottage; my cheap old Kmart parking-lot cat.

Julianna held Frank in the backseat while I drove too fast to the animal hospital clear over in Cadillac. She held him tight so he couldn't move at all, stroking softly between the ears where his face peeped through the towels. Blood soaked through the feed sack, onto her hands and shirt. Turning onto 55, he kicked and fought with his good leg, but she kept him pinned. When I glanced in the rearview mirror I saw a large smear of blood on her temple where she had brushed the hair out of her eyes.

"Wipe it off," I said.

"What?" She looked up from Frank to me, confused.

"You got blood on your face," I told her in a harsh voice. "Goddamn it, wipe it off."

Julianna rubbed the side of her face into her shoulder as best she could, making it worse. I kept my eyes on the road, unable to bear the sight in the backseat. Fought to keep the wheel steady as we flew into the city limits.

"His eyes are closed," she said, trying not to cry.

"Almost there."

Two hours later I stepped outside the lobby and bummed a cigarette from an attendant on break. Julianna had phoned her mother to tell her where she was. Mercifully, Doreen said okay without asking to speak with me. I had handed over the number of my regular veterinarian in Riverton, along with my credit card, and told them to do whatever they had to do. It was an animal hospital, the emergency clinic, so there was a steady flow of panicking people bearing pet carriers or, worse, clumsy makeshift bundles like Frank's. I longed for the quiet of my vet's waiting room, the routine check-ups, the Toothy Treats handed out. I went back inside, where Julianna and I distracted ourselves playing hangman with a pencil and paper copped from the front desk.

At 7:15 a short young man in scrubs invited us into a separate anteroom. Oh God, the bad news room. Julianna stuck to me like a burr. Frank was alive. Loss of blood, severed muscle, nerve damage, shock. Wait and see. Best to go home.

"Can I see him?"

He smiled with a gentleness rare in doctors. "Frankly, I don't—"

"No pun intended," I said.

"I'm sorry?"

"Frankly," I said. "His name is Frank."

The man smiled again. Probably used to erratic behavior by now.

"I don't think it would be good for morale to see him right now." Which raised images I could have lived without. He glanced at Julianna to include her in the conversation. "Besides, he's out cold."

On the drive back to Riverton Julianna was quiet, staring out the side window.

"I'm sorry I yelled at you on the way over," I said.

"That's okay." She leaned her head back against the seat and closed her eyes, like a person much older than twelve and a half. I wasn't sure if it was Frank bothering her or something else.

"It scared me when I saw the blood on your face." My voice shook a little, just mentioning it. "So I'm sorry."

"We gotta bury that thing," she said, eyes still closed. That thing. The dog lying dead in the backyard.

"I guess so," I answered. I wished I had my cigarettes with me.

"Let's stop at the Little Skipper first," she said. "I got six dollars."

After eating we drove back to the cottage. Dusk was starting to shroud the day. I pulled the empty feed sack out of the trunk and sent Julianna to the work shed for a shovel. She sat on the edge of the grass as I dug a hole out under the pines. I used the heel of my foot to roll the carcass onto the feed sack, then dragged the whole thing over to the grave. Tried not to look at the flies that already swarmed around his head. He rolled in with a dull, unnatural whump. We picked a couple of wildflowers at the edge of Millers' field and scattered them over the carcass before I filled in the hole. Dirt slid off the shovel and landed with a slap on the corners of the feed sack, the loneliest sound in the world. Julianna walked back and forth on the loose mound to pack it down. I hoped like hell that she wasn't going to want to say a prayer. She didn't.

Back in the cottage I put away the gun and we washed up. Julianna sat at the table while I reached into the cupboard and pulled down a bottle of Jameson's and two shot glasses. Poured a full one for myself. For her, a dribble of liquor into a shot of water. I sat down heavily and handed the drink to her.

"Knock it back all at one time," I said. We did. "You ought to get Eleanor Prudhomme home before it gets much darker."

She had brought her fishing hat in from the backyard. She sat with it on her lap, flipping the brim up and down. "I was thinking maybe I'd spend the night," she said, slipping the hat on so it covered her eyes. "You might need some help if anything happens."

"Sure," I said.

"I'll call my mom." She jumped up and reached for the phone. I went in the bathroom and closed the door. Scrubbed my face and hands again in the running water. Didn't want to hear the conversation. A knock on the door.

"Yeah?"

"She wants to talk to you."

I dried off and took the receiver. "Hello?"

"You sure it's no bother?"

"I could use the company, to tell the truth." I was unreal, without gravity. This was John's wife.

"I'm sorry about your cat," Doreen said. "Is he all right?"

"Won't really know for a while." *Don't be so goddamn nice to me.* Under the table, I could see Sock Buddy lying on the floor. "I'm going to call over there later."

"I told Juju it was all right so long as she wasn't in your hair."

"Not at all," I replied.

We watched the Nature Channel and ate red popcorn balls that we made with Karo syrup and food coloring. I called the clinic twice, spoke with some nice people. Veterinarians must go through some intense niceness training. Frank was doped up and feeling nothing. As we tucked sheets into the couch for Julianna's bed, it occurred to me that John might call or even show up. I could hardly bring myself to worry about it. Loretta was worn out from worrying about her little cat.

Shortly after midnight Julianna lay under a sheet scattered with pink rosebuds. A blanket lay folded at her feet. She had borrowed one of my old nightgowns, flapping the sleeves loosely over her hands and crying, "I'm shrinking! I'm shrinking!" Now she lay there on her back, fingers plucking at the rosebuds, not sleepy yet. I sat in my armchair by the front window. All the lights were out except for the dim glow of the reading lamp on the table beside me.

"I'm behind schedule now," she said in the dark. "I'm gonna have to ride my ass off tomorrow."

"Don't swear," I said, quietly sipping a beer. She was silent for a while, plucking the sheets.

"Did your mom and dad ever fight?" she asked.

"All parents fight," I said. "It's normal. Don't let it get to you."

Mom hollering, Dad's quiet refusals, denials, disappearances. Stacy's attack on them earlier in the evening. I wondered about the scene that had taken place when John showed up at home earlier that afternoon. I hadn't thought about it before, didn't want to now. Maybe Julianna had been out, hadn't seen or heard it. But she'd been distracted and unhappy all night.

"It's normal," I said again.

At 3:45 A.M. a cold shadow darkened my window despite Julianna dreaming in the next room. His weight was heavier than ever, inexorable. Tonight would be a bad one. The paralyzing chill ran down my chest, through my veins, in my bones. Blood on Julianna's temple. I closed my eyes. It did no good. The red warmth seeped into her hair. She was looking at me. The wound on her head darkened until it was nearly black on her temple, and it was Jen Colby. Then she was gone and there was only the door. The same door over and over that I had to reach out and open. Birds sang somewhere and I shivered in the cold.

Last February we had a freak thaw. Spring arrived out of nowhere and gave us a week of warmth and sunshine. The Colbys were the last stop of my bus route for the Abraham Lincoln Elementary School. Theirs was a typical mobile home up on cinder blocks, with a few geraniums brightening the front. Jen Colby's older brother and sister, in the fourth and fifth grade, were sitting well apart from one another, though the bus was empty but for them. The Colby kids never sat together. The girl climbed out first, stone-faced. The boy stopped a few feet from me.

"Would you come see about my sister?" he said softly, looking at his feet.

"What?" I leaned over to hear him better.

"My sister needs some help."

"Well, I'm sure your mom took her to a doctor," I said. It was
my last stop and I wanted to get home. He didn't say anything
more, just looked at me like he was never going to forgive anyone in the world ever. He climbed down the steps and joined his
sister, who had waited for him, face turned toward the house.
They stood there not moving.

I pulled the bus off onto the shoulder, slammed her hard into
park with a muffled curse, and killed the engine. Climbed down
into the yard and rehearsed what I would say, how I would jus-
tify butting my nose into their privacy. A polite inquiry, a polite
rebuff, and I'd be on my way. I mounted the cement-block steps,
squinting in the bright sunshine. Crocuses spread a carpet of
purple across a corner of the front lawn. It was a day to take
your jacket off and let the sweet breeze hit your bare arms, a
day to walk out to get the mail in your bare feet. I knocked on
the aluminum screen door. The boy and the girl stood behind
me as if it weren't their house.

"There's no answer," I said pointlessly to the boy. He had a
tooth turned crooked at the front of his mouth, an overbite. He
kept his eyes on the door.

"Try again," he said.

I knocked harder. Rang the bell. The girl pulled a key out of
her book bag, unlocked the door, and held it open for me.

"Mom?" she hollered. There was no answer. Inside the house
it was utterly silent.

"Mrs. Colby?" I said politely. That got no answer either. I stepped into the front hallway. The house smelled newly rinsed, like houses do when the windows are opened after a long winter. The boy and the girl were behind me, still holding their book bags. Maybe their mother had taken Jen to see a doctor like I said. I couldn't remember whether I'd seen a car in the driveway or not. I looked in the kitchen. Tree branches rustled through the open window. The house had a weird stillness like it was holding its breath. Something was turning absolutely, horribly wrong. All three of us could feel it. The warmth outside had not penetrated the inner reaches of the house, as if the chill were permanent. I wished Mrs. Colby would show up. I told the boy and the girl to sit at the kitchen table and stay there. They dropped their bags on the spot and sat dumbly. I walked down the hallway. Nothing stirred. I passed a small bathroom. Dirty towels lay bunched on the floor. Dried toothpaste splotched the rim of the sink. My feet traveled farther down the hall, the rest of me carried along reluctantly. I passed two closed doors and came to a third, open.

I stepped in and looked around. One bed was perfectly neat with stuffed animals sitting orderly against the pillow. The other bed was unmade, blankets dragged halfway to the floor and sheets all untucked at one end. No pillow on the bed. A Hello Kitty plastic purse lay on the floor. Dirty clothes were scattered around. A naked Barbie sprawled with her hair wild and one leg missing. The stillness in there was stifling, even with the window open. For the first time in my life, I thought that maybe there were evil spirits, and that I had stepped in the middle of one. There was no other explanation for the prickly fear. My lungs squeezed down to the size of lemons. I couldn't take in any air.

To my right the closet door was ajar. The corner of a baby blanket stuck out of the threshold. Tangled in the blanket was a dirty sock with a large hole in it. A toe poked through the hole. The toenail was dark blue. A fireball rolled through my veins from neck to fingertips, leaving a wake of tingling heat. I thought, "I am seeing something that I'm not supposed to see, and now I will never be allowed to leave here." I took a step toward the closet door, opened it and looked in. Jen lay curled up on the floor of the closet in a nest she'd made out of dirty clothes, the old baby blanket, and some towels. Her head lay on the pillow she'd taken from the bed. She wore pajama bottoms that were too small for her, skinny as she was. Her hair hadn't been combed in days. There was a series of welts on her upper arm. Something swollen, purple and black, stained the hairline at her temple. A trickle of dark blood had crept from her ear to her jawline. I knew without touching her that she was dead. A bird sang outside.

"It's okay," I said to her. "I'm here."

Lying near the pillow was a package of saltines with a few crackers left, some crumbs on the floor. Broken crayons scattered around a single coloring book, *Disney's AristoCats.* A ragged stuffed rabbit lay under her arm, gray and furless from too much love. And in the corner was a small plastic wastebasket that she had used instead of going down the hall to the bathroom. Her mouth was open slightly, as if she had a cold and were breathing through her mouth. The sock with the toe sticking out had a Nike logo on the cuff.

I wanted to grab hold of her ankles and drag her out of there, out of that dark narrow space. I wanted to hold her on my lap and tell her someone was here with her now. At least lay a hand on hers, give her one moment of not being alone in all that still- ness. But I walked out of the room without touching a thing. Returning to the kitchen, I picked up the phone and dialed 911. The boy and girl listened as I told the operator it was an emer- gency; I had a sick child on my hands. Gave my name, location. Told her she better send the police as well, then hung up. I sat down at the table with the two kids.

"Your sister's sick," I said, not looking at either of them. "I want you to stay right here until somebody comes to help."

"Where are you going?" asked the boy.

"Nowhere," I answered, surprised. "We'll just wait here."

I held my hands in my lap and looked at the boy's soccer schedule posted on the refrigerator. A box of Cap'n Crunch sat on the counter next to a recipe cut out of a magazine. We heard tires outside. The girl jumped up and went to the door.

"Mom," she said.

I didn't get up. Patricia Colby came into the house, into the kitchen. She had thin hair back in a ponytail and she carried a grocery bag from Foster's Supermarket. She stood looking at me with her mouth slightly open like Jen's in the other room. I remembered my earlier dread of embarrassment as she stared at me. I was far on the other side of etiquette now. "I'm just here until help comes," I said at last. "Your little girl is sick."

"Who let you in here?" she asked. Then she turned on the girl. "You let her in here?"

"I made her," I lied.

A siren called from far away, getting closer. Just here until help comes. Just here until somebody comes along to take charge, take action, take over.

"Your girl is sick," I said again. The right word refused to come.

"What are you talking about? I don't know you."

"Something's wrong with her. She needs to see a doctor," I told her. She started toward Jen's room as a siren screeched to a halt outside. I opened the screen door and said, "She's down the hall."

It was a young man and a young woman, wearing medic uniforms with short sleeves and official patches sewn here and there. Other sirens were approaching. A pickup truck with a single red light on the dashboard swung into the yard. Volunteer fire department. Carl had been a volunteer fireman but quit when he married Amy. Soon there were vehicles parked all over the road.

I returned to the kitchen and sat with the brother and sister. I heard their mother repeating, "What's going on? What's wrong?" Her voice became shrill with panic.

Several volunteer firemen poked their heads around the corner to look at me and the two kids. At one point I recognized Toomey Sherman's voice in the confusion. I grabbed onto the familiar sound of it. A police officer came into the kitchen. The boy and the girl kept their heads turned away, not looking at him or me.

"Are you the one who called?"

"Yes."

"Are you a relative?"

"I'm the bus driver."

"I need to ask you a couple of questions."

"Can we go outside?" I asked. Someone came to sit with the kids to keep them from going down the hall, as if they would in a million years. The officer and I went into the backyard. He asked me questions and I answered them.

Finally he asked, "Did the other children indicate any problem this morning when you picked them up?"

"No."

"Did you have any reason to suspect that abuse was taking place in the house?"

"No," I answered. "None."

Back in my bedroom, the Night Visitor rose to his haunches. He was a long time leaving, while I lay there shivering. I waited until the count of one hundred and pulled aside the covers. The cold he left behind was so deep, I had to steady my legs to get out of bed. In the living room Julianna lay on her back with an arm draped off the couch like a dying opera star. There was no Frank rubbing against my ankles. I dialed the animal hospital and got a sleepy young woman. Frank was stable. If anything changed she would call me. I poured myself another shot of the Jameson's that sat on the counter. Stood looking out the kitchen window at the ghost version of me looking in. It was getting worse instead of better. I had a queasy feeling of dread thickening to fear. I stood there thinking until the first breath of dawn stained the neighboring woods. Now it was Thursday; the trial was one day away.

14

Amy was out the door as soon as I pulled into her driveway. She slammed the door of the Merc harder than necessary and tossed a new pair of pinking shears onto the seat between us.

"What's the matter with you?" I asked.

"He's a prick."

I wasn't going to touch that, so I said, "Thanks for the scissors."

"Welcome."

I backed out of the driveway, eyes on the nasty curve thirty yards to the right, as Amy said, "You look like hell, I have to say."

"Tired."

"How's Frank?"

"They got him all sewed up. Looks like Franken-kitty."

"No pun intended," Amy added. "I got this for him." She set a little present on the seat between us. It was tied with a yarn tassel.

I had called Amy earlier to tell her I'd be late and why. Julianna and I were up and out by 8:00 A.M. She rode Eleanor home, while I drove to Cadillac to check on Frank. He was awake. I gave him Sock Buddy. He twitched his ear and gave me his evil eye.

"They don't know yet if he's going to be able to use his front legs," I said after a few minutes. "If not, they want to put him to sleep."

"Jesus," said Amy. "Couldn't we rig up a cripple cart like Harley did for BooBoo?"

"They said it would be more humane." I could see Frank whirling around the cottage in a two-legged cart, a little pirate flag flying off the back end. What I could not, would not, see was Frank dead. I remembered the feral dog from yesterday, his forepaw dragging through the grass as I hauled him toward the homemade grave.

"You bring the paper?" Amy asked.

"Got it right here." I patted my Bicentennial bag. She pulled it out and turned to the classifieds for garage sales.

"I guess you heard about Stacy."

"Yeah. Congratulations," she murmured. "How's he look?"

"Like he'll live."

"Hmm." Then suddenly she said, "Forget the New Orleans trip."

"Okay," I replied. She waited, then she answered the question I wasn't asking.

"Carl wants to stay home this year."

I'll bet. She turned her head and looked out her window. "He mentioned he saw you the other day," she said.

"Who?"

"Carl. Said you came in for some bait."

"Uh-hum."

"Your nails look great," she said. "What's the occasion?"

"Just screwing around," I said, flushing dark. Here I'd been waiting for a chance to talk to her about John and suddenly I couldn't even look at her. Then we were quiet, each with our own thoughts, until I pulled into the Lake Crest Café. "Here we are."

"You okay?" she asked, watching me.

"I'm hungry. Come on."

We settled into our usual booth like every other Thursday morning for the past dozen summers. Tammy tossed a couple of menus on the table followed by two cups of black coffee.

"Give me the Scramble Ranchero," Amy said without touching the menu. Tammy was Amy's older sister and there was no love lost between the two.

"Biscuits and gravy," I said to Tammy.

"Side of bacon?"

"Yeah."

She put her order pad in her pocket and said, "So it's tomorrow, huh?"

"What is?"

"Pat Colby. I hope she fries."

I looked at the salt shaker near my hand and couldn't think what to answer. Amy broke in, "You don't know a thing about it, so shut up."

"She turned around with a cast-iron skillet in her hand and *accidentally* hit the kid upside the head?"

"I said shut up about it."

Tammy was talking loud. I wanted to tell her to shut up myself. Amy picked up the menus from the table and shoved them at her sister. "Get our food, will you?"

Tammy disappeared. "Every asshole has their theory," Amy said. "Sorry you had to hear it." She tapped out a cigarette, slid the pack across to me, watched while I lit one.

"Thanks," I said.

"You're welcome" was her only comment.

I pulled a pencil stub from the pocket of my shorts and got to work on the classifieds. My hand shook.

"What've we got this week?" she asked.

"There's one on Maple that looks good."

"All you're going to get is baby clothes," Amy replied. "You know how many kids live on Maple?"

We settled into quiet. I circled some ads while Amy stared absently out the window. Her cigarette lay in the ashtray untouched. The long ash curled like a gray caterpillar until Tammy brought our food.

"Mom just called," she said to Amy. "She wants you to call her."

"Why?"

"Maybe because she never hears from you. Don't ask me." Tammy clattered our plates onto the table and left.

I put the pencil down to eat. Amy was still staring out the window, a million miles away, when a bell tinkled above the door and Toomey Sherman came in. He pulled off his LaRue's Contracting cap and tucked it under his arm.

"Hey, Tammy."

"Hey, Toomey."

"They ought to get married," Amy muttered. "Name their kids Timmy and Tommy." I had to laugh.

He stopped at the table. "Morning, ladies."

"How you doing?" I asked.

"Gotta be doing all right when it's this nice out, okay." He stood nodding, pulling his hands in and out of the pockets of his windbreaker.

"Enjoy it now," Amy told him. "It'll be hotter than a blister in a few hours." She took a bite of her Scramble Ranchero. He started to step away.

"How's your house?" I asked him.

"Oh, it's a lot of work, you know." He put his cap on, then took it off again. "I'm wiring it now. You come out and see it when I'm done, okay."

"I will," I said.

He chucked me on the side of the arm and went over to the counter. Swung one wide leg over the stool like he was mounting a horse.

"He's sweet," Amy said, a little dismissively. "We had him and Harley over for euchre the other night. He brought us a whole case of Bud and five bags of chips."

It was Toomey Sherman who drove me home from the Colby house the day I found Jen. I had been questioned by three different people, one with a uniform and two without. Someone made arrangements to return the bus to Lincoln Elementary. Toomey said maybe he ought to take me home so I wouldn't have to ride in a police car. We climbed in his 4x4 and off we went. I stared at the red volunteer fireman light on his dash that was no longer flashing. Felt like I was in a space capsule, sealed off.

"Let's drive for a while," I said.

"I'll show you my house, okay." He'd bought a lot on the other side of the lake. It was still just a big hole they'd dug and a bunch of wooden stakes to mark the foundation. "Okay, see, there'll be the kitchen, and you walk right through here, bang, and you're in the living room." He counted off the distance with his feet, spreading his arms to form walls. I walked over mounds of dirt until my legs gave out and I sat down on top of one.

"And then this is the view, okay." He had his back to me, facing the lake with arms outstretched as if he were hugging the entire shoreline. I took off my sneakers and dug my toes into the pile of dirt beneath me. It was warm from the sun beating on it all day.

"You'll get your clothes dirty," Toomey said when he turned back to me.

"I don't care," I told him.

He dug in his pocket and brought out a couple of Tootsie Rolls, handed me one. I filled my mouth with the gritty, rubbery chocolate. Wiggled my toes deep in the dirt, nailing myself to the earth. I wished I had my old bike to ride. Amy and I used to ride our bikes all over this county, as far away as Cadillac once. This was a good day to be on a bicycle, winging through patches of shade into the pink sunlight. I couldn't think what I'd done with that bike. Maybe Toomey could drop me off at Mom's house. I could dig through the garage, see if it was there. I'd call Amy and we could go for a bike ride out to Cedar Hill Cemetery, or the Jefferson Speedway. Just ride around until our legs fell off.

Toomey stood off to one side, giving me privacy. New green leaves glittered in the sunlight. I stared up at them, frowning. How could they be so lovely after what I'd just seen? As if God took as much pleasure in a six-year-old corpse as a budding cherry tree. I lay back on the mound of dirt and stared up at an empty sky. God had made the world in a moment of curiosity, then wandered away like a child from a broken toy; no one to take responsibility for what was left behind.

"Toomey, come here a second, will you?"

He climbed up beside me and sat down, getting his own clothes dirty. I don't know what he'd seen on my face, but he took my hand and held it in his own. It was large and blistered and attached to a beating heart. I leaned over and kissed him. We moved down to a clean patch of grass. With the woods surrounding us and the lake behind it, no one saw the two bodies that came together. As soon as our breathing was back to normal Toomey said, "Time to go, okay."

"Okay." I stood up to put my clothes on. The grass was miles below me. I bent over and vomited a river of lunch that pooled at my feet. I looked at it in surprise, and another wave came. Toomey stood beside me and held my shoulders. He gave me his denim shirt to wipe my mouth. My sneakers were spattered. It took a long time to finish. He got me dressed and back in the truck. We drove with the windows down to get some air on my face. I'd strained my stomach muscles and burned my throat raw. I was going to need help getting into the house.

"I won't tell anyone you barfed," Toomey said in an offhand way. Meaning, I won't tell anyone anything.

"Thanks."

"They're gonna put that woman in prison, okay."

I didn't know what to say to that, what to think of that. Neither of us said anything more until we pulled into my driveway. Mom's blue Escort was parked alongside the cottage. She came out to the truck and had her hand on my elbow, helping me out.

"Toomey, thanks for getting her home," she said into the truck. He must have called her from the Colby house. I didn't hear any more of the conversation. I could see Frank sitting in the living room window, looking out at me. His mouth made a silent meow. The window was closed and he was inside. I wanted to be inside too, where he was. I said good-bye to the truck and I walked and walked to the front door and then I was inside and Frank was on my lap and the windows were closed and God's beautiful spring day was shut out for good.

"And he obviously has a crush on you," Amy whispered.

"What?"

"Toomey. He has a little crush on you." We were still in the diner, and Amy was smiling at me, but the smile had an odd edge to it. She picked up the pencil, started circling more garage sales. "We'll start at Waterman Street and work our way west," she said.

I dug into my food. Out the window, across the street, I caught a glimpse of wide shoulders and dark hair walking into Dudley Hardware. I leaned forward to look, but it was some man I didn't know.

"Mary?"

"What?" I asked, my mouth full of gravy.

"For the third time, do you want more coffee?" Amy was visibly annoyed.

Tammy stood at my elbow with a full pot. I nodded. She poured while Amy pushed her plate away and scowled at me.

"What's the matter with you?" she asked.

"Me? What's with you?" I had never seen her so irritable.

She waited until Tammy left, then said, "I'm having a little trouble, thanks for asking."

"What trouble?"

"Carl."

I took a deep breath and let it out. "What?"

She waited until she'd poured more Half 'n Half into her coffee. Then she said, "Is there something you want to tell me?"

"About what?"

"About anything."

"Well." Here was the moment for me to tell her about that woman in Traverse City. "No."

"We haven't had sex in four months."

We both stared at the spoon she was clanging softly around in her cup. When I looked up there were tears hovering on her lashes. This was my best friend and she was crying. But the words of comfort wouldn't come.

"Tell me the truth, all right?" She grabbed a couple of paper napkins and blinked hard to get the tears back inside.

"Amy, I'm sorry—"

"Oh God," she said, bringing her fist down so her spoon clattered in her cup. "Just say yes or no," she said quickly. "Are you seeing him or not?"

Between thoughts of Toomey and John, I was slow to catch on. "Who?" I asked.

"Carl," she said. "Who the hell do you *think*?"

The whole forsaken universe jolted to a stop. Her words sank in. Then everything resumed.

"No, I'm not seeing Carl," I said, trying to laugh it off. But Loretta rose up out of the booth and said, "Is that what you think of me? That I would steal your husband?"

The click-clack of diner noise stopped. Tammy watched from behind the counter. Every eye in the room was glued to our table. Amy looked up at me with her chin set, waiting for me to sit down. When I didn't she said, "Can we please discuss this later?"

"Discuss what? What an asshole you're being?"

"All right," she said, and took a deep breath. "Forget—"

"I can't believe that after knowing me all these years, you would think that I was no better than you."

Well, that did it. That one landed. The silence in the diner swelled around us. Amy's face was sharp and white. "Of course not," she said. "You're the Great Solitary Martyr."

"Martyr, my ass."

"Not one bleat out of you when he left. God forbid."

"What did you want me to say? Please don't take my husband?"

I needed to sit down. I needed to shut up. I needed to get out of there, but I'd stepped off a cliff, and there was no scrambling back.

Amy said, "If you were a true friend you'd have told me how you really felt."

"If you were a true friend you'd have come to me yourself and not left me to hear it from him."

My lips were moving, but all I could think was how this was

the sort of scene I'd normally want to tell her all about later over the phone. I could even hear her laughter: "You said *what?*" But it was not later, it was now. And Amy wasn't laughing, she was slipping farther away with every word.

"Why didn't you say so then?" she asked, throwing her napkin on the table. "Why?"

"Are you going to make this my fault?"

"Because you'd rather die than open your mouth and admit you feel anything."

"Stop it, Amy."

"Then you might be human like the rest of us."

"No," I said. "Even at my worst I could never, ever be like you." I turned around and walked. Hit the door hard with the butt of my palm.

"That's right, leave." Amy was actually shouting after me. "Run home and have a drink."

I had a moment of panic imagining my keys lying back there on the table. There they were in my pocket, then in the ignition, and then the Merc was moving. One thing I did leave on the table was my cigarettes. I pulled into the Gas 'n Go, put a five on the counter, and left without my change. Had the Kool lit before I was out the door. Swung the Merc onto the street looking for someone to crowd me so I could ram them. I caught a flash of fluorescent yellow nailed to a tree and hooked a quick right; a sign for a yard sale two blocks down. As if I'd spent these past seven years plotting to get him back. As if I hadn't had a life outside of them. As if I'd been paralyzed all this time, freeze-dried into a bitter little bean of jealousy.

I eased the Merc politely to the curb. Approach respectfully when you're about to enter someone's yard. They had three tables set up, a good sign. Lots of clothes hung on hangers along the fence. I stopped at the first table. Travel clock, hot rollers, rusted *Dukes of Hazzard* lunch box.

"Morning," I said.

"Gonna be a nice one," replied an older woman seated in a lawn chair. Next to her, another woman the same age nodded and smiled.

"Browse all you want," she said.

On the second table I spotted a cracked porcelain teapot in a wisteria pattern for seventy-five cents. I picked it up and moved on. Off to the side was a plastic freezer bag full of old jewelry. I picked it up, examined the jeweled brooches in the shape of lizards and parrots. Amy would love this, and it was only two dollars for the bag. A little black hole opened in my stomach and then snapped shut again. I set the jewelry back on the table and moved on. Best not to think about it. A shoebox full of twenty-year-old Simplicity dress patterns. A nickel each. Maybe Sharon could use them. "How much for the whole box?" I asked.

"A dollar?" asked the first woman.

"Fifty cents," I countered. She nodded.

"Can I set this stuff over there?" I asked. "I want to keep looking."

"Here, I'll take it," said her friend, who heaved up out of her lawn chair to collect my purchases. A disheveled miniature poodle skipped across the driveway to say hello to my ankles.

"Hey pooch." I lowered one hand for him to sniff, scratched the back of one ear. He head-butted my leg in a friendly way and sat down, tail thumping.

"What?" I asked him.

He thumped harder. I thought of Frank at the vet. Normally, at this hour, he'd be deep in his mid-morning nap at the foot of the bed, Sock Buddy lying nearby. He'd give me hell later when he smelled poodle on me. At the third table I stopped still. It was an entire picnic table covered in glassware: a full tea set in a pussy willow pattern, three glass shepherdesses, a set of four liqueur glasses in frosted crystal, and random teacups with saucers. Everything from highball glasses to poodle figurines. And best of all, half a dozen delicate blown-glass bud vases.

"I want everything here," I said, gesturing to the table.

The two friends broke off their conversation. The owner looked at me blankly, looked at the table, then back at me.

"How much you give me for it?"

"Ten dollars," I answered.

She shook her head. "The sherry glasses alone are a dollar each."

I looked again at the table. There were some nice pieces, I could see that. I busied myself looking at individual prices. She stayed quiet, letting me figure things up in my head. This was more than I could afford.

"Got newspapers here to wrap it all up in," said her friend, who'd already done the job on the teapot. Two old friends, probably knew each other since grade school.

"Fifteen," I said warily.

"Twenty?"

"Eighteen," I answered decisively. "You can keep the coffee mugs." They were ceramic, no good. "And throw in the *National Geographic*s." They conferred in their lawn chairs and agreed to the deal. The three of us wrapped each piece of glass carefully and filled two boxes, which they helped me lug out to the Merc with the poodle trotting behind. I forked over the $19.25. I was in no position to be dropping twenties like gumdrops but I deserved something good from this crappy morning.

On the way home I saw a green Cutlass waiting at the light on Chessman Road. Bubbles raced through my veins as I pulled up alongside, but an older man was at the wheel, his mouth moving to the radio behind a closed window. I stopped in at Sullivan's Appliance to look at answering machines. They were cheaper than I expected. I chose one with the simplest face, the fewest buttons. My God, what did people do with all of those buttons? I put it on my credit card. I'd been whipping the card out a lot lately.

I got everything safely home. Carried the boxes out back to the work shed. I unwrapped each fragile gem and lined them up lovingly on the shelves. The phone rang in the house. I threw the newspapers and boxes in the burn barrel and went inside. I'd apologize first for overreacting and then we'd find something funny about this. I grabbed a Stroh's out of the fridge and carried it to the table. Cradled the receiver while I poured myself some happiness. "Hi."

"Hey. It's John."

"John," I said as I dropped into the chair, my hip clearing the table this time. I rubbed my forehead with eyes closed. My chest felt tight. For Christ's sake, I could be cool as silk when someone was tossing abuse at me, stoic and glacier-eyed all the way home, only to fall apart at the first kind voice.

"You okay?"

"Yeah," I said. "Just glad to hear from you."

There was a pause on his end, then he said, "Were you thinking you wouldn't?"

My turn to pause. "Actually, that never occurred to me."

I could hear his laughter like it was coming down an empty corridor. "How's your cat?" he asked. Who had told him, Julianna or Doreen?

"He's doing fine. He'll be fine." He had to be.

"I'm getting off here at four-thirty," he said. "Then I'm taking Juju up to the fair. Any chance you're going to be there?"

"I play tonight." Shit.

"What time?"

"Six-thirty."

"If you stop by the fairgrounds before the game I'll buy you a hot dog."

"With chili and onions?"

"And mustard and sauerkraut and melted cheese if you want."

The scene in the diner faded farther with every word. "Just you and Julianna?"

"Just us two, wandering around looking for our lost friend."

At the words *lost friend,* the hole in my stomach gave another little gulp. I ran my fingernail along the metal rim of the table.

"I'll see you there," I said. He was happy. I could feel it cartwheeling across the telephone line.

"I have a cell phone here at work," he said. "It's always in my pocket. No one answers it but me."

"What's the number?" I fished for a pen and wrote it on my hand. After we hung up I sat with an elbow on the table, the ink-stained palm cupping my chin.

Amy and I held a yard sale together two summers ago. And we'd gone to yard sales together since we learned to ride bikes. One year we bought a deck of cards for a nickel and spent the rest of the summer playing cribbage every waking minute. We'd climb into the open space beneath the old pine in her backyard. The tree was so old the branches drooped so their tips swept the ground. If we crawled through the curtain of sweet-bitter needles, we were in a fort high enough for us to sit up straight. We played by flashlight when it grew dark. That's where we were sitting the night Amy told me that her mom and dad were getting a divorce. Our flashlights cast faint, jumpy shadows against the trunk.

"He's not coming home anymore," she said. "I'll get to visit him whenever I want, though."

I looked how I felt. The carpet of dead needles scratched against my bare legs. "Where is he?" I asked, not looking at her face.

"At my Aunt Joy's house for now," she told me, dealing out the cards. Her fingernails were bitten short, painted hot pink. "But he's moving into Pineview."

Pineview Apartments. They were the only apartments in Riverton. They had parties there, and people called the police because of the loud music. I tried to picture Mr. Richardson at a loud music party. My heart was jumpy like the shadows.

"There'll be an extra bedroom with bunk beds and we can go visit whenever we want," she repeated. I thought she meant her and her brother and sisters. She was staring at me. "Okay?" she asked.

I mumbled, "Sure," into my knee.

"What?" She kept looking at me. In the dark, in the greenish flashlight glow, she kept looking at me. I was never, ever going to spend the night at the Pineview Apartments. Not even if both Mr. and Mrs. Richardson were there, which was impossible because they were getting a divorce. My lungs swelled up and I held my breath. Oh God, it was happening right next door to me. Suddenly Amy was hitting me. "I don't care. I'll get double Christmas presents," she said. "And birthdays too."

I couldn't breathe, couldn't say anything, couldn't hit her back. We were both suffocating in that pine cave. I clawed at the branches, her fists on my back until I hit the sweet open air. It was deep dark with no moon. I ran across our backyards, around the ancient honeysuckle bush and the Brickhams' mulberry tree. I felt with my hands for the side of our garage. I could still hear Amy back there in the dark.

"I don't care, I don't care," she kept saying, even after I stood there and counted to fifty. I wanted to go back and tell her yes, I'd spend the night with her at her dad's any time she wanted. I wanted to tell her she could have the top bunk. I wanted to go ask her to stay the night at my house. Instead I went into the kitchen, where Mom was scooping out peach ice cream for Dad. "Where's Amy?" she asked.

"She had to go in for her bath," I said. Mom set out a bowl of ice cream for me and I sat there with Mom and Dad at the kitchen table, thanking God that we were a normal family, that no one was going to Pineview.

I copied John's phone number on a gum wrapper, poured a second beer, and set to work on the answering machine. I spent the rest of the morning cooking up a pot of chili to get me through the weekend and recording various outgoing messages.

"Mary Culpepper moved away. No forwarding number."

"If it's John, leave a message. Everyone else leave me alone."

"This is Mary Culpepper. I'm sorry."

Mustn't be clever or coy, inviting or hostile. Got it on the seventh try. When I was all done setting switches and testing, I gazed at it skeptically. I would call Amy after lunch, iron things out. Around one o'clock I tried the chili. There I sat at the table alone, without Frank, leafing through the new *National Geographic*s. I chopped up another half onion and tossed it in the pot, kept it simmering while I lay down for a little while. Dreamt about miniature children left rotting in the backyard by the woodpile. Woke up breathing hard from trying to bury them all. I lay there with my eyes on the ceiling, thinking about what lay before me the next day. The knot of dread was growing stronger, as if I were the one on trial. In a few hours I would see John; no need to think ahead any farther than that.

15

I ran over to Cadillac before going to the fairgrounds, which left me no time to call Amy. The rain from the past several days had worn itself out. It was looking to shape up for a fine Labor Day weekend. I climbed into the Merc and pushed the button so the rear window glided down. Everything was breeze-filled and eager to hit the road. The scent of grass wafted up out of my Marion's T-shirt, faint so you'd have to be awfully close to catch it. I was wearing my creamy yellow bra-and-underwear set under the softball uniform. I had put on extra Carmex.

They put Frank in an examining room and left me alone with him. He still looked like he'd gone through the garbage disposal, but his spirits were better. I helped him unwrap Amy's present; a can of Fancy Feast gourmet turkey.

"This is for when you come home," I said, pocketing the can.

I dangled the yarn tassel for him. Slowly, gently, didn't want him popping his stitches.

"We want to keep him at least a few more days," said the doctor on my way out. "He isn't mending like he should be."

"He's doing great," I said.

"He's not regaining much movement," he answered with an apologetic smile. "Eventually you're going to have to think of what's best for him."

I thanked him for his opinion and fled. Frank was a mean, scrappy bastard who could kick the shit out of an adult woodchuck. He'd be back on all fours in a few days. I drove too fast back to Riverton. Jeff Richardson was taking admission at the main gate at the fairgrounds. He wore a green plastic money apron that said "Riverton Chamber of Commerce." "Two dollars," he said.

"I thought you and Harley were going out to shoot grouse today." I handed him two bucks as if we'd never been closer than a peck on the cheek.

"That Harley, he's a dumb son of a bitch," he answered. "Season doesn't even start for another two weeks."

Activity bubbled and swirled all around me on the midway. The puddles that muddied up the ground on Tuesday had disappeared. The desolate air of an abandoned circus was transformed with the milling of the crowd. A sweet, hot smell hit me and I headed for the nearest cotton candy stand.

"Mary honey, what can I get for you?" It was Mrs. Richardson, Amy's mom. I was surrounded by them on all sides.

"Cotton candy," I said, handing her a few dollars. "How's it going?"

"Oh fine, fine. Tammy said you and Amy were in for breakfast this morning."

"Yeah." Was this the phone call Tammy had mentioned while we were there? Or did she race for the phone as soon as I walked out of the diner?

I tore into the cloud of blue sugar and wandered down the midway with one eye peeled for a black wave of hair. Stopped at the raffle table and bought ten tickets for the Dodge Dakota they were giving away on Labor Day. I needed something to drive in the winter; road salt was eating the guts out of the Merc.

Where would you take a twelve-year-old girl at the fair? I scanned the Scrambler, the Rocket Slide, the Swings. Screaming heads whizzed by, impossible to tell one from another. I sucked a mouthful of sugar and watched the crowd move in a hundred directions all around me. Bells dinged, buzzers blatted, and everything moved at once. This was the first time I'd come to the fair alone. I was invisible in the midst of this chaotic rumble. I heard an engine roar on the other side of the grandstand; the prelims for that night's tractor pull. The smell of animals mingled with the food trailers. I stopped at the pay phone near the rest rooms and dialed my own number. Figured I'd test the answering machine while I was out. Four rings, and it picked up. A strange, stern voice said, "This is Mary. Talk after the beep." I was so surprised at the sound of myself that I stood speechless with the phone at my ear. I had no idea what to say. "Today's a nice day, so let's keep it that way," I said quickly, and hung up.

I walked over to the exhibition sheds; thought maybe I'd see how my zucchini bread held up. I slid in the far door and joined the traffic of bodies as they surveyed the goods. A tap on my shoulder. Sharon.

"Checking out your ribbon?" she asked.

"Why aren't you at work?"

"Have a game tonight."

"You've got to be kidding." The Sleazebag Inn finished last in the regular season, now they were in the semifinals.

"We're playing you guys," she said. "And we're going to kick your ass." She was on me like a bird dog as I walked over to the baked goods, keeping my attention on the shelves: bread, cookies, cakes. "I heard you had a good time up to Marion's on Tuesday night," she added.

Marion's on Tuesday night with John. I stared at the blue ribbon on my entry card. My cheeks and forehead burned under my visor. "What did you hear?"

"Is that the same guy that was over to your house on Sunday?" she asked in return.

"What did you hear?"

"That you left together."

We followed the current of the crowd through the building. Gingersnaps, spaghetti sauce, hard salami all passed under my eyes in a blur.

"Don't get mad," she told me. "I just wondered."

"Who told you we left together?"

"Doesn't matter—"

"Who told you?"

"Tammy Richardson."

God Almighty, that woman could start her own Mary Culpepper newsletter. "I'm getting a little sick of the Richardson clan."

"I told you that seven years ago," Sharon agreed. "But you

had to be a martyr." I stopped and looked at her. Amy's earlier words slithered back to life. "Don't hit me," she added.

"I'm not going to hit you, for God's sake." I unclenched my fist. We came out into the sunshine. Now would be John's cue to pop up out of the dirt, but a long scan of the area revealed only non-Johns.

"Mom's in the bingo tent losing her shirt," Sharon said. "You should at least say hi."

The evening was shaping up far different than I'd imagined. I pulled at the last hunk of cotton candy and shoved it into my mouth. Maybe I'd get lucky and choke to death. We made it to the bingo tent without running into anyone. I figured maybe I could get Sharon into a game and then slip away unseen. Large fans blew at one end of the tent, but it was still stifling. The caller hollered into a microphone: "I-seventeen." Mom sat at a table with Peg Monroe and her mother. Sharon and I slid into the seat beside her.

"Good God," Mom said to me. "What happened to your mouth?"

"You look like *Night of the Living Dead*," Sharon added. She dug a mirror out of Mom's purse and held it up to me. My lips and tongue were stained dark blue.

"Blagh," I said, then wiped my mouth hard with my T-shirt.

"B-fourteen. B-fourteen."

Mom was playing four cards at once. She held her hand up for us to hush while she scanned the numbers.

"What's up, Mary?" Peg Monroe was helping her mother play two cards.

"You playing tonight?" I asked.

"If I can get her home in time," Peg answered, stacking bingo chips into a tiny tower on the table.

"I'm wearing a catheter now," whispered Mrs. Monroe across the table.

"Nothing wrong with that, Judy," said Mom, eyes on her cards.

"It's better than the alternative," Mrs. Monroe answered darkly.

I wondered what the alternative was. I looked at Peg, who rolled her eyes and added another chip to her tower.

"N-thirty-six. N-thirty-six."

"Bingo!" shouted a man at the front of the tent.

"Oh for Christ's sake," Mom muttered, clearing her cards. There was a break while the cashiers came to collect money for the next game. Mom ponied up for two additional cards. Sharon bought one. "Did you see your ribbon, Mary?" Mom asked.

"Yes."

"You don't sound very happy about it."

"I'm happy." I gave her a dark blue smile. "I just stopped to say hello. I'm gonna take off." Mom looked up, surprised. I was usually good for two or three cards myself. "You're not coming to the game tonight, are you?" I asked her.

She shook her head. "What time do you have to be at the courthouse tomorrow?"

"Ten o'clock," I said, as if I were really going to show up and testify, as if the whole thing weren't just a bad dream about to go away.

"Pick me up on your way," she said without looking up. The

caller started a new game. I slid out after a "See you later" to Peg who looked about ready to shoot herself. Once free of the bingo tent I stood still in the heat and the sawdust. What had I thought was going to happen? I couldn't walk around the goddamn Kassauga County Fair with a married man and his daughter without being noticed. I'd run into someone I knew every ten feet. A grim, gray curtain settled over me. It didn't end there. I couldn't walk around the fair with him. And there were a lot of other things I couldn't do with him. The words *married man, married man* dropped like lead pellets on my head. I was moving now, strolling along the rows of carnival games. I should go home, but I had a lot on my mind. John was the only thing that could make it all go away for a few hours. And I missed Julianna.

All around me kids swarmed like hyperactive bees. Teenagers were clustered in groups of girls, groups of boys, the occasional lucky quartet of a double date. The little ones were slipping like quicksilver out of their parents' hands. And sure enough there he was, the perennial Lost Little Boy at the Fair. About four years old, he was a frozen island in the current of bodies. Even at that age he tried to hide the fear, but his eyes were getting larger and larger, and panic was about to flow over.

Mom lost me in Kmart when I was no more than five. She'd always warned me that if I wandered off and got lost, she'd leave without me, and the police would come and drag me off to an orphanage. So when she disappeared in Ladies' Outer-wear I hid in a rack of winter coats until a tall man heard the crying, pulled me out, and walked me up front to the manager's booth. Dad would never have left me to the orphanage. I'd given up hope of ever seeing home again. I was so filled with terror and despair I couldn't even remember my last name. When Mom showed up to claim me she had a white face and an angry mouth.

"Don't you *ever* do that again," she said on the way to the car. "You're damned lucky; I was halfway out the door when I heard the announcement."

And now, looking at this kid at the fair, Loretta began to whimper. I was ten feet away from him, watching his head move this way then that. Too small to see up to the faces, his gaze was bouncing from one unfamiliar knee to another as people drifted past him. Didn't anyone else see this? My eyes swept the crowd, searching for any agitation, anyone looking frantically around. No voice urgently called out a name. Then the kid started up with a moan that built to a shriek. I went toward him, through the folks who'd stopped dead to look. I was a few feet away when a girl appeared behind him and grabbed his shoulder.

"Hush up," she said over his crying. "Sammy! Hush up, now." The girl looked young enough to be in high school. She bent over and picked him up roughly, balancing him on one hip.

"Is that your kid?" I asked her.

She looked up at me, startled. "Yeah."

"Where the hell were you?"

She turned the boy away from me on instinct. "What's your problem, lady?" she asked.

If she hadn't been holding the kid, I would have knocked her on her ass. Instead I put distance between us, fast. People just had these kids willy-nilly; anyone could squirt one out. No training, no IQ test, no rules to memorize or entry forms. No one was overseeing things. No one was taking any goddamn responsibility for any of this. I was near the livestock grandstand. Hurried to the bleachers figuring I'd watch some cattle judging, cool my heels with the adults. I was halfway up the bleachers when I heard my name. Julianna sat next to her father at the far end of the bleachers, waving at me to join them. She looked absolutely twelve years old and absolutely invincible. John pulled his sunglasses up to rest on his head and smiled as I sat on the opposite side of his daughter. Everything was going to be all right.

"How's Frank?" Julianna asked.

"Doing great. He said to tell you hi."

"Donna's in the pageant, remember?" She leaned over to whisper in my ear. "Thank God you're here. You missed half of it."

Donna. The cousin with her period and her father's Corvette. I looked at the stage. It was the Miss Kassauga County Pageant, livestock judging of the worst stripe. And if Julianna's cousin was onstage, then more of her family was in the stands.

"This is Mary," Julianna was saying to a woman seated in front of her. The whole world turned electric white; I thought it was Doreen. "This is Aunt Sophie," Julianna was saying. "And Uncle Ted."

Relief rendered me saucer-eyed and stupid. I nodded. Uncle Ted nodded back genially enough. All I had was a quick impression of a large, beefy pink man. Sophie was something different.

"Hello," she said. Small, dark, she was a female carbon copy of John. Her eyes sloped down at the outer corners, making her look sleepy and shy. They focused somewhere around my chin, glancing off to the side once or twice at nothing.

"Hello," I managed, hoping my mouth was no longer blue.

"Mary's my friend," Julianna told her, explaining me neatly. Aunt Sophie smiled a tiny sunbeam at my chin and turned around to face the stage. There was something wrong with her that I couldn't pin down, as if an angel were tangled in a human shell and beating its wings to get out. Julianna swatted at my elbow. "There she is. In the blue."

A line of girls moved across the stage in long formals. I looked at them with all my might. No power on earth could have dragged my eyes in John's direction with his sister and his daughter nearby.

"You missed the talent part," Julianna whispered quickly. "Donna did her baton routine. She didn't mess up once." She turned her attention back to the stage. The host, a DJ from WKJF, congratulated all of the girls for something or other. Donna looked older than fourteen in all that hair and makeup. She was large, beefy, and pink like Uncle Ted. The dress was electric blue polyester. It had a halter topped with a sequined choker. The fit was a little tight, so she bulged around the armpits, but her posture was perfect. Her hair was pulled back in a tucked-up French braid, the obligatory finger curls dangling like mice in front of her ears. She was working hard at it: the walk, the smile, the shoulders thrown back and hips turned at an angle to minimize body width. She was never going to be a fashionable girl or a popular girl. No contestant in the history of the Kassauga County Fair had ever been considered anything but a geek. The horse barn girls wouldn't be caught dead on that stage. Homecoming Queen was their racket, something these girls would never be.

Amy was on the Homecoming Court all through high school.

She was friendly with everyone: the nerds, the jocks, even the burn-outs.

"The trick is, you have to look people in the eye when you talk to them," she told me. We were out by the football bleachers, cutting class and sneaking a joint. "Look at 'em like they're the only person in the world." She crushed the butt under her toe. "Even if it's just Toomey Sherman."

Senior year she lost Homecoming Queen to a girl who'd only just moved to Riverton the year before. She and I skipped the big dance, spent the rest of the night in her bedroom while she cried as if she were about to die.

"I don't understand," she said over and over. "What's the matter with me?"

"You're just disappointed," I said like a jerk.

"I don't mean that." She pulled her head out of the crumpled dress that she'd thrown on the bed. "Why didn't I win?"

"Amy, ten years from now you won't even remember this."

"I'm not like you, okay?" She sat up and looked at me like she hated me. "Maybe you don't give a crap what anyone thinks, maybe you're the Lone Rangerette; but *I need to be popular.*"

I stayed up all night with her. Did everything I could to make her feel better while inside I glowed with the memory of what she'd called me: The Lone Rangerette.

And now Julianna was watching her cousin in this beauty pageant like she was a movie star. When Donna stepped up for her interview, Julianna pounded her father's knee and elbowed me hard in the arm.

"Donna Melnick, fourteen years old, daughter of Theodore and Sophia Melnick of Manton," said the WKJF announcer.

Donna smiled on cue. Her eyes were a little wild behind the blue eyeliner.

"Can you tell us about your hobbies and interests?" he asked.

Donna leaned into the microphone like a pro, eyes fixed on some imaginary face in the sparse crowd. "I like to ride my bike, work on my computer, and visit with my friends." The host started to ask the next question. "I also play the clarinet," she added quickly.

"And what are your plans for the future, Donna?"

"Well . . ." And here she stopped and gave it some thought, as if the future were some new and bizarre idea. "I'm going to attend high school this fall," she said carefully. "And in four years I will graduate and become a nurse."

She beamed out at the audience. Julianna's elbow bruised me from hip to shoulder. The judges smiled noncommittally. I pictured Julianna up on that stage in a couple of years, submitting herself to their scrutiny. I wanted to plug each one of them with my Remington. There were five other girls who took their turn answering questions, none of them older than sixteen. John leaned forward and looked at me. I risked a small glance in return. He gave me a tentative smile. For a second the rest of the world disappeared. I'm not sure what I gave him back; it seemed to make him happy.

"If I had one wish," the last contestant was saying, "it would be that I do more good in my life than harm."

The DJ patted her on the shoulder like she was a beagle and sent the girls back to their chairs while the judges did their dirty work. Uncle Ted turned around to ask John what time it was. A brief, pointless conversation ensued, killing time until the judges were done. I nodded and smiled earnestly, like a tourist trying to make friends in a foreign language. Aunt Sophie's sleepy eyes and little smile bounced off my nose, my shoulder, my ear.

"There's no way she's not gonna win," Julianna said. "It's so obvious."

She did not win, was not even the runner-up. When the smarmy bastard DJ asked the audience to "give the rest of these beautiful girls a hand," we clapped and stomped our feet. Julianna whistled until the other parents shot dirty looks. We waited in a subdued group near the back of the stage.

"I wouldn't enter that dumb contest if you lit a fire under my ass," Julianna said.

"Don't swear," John answered.

Donna appeared in her blue dress holding her baton, a duffel bag, and a single rose given as a consolation prize. She joined us with a quiet fourteen-year-old dignity. Uncle Ted gave her an awkward meaty hug, took the baton and the duffel bag, and said, "You did a good job, girl."

That was all it took for the shameful tears to come, and she buried her face in her mother's neck so no one would see them. Julianna stood next to them, indignant and sputtering.

"You were the best one," she told Donna's back. "You were better than them. You destroyed them!" John and I both stood there empty-handed and wordless. The girl who wanted to do more good than harm in her life, also carrying a single rose, walked by with her parents.

"And you didn't smile hardly at all," her father was saying. "You looked like you were at a funeral."

Uncle Ted said, "How about if you get changed, and I'll treat you and Juju to some fried ice cream?" Donna didn't want to change clothes. She wanted to go home.

"But we have to ride the Scrambler," Julianna said.

"I don't feel like it," Donna answered, not raising her eyes from waist level.

"What about the bumper cars?"

"I just wanna go home."

Donna was facing a heartbreak too big for fairground rides and, to her credit, Julianna shut up. I hung back as they said their good-byes. Donna and Uncle Ted headed for the exit gate, the blue dress drinking up dirt and dust along the hem. Aunt Sophie stayed long enough to kiss John on the cheek and hug Julianna somewhat fiercely.

"Well, we're going," she said. She was the shyest person I'd ever met. With a heroic act of will, her eyes rested on mine for a second. "It was nice to meet you." And she was gone.

"Well, God, everything's ruined!" Julianna cried as soon as her aunt was out of earshot. For a moment it looked like she would scream. She scowled from me to her dad and said, "Will someone *please* go on the Scrambler with me?"

Now it was someone's turn to answer. Now it sank in that I was alone with them. A strong urge to disappear overtook me. In Julianna's presence I couldn't look at John, could barely speak. I wanted to escape and moon over him from a safe distance. But there she stood, disappointed and upset and outraged and thwarted, so we walked toward the Scrambler.

"That other girl, she was horrible," Julianna declared, kicking at an empty Sno-Kone wrapper. "You should have seen her. She couldn't even dance."

I looked at Julianna, looked at the carousel with the flaming-maned horses, looked at everything but John. I thought I caught a glimpse of Sharon's dark blond hair and swiftly turned the other way. I was never going to get away with this. We stopped at the ticket booth and each of us bought enough for five rides.

"My mom's at work," Julianna told me all of a sudden. "She works at night."

"Uh-huh." Where the hell was the Scrambler?

"She's bringing me back on Sunday," she continued. "Can Donna come on Sunday?" she asked her dad.

"That's up to your mom," he answered. "Hurry up. They're loading now." Julianna ran ahead to get a place in line.

"I feel like I'm walking around naked," he said quietly. I nodded. We joined Julianna as she handed over the tickets, then she and I climbed into our seats.

"You get the outside, you're bigger," she instructed me. We pulled the safety bar toward us and settled in to wait. John stood off to the side, in the shade of the poultry shed. The crowd flowing past us contained countless faces that I'd seen year after year at the fair. Strapped in and immobilized, I felt as if each of them were eyeing me surreptitiously. How long since I was on any of these rides? Nearly twenty years. Amy and I rode the Cyclone over and over until we ran under the bleachers at the big grandstand, the roar of the monster tractors drowning out the sound of our puking. The carriage started to move. I took off my visor for safekeeping. In no time the centrifugal force had smashed Julianna against me. Our heads whipped back and forth, stomachs careened against our kidneys. I laughed helplessly as the air was sucked out of me. Julianna's weight grew greater as the speed increased. Never had she been more of a solid concrete fact, crushing me into the side of the carriage. When the ride ended I emerged giddy and off balance. Julianna was giggling. John met us at the exit.

"Where to next?" he asked.

"The Ferris wheel," she said.

"Let's do the Helicopters first," I suggested. John and I took turns riding with her on the Hornet, the Bullet, the Swings, the dear old Cyclone. Occasionally his arm brushed against mine, exquisitely unraveling my nerves.

"My mom won't go on the rides," Julianna told me. "But she kills me in the bumper cars." I thought of how much fun Doreen would be in the bumper cars. Almost wished that I could be there again on Sunday with her and Julianna and Donna. I stopped looking over my shoulder for familiar faces. Decided that nothing could hurt Cinderella at the ball, and it was still twenty minutes before I had to leave for Everett Park.

We found an empty picnic table and sat down. "We got four tickets left between us," John announced, handing out chili dogs and drinks.

"The Ferris wheel!" Julianna cried, mouth full of onions. "We can all three fit in one seat."

"I have to leave pretty soon," I answered.

"Why?"

"I'm playing softball tonight." On another planet, in another lifetime. The chili dog was about the best thing I'd ever eaten in my life. It landed on top of that cotton candy and the two of them did a little happy dance in my stomach. Carl and Amy were approaching our table. It took a few seconds for it to sink in, but it was clearly Carl, and it was undeniably Amy, and they were stopping at our table. I had planned to call her when I got home. But now, in a moment of insanity, I pretended not to know them.

"Mary?" Carl said finally.

I looked up, surprised. "Hello."

"Hey, Carl," said John amiably. Hair prickled in my scalp before I realized that of course they knew one another; they played on the same team.

"This is Carl's wife," I told John.

He stood up as Amy thrust her hand out. "I'm Amy," she announced.

"John," he replied. "And this is Julianna."

Julianna looked annoyed at the interruption. Oh, I loved that kid. Reluctantly I turned my attention back to the adults, grateful that I hadn't had a chance to tell Amy about any of this.

"You play for Sizemor, don't you?" Amy asked.

"That's right." John was his usual friendly self, completely at ease. "Do you play?" he asked her.

She gave a tinkly laugh and said, "No, I'm just a fan. I like to watch from the sidelines."

"Amy was a cheerleader," I added. Julianna's cat eyes narrowed.

Carl looked at me as if I hadn't finished my homework. "Don't you have a game tonight?"

"Yes," I said. "If you'll excuse us, we're going to ride the Ferris wheel." I stood up, forcing Amy back a few steps. Julianna shoved the last piece of chili dog in her mouth and stood up as well.

"Very nice to meet you, Julianna," Amy said. Julianna's mouth was full, so she nodded and gave a little wave. Amy had been trying to catch my eye. One little smile and the stupid fight would be forgotten. I couldn't look at her. "So, John," she said, "we'll see you up at the ballpark?"

I didn't hear his response because I was humming a little tune in my head, turned away from them. John waited until we were out of the picnic area before saying, "How do you know them?"

"My ex-husband and my best friend," I said.

It took him a moment or two, then he said, "Oh."

"My best friend moved to Florida," Julianna offered.

"You are two of my favorite people," I said.

"In the whole world?" she asked.

"Yes."

We arrived at the Ferris wheel. It loomed silver and sinister above our heads. "You're not gonna chicken out, are you?" Julianna watched my face. "It's our last ride," she added.

I had told Amy and Carl that we were riding the Ferris wheel. I had no choice. I said, "Don't tilt the seat."

We climbed into the creaky broken-down carriage that lacked any safety features that I could see. Julianna sat in the middle practicing her Queen Elizabeth wave as the earth dropped from under us. The stomach dance between the chili dog and the cotton candy was no longer a happy one. We lifted, paused, lifted, paused, as more people were loaded into the death trap. With every stop the seat swung to and fro wildly. Julianna leaned forward to look down, nearly tumbling us clear to hell.

"Don't tilt the seat," I said again quietly. She immediately sat up. We lurched backward. I looked down at my hands gripping the handle bar. They were translucent and clawlike. John had his arm along the back of the seat, across Julianna's shoulders. His fingers brushed my shoulder. "You okay?"

I shook my head an inch or two.

"You gonna puke?" Julianna asked politely. Again, a tiny shake of the head. Then we were moving in earnest. We careened up the back, hurtled over the top, and sank sickeningly down the front, down down down. Julianna twisted around to look behind her, but I shouldered her back into place and pinned her there with an iron elbow. What had I been thinking? Reckless careless stupid thoughtless dumb. Up, up, up until there were no visible supports and then we were at the top. The sun was too close to my face. There was nothing to hold on to, just endless open space all around me. We hung there in terrifying blue nothingness, only to sink blessedly toward the earth again.

"Wow," Julianna said at one point. "Mary's flipping out."

"I'm fine." I kept my eyes on my John's plastic ring, not daring to look over the edge of our carriage.

"Look!" Julianna pointed suddenly off to the right. "There's Mrs. Chapman."

"Where?" asked John.

"In the orange dress." Julianna pointed more frantically and I sent my elbow more firmly into her gut. "See her?" she cried. I saw veins, skin, knuckles glowing white.

John spotted her. "Julianna's teacher last year," he said to me.

We stopped halfway down. I looked up, encouraged by the fact that we were no more than fifteen feet up; at worst I would break a wrist. I looked for an orange dress, but what I saw was Sharon staring up at me. She was leaning against the Dodge Dakota raffle booth, sipping her giant Coke and waiting for me to come back to earth. We finally hit bottom and the attendant opened the sad excuse for a safety bar.

"That was great," Julianna said, scrambling out behind me. "You almost totally barfed."

Earth, earth, earth, dirt and sawdust. I wanted to fall down on it, embrace it, roll around in it like an unsaddled horse. John was right beside me as we came through the exit gate onto the midway. Now was the time to say good-bye. Sharon was blocking our way.

"Hey," she said, and waited. Once I got them all introduced, Julianna informed her that I damn near puked on the Ferris wheel.

"She did once," Sharon answered, earning the instant esteem of Julianna.

"No kidding?"

"Right over the side, all over everyone."

"It wasn't all over everyone," I said.

"You had your eyes closed," Sharon replied. "You didn't see it." Oh yeah, let's all laugh at Mary.

I turned back to Julianna. "I gotta go," I told her. "I have my softball game."

"Crap," she answered. I looked at John. Would I see him later? I cringed, hating myself.

"It must be love," Sharon said, walking along beside me after we'd said our good-byes.

"I don't want to hear anything out of you."

"I about fell down when I saw you on that thing," she continued.

"Where are you parked?"

"Over by the billboard," she said. "He seems nice."

"Drop it." I wasn't going to let her take rabbit punches at him or Julianna. We walked out the main gate, through the field filled with parked cars. A logging truck tore past us, speeding down Route 108.

"I saw Amy," Sharon said casually. "She asked me about him."

"For Christ's sake," I grumbled.

"Don't you want to know what I told her?"

"No." We were coming up on the Merc. Sharon maintained a determined silence. I opened the car door and stopped before climbing in. "Okay. What?"

She smiled and kicked lightly at the front tire. "I told her he was our cousin visiting from the Upper Peninsula."

"You asshole."

"So she asks me, if he's your cousin visiting from the U.P., why's he been playing ball for Sizemor Septic all summer? So I asked her, if you already know who he is, why are you asking me?"

Sharon had always had an unwavering dislike of Amy that I never understood. Tonight I savored it like cheap candy. I was alone for the precious fifteen minutes it took to drive to Everett Park. I remembered how he had seemed anxious when I said good-bye to his sister, the way he had looked at me when I said I would ride the Scrambler with Julianna, how he'd concealed a smile when I announced that Amy was a cheerleader. His presence, which I could barely stand in the moment, came flooding into the car as I lifted the dashboard lighter. My stomach was still doing the Virginia reel after the rides, but I was happy. Memories of his mouth under mine, his hands setting fire along my hips, they flew like bright-colored ribbons out the window of the Merc. If they were red warning flags, waving wildly in the back of my mind, I didn't want to know.

I took the long way to the park. Notions of wrong seemed out of place, didn't apply to this sense of well-being that he gave me. One of the things I liked most about him, he was terrible at hiding his feelings. Relaxed and at ease with everyone else, there was an awkwardness that showed up when he was dealing with me. Me, who'd seldom inspired more than a tolerant affection in anyone. He looked both anxious and relieved to see me when he lifted up his sunglasses on the bleachers. He nearly dumped chili on my lap when he handed me my hot dog. Never, not even when I'd wielded makeup and dresses in the Girliest Girl Club, had I felt that kind of power. He had gotten tongue-tied when we said good-bye.

Him. "Thanks for . . . you know. It was fun."

Me. "Yeah. Uh, see you later."

All these thoughts of John made the day swell with complacency. The afternoon was beautiful. Mad Dog Mahoney and Jen Colby and all of tomorrow were far in the distant future. What had I been so nervous about? Lines of blue spruce marched in formation as I flew past Anderson's Christmas Tree Farm. Sheets flapped lazily on somebody's clothesline. Julianna never needed to know. She and I were buddies, and that didn't have to change. My softball mitt was nestled happily at the bottom of the Bicentennial bag. I couldn't wait to play ball. Sharon and the Sleazebag Inn were going to get an ass whipping.

I took my time stretching and warming up at the ballpark. Flopped down on the grass and worked on my calves. Then I lay on my back and stared up at the sky burning itself away in the heat. A dragonfly landed on the rim of my visor. I didn't move, didn't brush him away. It was hard to see him perched there a few inches from my nose. Dragonflies routinely landed on the open pages of my book at the beach, refusing to move even when I touched their iridescent backs. Something about the printed page a dragonfly cannot get enough of. I looked at his wings slowly rising and falling with nothing behind them but empty air; nothing on earth but me and this dragonfly floating in an endless scorched stretch of blue. I wouldn't be the first to move even if they had to play the game without me. Peg Monroe tossed her mitt down nearby.

"Got the old bitch home," she announced, dropping onto the grass. "Would you believe she won sixty bucks?"

The dragonfly took off, only to come back halfway through the second inning. He hovered between first base and home when Sharon came up to bat. He dashed wildly straight up and down like he was working up the nerve to make a dive for me. Sharon's bat cracked. A simple short hopper, it would have been an easy out if I'd been paying attention, but Carla Fitch's throw went right past me. Sharon rounded off and flirted with second base. Suzanne O'Dell fielded the ball on back-up and had her covered.

"Shake it off," Suzanne yelled to me, throwing in to the pitcher. "Shake it off, let's go." Suzanne O'Dell was getting on my nerves. Sharon stayed close to the base. Angie Calloway and I were known in the league for picking runners off at first.

"Yup, it must be love," Sharon muttered, adjusting her cap. I watched the next batter approach the plate. The dragonfly had gone for good. "I want to hear about this fight you had with Amy," she said.

"Who told you?"

"Rebecca Whitehurst in left field." The pitch was high. Ball one. "Her mom was at the diner this morning."

"Then why don't you call and ask her about it?" I asked. Angie let fly with a fastball.

"Are you really fooling around with Carl?"

The bat cracked and Sharon took off running while I fielded the ball, turned on one knee, and fired it to second as Sharon went down for the slide. I didn't hear the call, scrambling back to first. The ball came hurtling at me like a small furious ghost. I made the catch and shouts erupted. Toomey called them both out. I had redeemed myself after fluffing Sharon's single. I wished that John and Julianna had been there to see it. Few things on earth prettier than a clean double-play. Never mind that I'd been aiming at the back of Sharon's head.

At Marion's afterward I did a quick scan of the crowd. No John. Sharon launched another assault in the middle of a game of pool. "Come on," she said as I returned from the bar with a fresh Stroh's. "I've waited years and I want the blow-by-blow."

"It was no big deal." I turned away. I remembered Stacy's revelation about Sharon having had sex recently. Silent as a tomb about herself, but my private life was open season.

"What're you all pissed about?" she wanted to know.

"Why would you think I was sleeping with Carl?"

"Oh, come off it. You're practically married to both of them." Sharon chalked her pool stick with one hand. "I don't get you guys." She hit a ball into the far corner pocket and stood considering her next move. "It's sick," she added.

"It's none of your business."

"Gee," she shot back. "Really?"

She bent over, studying the angle of the balls. I was overcome with an attack of boredom that nearly knocked me over onto the peanut-scattered floor.

"I'm going home." I set my beer down on the edge of the pool table. "See you later."

"Hey," Sharon stopped me. "I gotta take care of Stacy tomorrow."

"So?"

"So call and tell me how it goes."

"Yeah. Okay." I made a push for the front door and the evening breeze. Filled my lungs with it on the way down the block where the Merc waited, dark and patient.

Back at the cottage a little red light blinked nervously up at me from the answering machine. Five messages! Frank was dead and they'd been calling me all night. I swore loudly, yanked the instructions out of the utility drawer, and read them again. Didn't want to accidentally erase five goddamn messages. I gingerly pressed the PLAY button and waited. The beep made me jump. A strained, artificial voice said, "Today's a nice day, so let's keep it that way."

I'd forgotten. It'd been hours ago. No one could have remembered, but the merciless accuracy of technology had preserved it. Now I had this thing on my counter, this recorder of words and events, there would be no escape from myself, ever. I pressed ERASE, thrilling at the finality of it. "You can preserve," I thought. "But I can erase."

A second beep. A click. Someone hanging up. My jaw clenched. Third beep: "Mary Culpepper, it's Melanie Mahoney. Just a reminder I'll see you at Courtroom B at ten sharp tomorrow morning." This machine was a big mistake. It held out the promise of possibility but delivered only cold, unimaginative reality. I pressed ERASE again, preparing myself for the bad news about Frank to round out the miserable goddamn night. I could see him watching an ant work its way across the kitchen floor. He'd sit calmly upright, his front paws drawn in tight to his hind legs like an Egyptian god, ears tilted forward like sonar disks. Please God, wake up for once and do something; let him be okay.

A fourth beep: "You finally broke down and got one." It was Amy, sounding breezy and casual. "Give a call when you get a chance, so we can chat."

I hit ERASE. Pressed my palms flat on the Formica countertop. Looked miserably at the whorls and wrinkles that made up my knuckles. The fifth beep felt like some exotic form of torture.

"Hi, it's me . . . uhm, John."

I expelled all the air I'd been hoarding. Bent over the counter and dropped my forehead down to the cool surface. Frank had been spared one more night, and John had called even though I'd seen him just a few hours before. When was the last time I'd been reduced to this over a man? Never, I realized with surprise: never. I was falling down a steep and slippery slope with nothing to grab on to. I remembered the black, lonely ride four nights ago, when I stepped out of a Hopper painting with a cigarette in my hand, when I had decided he was the distraction I needed, whatever the price.

"I was calling to see how you did tonight," the machine said. Tonight? Oh, the game. We won. "I'll try you tomorrow. Maybe we can get together later on."

16

When the alarm went off at 8:00 Friday morning I was already up and dressed in my yellow linen dress, on the phone with the animal hospital. No change either way. I sat flipping through *National Geographic*s and wishing my stomach would stay still. Something niggled at the base of my skull, knocking to get in. Something about Jen, little discrepancies I couldn't put my finger on, like she was blending with a movie I'd seen or a book I'd read. I took out the notes from my meetings with Mahoney. After a minute I tore them to pieces and threw them in the trash. Nothing was making sense. Even with the windows open I couldn't get a breath. I got up and poured half a beer to settle my stomach. When I arrived at Mom's house an hour later, she dithered forever about which shoes to wear.

"The navy pumps are all frayed at the heel," she said. I stood outside her bedroom door, willing her to hurry up. "But if I wear the white flats I look like an old lady."

"No one's going to be looking at you." It came out sounding harsher than I meant.

Morning talk-show chatter filled the car. I flicked the radio off. Mom was quiet. A station wagon overflowing with children passed me on Route 108. They were dirty and wild-haired and having a great time waving out the back window. I gave them a toot and they laughed, their mouths wide and snaggle-toothed. It was a painfully clear day. Wheeling hawks scanned the fields with their black-bead eyes. The Labor Day Festival started today, and we were playing in the tournament finals tomorrow. If this weather held, half the town would turn out with sunblock and shades, basking in the perfect capper to the summer.

"Stacy's going home this morning?" I asked.

Mom turned her head toward me, torn out of some faraway thought. "I told you she was," she said.

"I'm not going to be able to baby-sit her tomorrow," I said. "I have the tournament."

"Ruther can handle it for one day," Mom replied. "Sharon's there right now. I'll go over tonight."

"Okay."

She fumbled and fussed in her purse, looking for something. "Did you have a nice time at the fair yesterday?" she asked.

"Yes. You?"

She pulled a brush out of the purse and sent it rigorously through her hair. "I won twenty bucks." Brush, yank, tug, she was really giving her head a work over. "Sharon mentioned that she met a friend of yours." My pinky ring winked up at us. My nails were still looking pretty good despite the chips. Mom gave a final, vicious tug at her bangs, whipping them up and back.

"I hate this goddamn thing," she said, then threw the hairbrush out the car window and into a ditch.

"What was that for?" I asked, startled.

"I hate that goddamn brush, that's all." Then a moment later, "I have to say, I never thought my own daughter would behave like those bar girls your father used to run around with."

The car stayed on the road; the sun continued to dazzle. But everything dear and familiar about the Merc's interior was suddenly rendered unsafe, as if a gear shift could betray you or an oil gauge break your heart.

"You mean sluts, right?" Just shut up, Mary. Let it go. "Or whores?"

"Don't you mock me," she said. "And don't do anything in this town to embarrass me."

"Like what?"

"Go sleeping around with no respect for yourself. I raised you better than that."

"No you didn't," I replied. "And don't get all over my ass because you couldn't hold on to your husband."

Like an expanding gas, the words crowded all other elements out of the car. Mom turned to me like she was seeing me clearly for the first time. It was more painful than the misjudging and bullying. "Neither could you," she said.

Then she leaned her head against the seat. Fists of wind reached in the window and lifted one lock of her hair. I turned the radio back on with a shaking hand and let the mindless chatter fill the space between us and the courthouse.

When we arrived I walked through the doors like a general; no nonsense, let's get it over with. Goose bumps rose despite the morning sun already blazing full tilt outside. The chill was pervasive, the same deep cold as the Night Visitor, as if he were roaming the halls looking for me. I rubbed my arms to wipe away the goose bumps. I was shown to a small annex room, the holding pen. Mom stayed glued to me despite our silence.

Once seated, I was exhausted. I'd lain awake most of the night with that oppression of stone on my chest, the merciless flashes and snippets: the sun shining through her thin arms as if her skin were translucent, large eyes in a tiny pale face. But there had been no sunlight in that darkened closet. How could it have shone through her arms? And her eyes had been closed, not open. I shook my head like I was swatting away a fly.

I was encased in a glass fishbowl looking out at the rest of the world. If I tried to speak, only bubbles would emerge. Something was tangled up in my head. I saw Jen climbing on the bus with an elbow swollen and discolored. I saw her with an ugly burn on her fingers, no coat in November, a cut on her lip. Sometimes she looked like she hadn't washed in days. Were these real? Had I made them up? I saw her with eyes wide open. They were ringed with blue shadows and they were looking at me.

"Mary?" Mom's voice was tinny with concern. "You want some water?"

I shook my head again, rubbed my forehead, tried to piece it together. I was seeing more than just that one day last February. My brain scrambled back to safety. Every family had a kid who was too small, shy, a little clumsy. Sharon went to school half-dressed for years; she wasn't neglected, just stubborn. It's not like I ever saw Jen with a cast on her arm or a black eye. It's not like there was ever anything wrong with the other two kids. The more I reassured myself, the higher rose a tidal wave of dread and certainty that cut off all my air. Underfed, hair uncombed, accident prone, extremely shy. And the bruises, the ugly pictures night after night, they flooded my memory. Why hadn't I seen it sooner? How could I have been so blind? For at least a year it should have been obvious—

Did you have any reason to suspect that abuse was taking place in the house?

No. None.

Some sort of magical veil was being torn apart. I crossed my arms, brought my head down to my knees. Jen Colby seemed like a normal six-year-old kid because I wanted her to be. In the face of Mad Dog Mahoney's relentless badgering I had clung to the image of a happy little girl and now it was slipping away. I looked down at the pattern on the tile floor, wanting to disappear into it. If this was true, I couldn't live with it. I couldn't live. Mom sat beside me all morning, bringing me water or rubbing lightly between my shoulder blades while I tried to talk myself out of what I knew.

A pear-shaped man came in to tell us we had an hour recess for lunch. Mom and I went to the Lake Crest Café out of habit, like dumb animals. We were seated exactly one booth and twenty-seven hours away from my fight with Amy. My arms stuck to the hot plastic tablecloth as I ordered eggplant lasagna, the special of the day. Tammy Richardson wasn't working. Today it was Marcie, who'd normally yack our ear off, but that afternoon she kept her lip buttoned and brought our orders before the folks who'd arrived ahead of us. I sat with my head down, fork in my hand. Marcie was at the height of the lunch rush. As she flew by she whipped a clean handkerchief out of her pocket and slapped it on the table next to my arm. It was neatly folded with small daisies embroidered in the corner. I looked at it until Mom said, "In case you need it."

I tried not to think about Marcie giving that handkerchief to me; if I dwelled on people's little kindnesses, I'd start to cry and never stop.

"How's your lasagna?" Mom asked.

"The eggplant's slimy."

"I wondered." She left me alone after that.

Several hours later I was ushered into the courtroom. Mom followed discreetly behind. I heard the swish of her skirt as she slid into a seat near the back. I walked slowly toward the judge, staring all the while at the back of Patricia Colby's head. Her thin hair was cut in a shoulder-length pageboy. She sat round-shouldered with her head thrust before her like a defeated turtle. When I was near the witness box I glanced over at the jury. In the second row sat Kurt Backhaus. He had graduated a year ahead of me. Was a star on the varsity wrestling team until he broke his opponent's elbow in a match. "Pop," it had echoed through the gym, and he quit the next day. Every familiar face made my head shrink smaller. By the time I got to the witness box I would look like a Dr. Seuss character, with a head the size of a walnut, yammering accusations in a tiny hysterical voice.

There were people in seats with notebooks and ravenous faces. Each witness was a raw chunk of meat for them to carry back to their newspapers. Soon I would be written about, quoted, gobbled up. I glanced at Mad Dog. *If there's anything you want to add to your story, now's the time to tell me.*

I could turn around and leave before I was sworn in. Quietly, no commotion, to hell with the subpoena. Frank would be there at the kitchen door when I opened it, all healed and good as new. He'd rub himself against my legs and flop onto his back to slide down the front of one ankle. I'd have that chili for dinner, with melted Velveeta on top, maybe work on the baby quilt I'd started for Turd Ball.

I raise my right hand, though I'm left handed.

If I went home now, I could take a light nap and then turn on *Mister Rogers' Neighborhood* and spend a half hour with Lady Elaine and Daniel Tiger. Maybe take another of those scented bubble baths, really go at my skin with that loofah thing.

"State your name, please."

By then the mail would have come and I'd walk down the driveway to the mailbox and see the last of the year's hawkweed in the yard, the little white butterflies that traveled in trios like Bible salesmen. If there was a good breeze, I'd be able to smell the lake.

"Do you swear . . ."

The wild, decaying smell of lake water in the afternoon.

". . . Have a seat."

I'd go barefoot out there to the mailbox, squeezing my toes in the warm pebbly dirt. There would be *Car & Travel,* and the electric bill, a little higher than last month from running the fan in the living room.

". . . your occupation?"

Maybe I'd find a another postcard from Julianna. A picture of

Eskimos or just the whiteness of snow. *Freezing my ass off. Wish you were here.*

". . . the afternoon of February eighth when you . . ."

Nothing like sitting outside in the breeze after a nice long bath, flipping through the mail and petting Frank as he stretched out on the railing.

". . . when no one answered your knock, what did you . . ."

I looked ahead to John, the evening ahead with him, my reward if I lived through the day. Would he want to meet somewhere or just come over, pull his car around to the backyard?

". . . what you saw in the closet?"

I was almost through the worst of it. In my mind Julianna stood with her head tilted down, looking up at me under lifted eyebrows. Her serious look, just like her father's. She and I were at the beach. She turned to catch a Frisbee we were throwing around. When she turned back it was Jen Colby that looked up at me. The beach was empty except for us. Far away somewhere, someone's steady voice filled up a courtroom with her story. Far away in the courthouse, every face was turned to hear the witness's words.

"How did the other two children seem to you?"

Just a few questions left. I looked at Jen Colby standing on the beach beside me. I told myself again that she was a perfectly normal six-year-old. Just an unlucky kid who happened to get in the way of a cast-iron skillet while her mom was making scrambled eggs. A sweet kid, little shy, a little scrawny, and clumsy too. But nothing really wrong with her. No one would hurt their kid like that. I would never, never have done that to the Shrimp.

"Did you have any reason to suspect that abuse was taking place in the house?"

The beach disappeared. So did Jen. I was in the courtroom with a question hanging in the air. Just one little word would get me out of there forever. My eye shot to the window, seeking escape. There outside the streaked glass was the Night Visitor. A cold little shudder ran across my shoulders. In the harsh afternoon light he looked crumbled and worn. For the first time I saw his face. He was watching me.

"Miss Culpepper?" Mad Dog stood six feet from me. "Did you have any reason to suspect that abuse was taking place in the house?"

"Yes. I had reason to suspect it."

There were no audible gasps, no outbreaks of whispering all over the room, just a slight rustle of paper from the defense table. Folks continued to look at me, unmoving and silent. I kept my eyes on Mahoney, who was staring at me with her mouth slightly open.

"Would you please be more specific?" she said.

I told her everything that I had been seeing every night for months. Each thing alone could be excused, but not when you added it all up. And Jen's brother and sister behaved as though she didn't exist, as though she were diseased and might somehow contaminate them.

Mad Dog listened with no reaction. All this time she'd tried to get someone, anyone, to dig something out of their memory that she could use against Patricia Colby. She'd come up against a wall of "Nope sorry" every step of the way. If I had spoken up sooner, she would have had an entirely different case. Her face was blank, but I could see in the slight vibration of corkscrews all over her head that she was furious. She asked for specifics when she thought of it, had me repeat a few things. I kept talking until I had only one thing left to tell, the hardest thing, the impossible thing. And even then I kept on talking.

The Colby kids were the first to be picked up on the route each morning, the last to be dropped off each afternoon. The morning of February eighth when I pulled up to their house, there was the boy and the girl waiting at the end of the driveway like usual, but no Jen. When they boarded the bus it was clear that the older girl had been crying. The boy climbed in after her. He looked scared.

"Jen still sick?" I asked. She hadn't been to school in a week. I could feel the older girl grow alert, listening from her seat two rows away. The boy flushed dark and went to his seat without looking at me.

I closed the door and put the engine in gear. I looked over at the house, at the sheet hung neatly over one of the windows for a curtain, at the small yard and the bikes leaning against a tree. Just one of a dozen identical houses on that road, but something was different. Something was wrong. I thought maybe I should go up to the door and knock. Just ask if Jen was running late and should I wait a few minutes? But I didn't want to make a scene. If there was something wrong in that house it was none of my business; some relative or neighbor would help. People around here took care of their own and didn't appreciate strangers butting in. I had responsibilities, kids to get to school. I drove away.

"I drove away," I said to Mad Dog, and then I was silent. She stood looking at me like there was something she was trying to remember.

"That's all," she said at last, whether to me or the judge, I wasn't sure. She sat down and the defense lawyer stood up as if they were on a seesaw.

"I'd like to read from the police report filed by Detective Richard Freemont on February eighth," he said. No one objected so he continued. "Miss Culpepper was asked if the other children had indicated any problems that morning when she picked them up. Her reply was no. She was then asked if she had any suspicion that abuse was taking place in the house. Her reply, quote, 'No, none.'"

He paused. He looked younger than me, but his neck puffed out of the collar of his shirt like a middle-aged toad.

"Did you deliberately lie to the police that day?" he asked.

"No," I answered.

"But you just contradicted your statement."

This wasn't a question, so I didn't answer. He looked at me for a long time. I looked past Patricia Colby's out-thrust head, past Mad Dog's impassive mask. There sat the ravenous people with notebooks. I could feel the little bites as they scribbled. Soon there would be nothing left of me.

"I'm confused," he said. "Did you or did you not have any reason to believe that abuse was taking place in the Colby house?"

"I did."

"Were you aware that there was a problem that morning?"

"I was."

"And are you aware that Jennifer Colby died between the hours of 10:00 A.M. and 2:00 P.M. on February eighth?" Mr. Puffy Neck asked almost gently.

"Yes."

"And you're telling us that you knew something was wrong as early as 8:00 A.M.?"

"Yes."

"And yet you did nothing. By your own admission, you drove away and left her there to die."

And although this too was not a question, I gave him the answer. "Yes."

■   ■   ■

Four hours later I finished a beer and brought the second-day chili up to a low boil. Laid strips of Velveeta across the surface just as I'd promised myself. First I would eat, then I would plan how to live through the rest of the night.

I had dropped Mom off at her house and gone straight to Cadillac. Authorized more surgery to repair a shoulder tendon. Scheduled it for Sunday. If this didn't get him walking, they were out of ideas. The doctor once again talked of the possibility of euthanasia. When I was in sixth grade and the teacher discussed euthanasia I thought she said "Youth in Asia," and I didn't understand what the problem was and what they could have done that was so wrong. Frank was withdrawn, looking at me as if I had done this to him.

I came home to three messages from Amy and one from John. He'd sounded distracted, annoyed. "Something came up." He'd try to come by later, at least call. The metal spoon clattered against the stovetop. The cupboard door slammed harder than necessary. *Something came up.* I needed him now, not maybe later. Sat down at the table without Frank in the chair opposite me and ate, willing the phone to ring and break this sadistic solitude. Tried to unclench my stomach enough to eat. All the way home from the courthouse Mom had repeated "You did the right thing; you told the truth" with such superficial conviction I nearly drove into a tree to shut her up. Once she climbed out of the car, the corridor of silence was worse.

Amy's three messages: The first at 10:30 A.M., still just wanting to chat. The second at 3:00 P.M., "If you're not speaking to me, at least have the courtesy to tell me so," which struck me so funny I choked a little on my beer. The third I had just missed at 6:10 P.M. Contrite, embarrassed, "I remembered what day it is. I'm a jerk. Call me when you get home so we can talk about it." As if I could talk about it. As if I could talk about it in a million years. I dumped the bowl of chili. Stood by the kitchen table and wondered if I could bring my head down on it hard enough to crush memories.

"We've heard statements from the Colbys' family doctor, several neighbors, and parents of Jen's little playmates." Here Puffy Neck had turned to the jury for emphasis. "Nobody saw anything like what has just been described." I knew what was coming, but it was like a phantom pain, a rumor of hurt. Turning back to me he said, "How can you expect the jury to believe your story over the testimony of the others, when all you're claiming is that you're not only a liar but a coward as well?"

Mahoney was on her feet barking and snapping. He withdrew the question and sat down. She briefly tried to repair the damage, but dismissed me soon after. Every person in the courtroom averted their eyes when I rose from the witness box. I looked toward the window as I left, but the Night Visitor was gone.

Where was John? Why wasn't he here? I opened another beer

and ran a bath. Bubbles, candles, something nice. But no breeze
flirted in the open window and no amount of scrubbing made
me feel any cleaner. The phone did not ring. I dried off and
opened the bottom drawer. A dusky blue satin nightgown slid
down the length of me and swirled around my ankles. He would
be here any minute.

I popped another Stroh's and carried it into the living room.
Flipped on the TV. Underfed women with poufy hair talked into
tiny phones.

"Is Megan there?" Ha ha.

"Is Stephanie there?" Ha ha ha.

"Is Brittany there?" Ho ho ho.

I turned it off and called the animal clinic, got the usual answer: Frank was resting. I put Jimmie Dale Gilmore on the
stereo to gain some equilibrium. His angelic wail blew through
the thin fabric of my nightgown. Listening to him, you could almost believe in a good world. The phone did not ring. Outside
the window, darkness fell.

The trial adjourned shortly after my testimony was over.
They'd pick it up again after the three-day weekend break. Mad
Dog had cornered me on the way out of the municipal building.
"In my office at eight o'clock Tuesday morning," she said, nearly
stabbing a finger through my chest.

Damn it, where was he? I went to the fridge for another
Stroh's. There were none left, and I had bought a twelve-pack
the night before. The clock on the stove said 11:00 P.M. How'd it
get that late? There was a light breeze coming in the window
above the sink. It prickled my bare shoulders, reminding me of
the small shudder that morning in the courthouse. Maybe he'd
meant later. Maybe he'd meant we could get together at the end

of the evening. "Later on." He was stuck at work, worried that I'd be upset with him. Maybe I should call, just to let him know it's fine, I'm here at home and he can call when he's done. I found the gum wrapper with his number on it and dialed. After two rings it picked up and Loretta clenched herself in joy. A woman's voice said, "The number you have reached is unavailable." Unavailable. He wasn't at work. I hung up.

Loretta squeezed a tiny egg of hope in her hand until it cracked. Her voice rose up loud from my chest. That fucking son of a bitch. That fucking miserable piece of shit bastard fuck. He was probably up to Marion's right now, knocking back a beer and charming the shit out of someone like Suzanne O'Dell, or even Amy for all I knew. And if he didn't get lucky up there, then he'd give me a call as a last resort. The dusky blue satin tore all the way to my knees with one yank. Out of the dresser came the rest of the underwear, the teddies, the short night-gowns, the honey silk wrap, all torn to a soft pile of rags at my feet. I gathered it all up in a paper bag with the candles, the loofah thing, the powder puff. Threw on sweats and a long-sleeved T-shirt. On my way out the back door I grabbed last week's *Riverton Gazette* and a can of lighter fluid.

Outside the stars whirled in a grand waltz above me. The contents of the bag slid noiselessly into the burn barrel, raising up a white cloud of ash. Crunch, crunch, crunch went the *Gazette*, wadded up and wedged down deep in the barrel. I shot the whole thing twice with the lighter fluid. I struck the match.

"Just stop," said a small voice inside. "Don't do this." But I was seized with a fierce, impulsive fury. No internal arguments were going to prevent this fire. Loretta looked on with empty eyes, her hands hanging at her sides. The flame caught and flared like jealousy. Lingerie melted as quickly as the cotton candy at the fair yesterday. Only yesterday. Time had both sped up and stood still in the past week. There wasn't a single molecule of last week's Mary Culpepper left. They had all been replaced by layers of calluses, wised up and repulsive. I leaned over the burn barrel. The heat rose up and seared my cheeks, my eyelids. I wiggled the gumball ring off my finger and dropped it into the flames. Watched the shameful pink melt with the rest of it as tires approached with a faint glow of headlights. Dumb, pitiful Loretta leapt hopefully to her feet. The headlights faded as the sound of tires receded toward the Millers' house. I fought the desire to plunge my hands deep into the fire as the anger shifted. It wasn't John's fault if I sat around all night dressed like a ridiculous slut, waiting for him to call.

It was Friday night. He wasn't at Marion's, he was with everyone else up at the Beer Tent outside the fairgrounds. I could see the small stage at one end, the space cleared for dancing, the sea of picnic tables. Everyone was drinking or dancing. Talk and laughter and cigarette smoke hovered a few feet over the crowd like the strips of mist that covered Lake Kassauga early in the morning. I could see John there. I could see that sleepy-eyed smile. He was scratching the side of his chin with his thumbnail and grinning at some woman whose thin laughter rose above the blanket of conversation. He had a beer in his hand, and I was the last thing on his mind.

I yanked open the door to the work shed. Firelight streamed in behind me causing my shadow to jump and dance. Plastic goggles hung on a nail near the door. I slipped them on, adjusted them tight, and grabbed blindly at the first shelf. Stretched back like I was throwing hard to third base and sent the glass figurine flying across the short space between me and the cinder-block wall. At the explosion my arm rose instinctively to protect my face. Needles of glass flew apart in quick, silver shrieks. Adrenaline flowed through me like desire. I reached up with two hands for more. Brought down a blown-glass bud vase that screamed high and thin when it hit the wall. My veins sang in response. Tiny slivers of glass filled the air.

I thought of Julianna, of the stupid, selfish waste of her trust; all for a one-night stand and this humiliation. Crash, crash, crash, a steady rhythm of explosions pitched faster and faster. I didn't deserve her friendship. All I deserved was someone like Amy. The thought of Amy ignited something that boiled and built momentum until seven years of fury rolled like lava down my arm. I sent more explosions against the concrete wall as the whole thing finally hit me. For Carl to choose Amy over me, it proved he was a weak, spineless bastard. A real man wouldn't need spicy Hungarian goulash. A real man knew the value of macaroni and cheese, goddamn it. Carl was nothing but an ig-norant alcoholic piece of shit. I hurled the glass faster. Con-descending asshole semiliterate patronizing prick. Faster and faster. Dishonest chicken-shit coward who wanted a manne-quin, a pretty doll for a wife. The magic veil that had torn apart that morning at the courthouse, it had hidden more than I thought. And it was dawning on me now, as the glass flew all around me, that my best friend Amy was a selfish bitch. So des-perate for approval, for everyone's love, that she strip-mined Carl right away from me. Wouldn't even tell me herself. After twenty years of friendship she'd left me to hear it from him. Why did I let it happen? Why was she still in my life?

The answer was closing in on me, the veil tearing apart in all directions. *I raised you better than that.* Mom had filled me with poison against all men, and women were worse, no one to be trusted.

"I hate you," I said in the darkness. "Hate you," as I swept an arm across an entire shelf. The crash sounded like the end of the world. I said it to Mom, who had used me as a club to beat her husband with guilt. I said it to Dad, who made me just one of many girlfriends to replace his wife. My wonderful, normal, average parents were so wrapped up in their selfish and hateful marriage that they chewed me up to spit me out at one another. People were supposed to cherish and protect their children. But Dad had loved me like one more pickup in a bar. And Mom had loved me like a soldier loves his gun.

I had learned it early on: Both men and women will annihilate you without a thought; love means being plundered and left for dead. And Amy had loved me all my life. Of course I had never questioned her behavior, of course she was my closest friend.

If I reached for one more piece of glass I wouldn't stop until I broke everything in sight, even the windows on the Merc. Breath came in acid gasps. I knelt there in the wreckage with Loretta pumping hard to keep up. My skin was hot all over where the slivers had dug deep. The geyser of scalding rage calmed to a steady flow. I pulled off the goggles that had fogged over with sweat. Regained my breath and stepped cautiously out of the shed, surprised to find the rest of the world intact. The northern night blossomed like a lustrous black rose all around me. I was tired and unraveled. A giant knot had come untied and my nerves lay in loose coils along the ground, all urgency gone. I left the mess behind me and drifted into the cottage, sat at the kitchen table. Missed Frank with a hollow ache. I kept the bottle of Jameson's at my elbow and refilled the glass regularly. The leaden flow of anger continued. I wondered how I would ever dam it up again. At 3:15 A.M. I opened another pack of Kools. At 4:30 A.M. the cigarette smoke was stale before it hit my lungs and the bottle of Jameson's was dry.

I could never say to Amy and Carl: *You betrayed me. You broke my heart. You have done the absolute worst thing in the world.* Just overused words. None of it conveyed the ache down to my fingernails, the deafening loneliness in taking the next breath. Worse than their betrayal was the fear that I'd lose them altogether, so I had sealed over any pain or anger. Now it was leaking out from a never-healed wound. All these years I'd pitied Amy's need to be loved. I enjoyed feeling superior to her, gloating in my stoic self-containment, only to find that I had needed love after all. And the final sickening truth was that the two people I needed most had loved one another more than they loved me.

I went into the bedroom and stood at the window waiting for the Night Visitor. Nothing but night stared back at me. I waited and waited. My cigarette was a small, fuming dot in a sea of dark. No one came.

I wished for my magic veil back again. Better to be blind and numb than to face this useless rage, this proof of just how alone I really was. Of all the people I'd been close to, the only one who hadn't hurt me was Julianna Coleros. And she was somewhere in the Arctic by now.

17

Saturday morning, the Labor Day Festival in full swing, and the tournament finals just hours away. I rolled out of bed still in my clothes from the night before, head pierced by a thousand needles. I'd agreed to drive with Mom to Kalkaska to see how Stacy was holding up at home. That was the reason Mom gave, but it was really just to see that baby. "I'm going to see that baby," she would say, as if there were a nationwide conspiracy to keep her from him.

When I flipped on the light in the bathroom I saw red dots sparkling across the backs of both hands, tiny pinpricks of blood like jeweled freckles. I patiently took the tweezers to each sliver. A half hour later my hands were glass-free but swollen and mottled and stinging like hell from the rubbing alcohol. When I looked in the mirror I saw a gash on my forehead. In the night it had bled like a bastard down my nose, making a stark portrait that stared at me in surprise. "Look at yourself," it said. "What did you do?"

Never mind that it was accidental. Never mind that facial cuts always bled buckets and looked worse than they were. I had been out of control, and this is what I'd done to myself. When I was admitted to Munson Medical last February my ankles had needed seven stitches from the glass shards coming off the steps. I took a shower, dug some makeup out the back of the bathroom closet, and dabbed tiny dots on my face. Smoothed it in to cover the evidence. Drove carefully to pick up Mom, but it was a shadow of me steering, talking, smoking; the real me was still sprawled on the bed at home. I couldn't look her in the face, couldn't stand to have her sitting so near me, but there was no other choice. I couldn't scream at her for ruining me before I even got started; couldn't blame my whole life on her. I could hear the answer: "Why are you dragging all that up now?"

I was hoping that she and Stacy would distract one another sufficiently for me to do a quiet fade into the background, but when Ruther led us into the bedroom Stacy started in.

"I left a message on your machine," she said as we came through the door. "I was beginning to think you weren't coming."

"We hit some traffic," I said.

"Did you know she got an answering machine?"

"No," Mom answered.

"So tell me all about this big fight," Stacy said.

"What big fight?"

"You and Amy. God, I wish I could've seen it. Lori said the whole restaurant heard every word."

"Lori who?"

"Lori, Ruther's sister. 'Lori who.' Give me a break."

"What fight?" asked Mom.

"Mary and Amy had a knock-down-drag-out at the Lake Crest."

"No we didn't."

"What did you girls fight about?" Mom asked.

"It's not like I pulled out the old twelve-gauge and let her have it," I added, flopping into an armchair near the bed.

"That's not funny," Stacy said to me. "You want to turn my milk sour?"

"What?"

"If you upset me, my milk could turn sour and make the baby sick."

"Maybe I ought to leave," I offered.

"Don't be silly," Mom said to Stacy. "Who told you that?"

Stacy tilted her head seriously. "Well, it stands to reason, doesn't it?"

"No it doesn't. Now both of you knock it off." There was a brief recess while we all regrouped.

"How are you feeling?" I inquired politely.

"Fine."

"Is it nice to be home?"

"Yes."

"Good."

Stacy ventured a peace offering. "How'd it go yesterday?" Mom gave her a warning look.

"Fine," I answered.

Mom picked a piece of fluff off the foot of Stacy's blanket and watched me sideways. "So you got an answering machine," she said.

"Yup."

"What finally made you give in?"

"So I can screen calls." Which was only half the truth, the hostile half.

"Why would you need to screen calls?" Mom asked.

"I don't need to. I want to."

"She wants to avoid Amy," Stacy interjected.

"How's the baby?" I asked as a diversion.

"Ruther's bringing him in so I can feed him," she said, beaming. In came Ruther with a very small thing in his hands. Stacy whipped out a breast like she'd been doing it her whole life. Turd Ball latched on for dear life.

"Ow!" Stacy said. "Watch it! Geez." She looked up at Mom and smiled like a madonna. "Isn't he great?"

"I'm going to lay down on the couch," Ruther mumbled. He looked like a cadaver. Finally, Stacy and Mom wandered down the lane of feedings, changings, burpings, and shittings. I maintained a pleasantly attentive expression while my thoughts jumped around at random. Frank was still resting quietly, according to a nice voice on the phone earlier. I would try to drive over there before the game that afternoon. Tomorrow I'd stay with Frank until the surgery was over. Would there be any messages on my machine when I got home? I hadn't done a good job of stretching out before the game Thursday night, and my shoulder still ached from my stunt in the work shed last night. Don't think about last night. A fly crawled in loops along the windowsill. No one had mentioned the cuts on my face, so I guess—

"Do you want to hold him?"

Mom and Stacy were both looking at me expectantly. Turd Ball flailed a fist in protest.

"No."

"God," said Stacy, throwing her head back against her pillow.

"Go on, Mary." Mom was gentle but firm. "It won't kill you."

She deposited the writhing thing, freshly fed, in my lap while reminding me to keep his head supported. I settled him against the crook of my elbow and waited for the screams to start. Turd Ball stared at the top of my head as if I had a herd of tiny giraffes up there. His eyeballs looked like gasoline scum on a pond. "What's wrong with his eyes?" I asked.

"What?" asked Stacy in alarm.

"There's this metallic film over his eyes."

"All babies have that at first," Mom reassured me. Stacy glowered. I kept the rest of my observations to myself. The fishhook-shaped scar from the forceps was fading nicely. The scales were reduced to scattered flakes here and there on his forehead. Not half as ugly as he'd been five days ago. The thing on my lap wasn't a week old.

"Hi," I said gamely. He arched his back. His face turned a dark red. "He's choking," I said, leaning forward suddenly in the chair.

"No, he's just shitting," Stacy told me grandly. "It takes a lot of energy."

Then he made a noise. He said, "Uphn aahng." All the while his eyes wandered among those tiny giraffes roaming the top of my head. Then he punched himself in the face.

"He likes you," Mom said. I frowned.

"Do you want me to take him?" Stacy asked.

"No," I answered. "He's all right."

She and Mom had been watching me closely. Stacy took a deep breath. "Well, I'm glad you feel that way," she said quickly. "Because Ruther and I want you to be his godmother."

If my mouth dropped to my knees, Mom's hit the floor. Twenty implications hit me at once while I stared at Stacy propped up on the bed. The question of my current mental stability, the fact that I was divorced and living in semihermitude, my stubborn refusal to swoon over her pregnancy, and of course the bitter conversation we'd had at the hospital a few nights before. Thousands of faults, large and small, that I believed had condemned me irrevocably in the eyes of Stacy and Ruther, all swept away in one unforeseen stroke. The baby had fallen asleep on me.

"What do I do?" I asked.

"Well, I guess the big thing is, you take him if Ruther and I both die." My eyes were saucer-sized. I couldn't blink or swallow. "But mostly you just, you know, be a good influence on him."

Mom interjected. "Traditionally, a godparent is a child's spiritual guide."

Spiritual guide? Stacy was watching me nervously. I was watching the baby. He farted wetly into my arm.

"Could you please say something?" Stacy finally asked. "It's kind of serious."

"Yes."

"You'll have to stand up with us at the christening," she added, as if afraid I would change my mind.

"Yes."

Mom asked for details on the christening gown and soon I

was forgotten. I looked down at Turd Ball, my godson with the fishhook-shaped scar. Well, we could play softball. We could rake leaves. I could show him my *National Geographic*s. We'd go for walks in the woods next to the cottage. I would teach him how to drive; I was a professional, after all. And teach him to embroider, whether Stacy liked it or not, so he could sew up the holes in his socks. I could buy him a drum set and drive his parents out of their minds. Turd Ball wiggled and turned his face toward my chest, overwhelmed by all my plans. He was tiny, uncoordinated, unable to do a thing for himself except shit. The world would brutalize him a thousand ways before he hit kindergarten. The first thing I would teach him was not to punch himself in the face.

Mrs. Baumann showed up to spend the day with Stacy. Mom and I drove back to Riverton and met Sharon in the basement of the First Presbyterian Church, where their rummage sale was already an hour old. There were about five billion lawn and garage sales all over Riverton that weekend, but the Annual First Presbyterian Rummage Sale was the acknowledged jewel in the festival's crown. Mom made a beeline for the children's clothes.

"It's ridiculous to pay good money for something he'll only wear once," she said, plowing into piles of tiny T-shirts alongside a dozen other women. Sharon had an armload of cotton print bedsheets for making summer skirts and blouses. She beckoned me over, happy to see me. Last night the whole town had been up at the Beer Tent, with me home alone and turned inside out; now I was a godmother. I was somewhere between the two extremes, trying to hold on.

"I already took two bags out to the car," Sharon said. "How's Stacy?"

"She's okay. Ruther's mom is gonna stay all day."

We drifted over to the shoe corner. Sharon slipped off one sandal and tucked it into her armload of sheets. "I stopped at the Lake Crest for waffles and made it here when they opened the doors at ten." She stuck her toe in a saddle shoe, then thought better of it. "You find anything yet?" she asked.

"No."

"You gonna look?"

I let out a sigh, sounding like Mom. "Yeah."

Then Sharon stopped browsing and looked at me for the first time. "Mom told me."

"Told you what?"

"About yesterday," she said. "Was it really that bad?"

I didn't answer. I saw a pair of red canvas slip-ons. Picked one up to check the size, too small.

"I'm sorry I wasn't there," she told me. "I wish I'd been there."

"Why?"

"Just . . . I don't know. Proud of you."

Something withered inside me. "Don't romanticize it," I said. "Besides, it's not over yet."

She laughed, picking up a pair of tan pumps. "God, you're such an asshole," she said, as if commenting on the price.

I wanted to ask her if she'd seen John last night at the Beer Tent. I would rather choke than mention him.

"Did you go up to the Beer Tent?" I asked, then walked away to look at toasters and ice cube trays.

"Jesus, it's a good thing you weren't there," she said behind me. My gut twisted, knotted, fell in a heap between my hip bones. He was there with some other woman. For Christ's sake, I was the other woman. He was probably there with Doreen. Pain and shame closed my eyes. I tossed off a "Really? Why?"

"Sharon, you want me to take those up front for you?" It was Mrs. Brickham. Her black beehive hairdo was covered by a straw hat embroidered with orange and blue butterflies, and a goofy apron hung around her waist. It was the uniform for all the First Presbyterian women working the rummage sale.

"Mom might already have a pile going," Sharon told her, handing over the stack of sheets and retrieving her sandal.

"How are you girls?" Mrs. Brickham asked. She smiled with black sparkly eyes like the shoe button eyes on my old Raggedy Ann.

"Great. We're great," said one of us.

"Bob's over behind the counter," she said. "So you be sure and say hi." Mr. Brickham was in the kitchen area with half a dozen other First Presbyterian men, serving coffee and homemade muffins for a dollar a pop. The thought of him handing me a blueberry muffin with his two-fingered hand made me suddenly so sad I wanted to lie under a table and weep.

Sharon and I were left with just a table full of glassware for company. I tried to keep my hands to myself as I contemplated how to steer the conversation back to last night. Still my index finger ran lightly over the fluted edge of a glass candy dish, making it hard to concentrate.

"You gonna buy that?" Sharon asked skeptically.

I yanked my hand away. To hell with it. To hell with him. I would not ask her. I would leave Everett Park as soon as we took the trophy. No staying for the men's game, no drifting up to the Beer Tent afterward, no dancing, no fireworks show at 10:00, none of the usual Labor Day festivities. I would spend the evening with Stacy and the baby. Ruther's mom would be there. Well, I could stop by anyway for a short visit, say hello to my godson. Then maybe I'd watch some TV with Mom. Didn't want to be near Mom. Maybe Carl and Amy . . . My jaw clamped tight. "Why is it a good thing I wasn't there last night?"

Sharon thought for a minute, as if I'd revived a subject that died hours ago. "Oh. Because Amy was going on and on, how she's worried about you. I wanted to smack her."

Was it possible to despise myself any more than I was about to? My hand rested on a glass salt shaker, just itching . . . "Was John there?"

"Your friend?" she asked.

"Yes," I seethed.

"I didn't see him."

Meaning she didn't see him because she didn't bother to notice if he was there? Or she didn't see him because he absolutely wasn't there and she would've noticed if he had been? I wanted to shake her until her ribs rattled.

"We can't call the kid Turd Ball anymore," I told her.

"Why not?"

"He's my godson."

Sharon was silent, looking at half-burned sand candles. Maybe she'd expected to be his godmother herself. The atmosphere had become heavy and complicated.

I said, "Stacy says I practically raised the two of you." Sharon looked up at me oddly. I went on, not knowing where it was coming from. "Is that true?"

Before Sharon could answer, a woman swooped at me with her arms full of doll clothes. It was Nancy LaFarge, the short-stop for Dudley Hardware. A small girl was wrapped around one of her legs. "I heard about it, Mary," she said to me.

"Heard about what?" I asked. Take your pick, these days.

"What you said yesterday," Nancy replied. "You know they live just down the road from us."

"Oh." I knew the LaFarge house: giant wooden butterfly nailed above the garage door, plastic wishing well spilling petunias in the front yard. The little girl was swinging from side to side against her mother's leg, staring up at me with her mouth open and slack the way kids do.

"I have to say, I was surprised," Nancy said. She stopped and looked at me, at a loss. Then she let out a little sigh and gave a puzzled, friendly smile. "I mean, maybe you've been watching too many talk shows."

"Why do you say that?" I asked, as Sharon swelled danger-ously beside me.

"Patty loved that little girl," Nancy said simply, as if love con-quered all. I looked down at Nancy Junior, who was now picking her nose behind her mother's knee.

"I don't watch TV much," I said stupidly. Then Sharon said something. Then Mom appeared. Then someone said some-thing else and I was walking away with Mom and Sharon on ei-ther side of me.

"Forget it," Mom said quietly. "That bitch ought to mind her own onions." But Nancy wasn't a bitch. If she honestly believed that love made you safe from your parents, then she wasn't vicious, just stupid.

"I'm hungry," I said while Mom and Sharon paid for their clothes.

"We're heading over to the sidewalk sales," Mom said. "You can get a bite then."

The sidewalks were thick with people, none of them moving above a crawl. Every merchant in Riverton had a table set up in front of their place piled with bargains. Mom stopped outside the House of Style, where Mrs. Richardson was getting a free beauty makeover right there on the sidewalk. I kept walking after a friendly wave. She was having lip liner applied and couldn't call out for me to stop.

"Tell Mom I'll be at Marion's," I said to Sharon before I shouldered my way out of the crowd and onto the street. I had to go a half block out of my way to avoid passing the bait shop. Carl would be out front selling lures and thermal socks. He wasn't the last person I wanted to talk to today, but he was in the top two. The sun sent sharp rays across the car hoods that rolled slowly by. The heat muffled my head in a pillow. A handful of Riverton High band members played Dixieland music at the gazebo across the street. Blue Light Sunoco had set up a helium tank, giving away balloons amid the gassed-up shrieks and laughter of the boys working the pumps. Everywhere I looked there were children shouting and playing, running around without any shells.

I ducked inside Marion's with my head beating a gong along the top of my eyebrows. It was pitch black inside except for the cool glow of neon from the silent jukebox. As my eyes adjusted to the dark, Marion slowly took shape on a stool at the bar.

Other than a few folks in a booth toward the back, the place was a tomb.

"You look like hell," Marion said.

"It's a nightmare out there," I replied.

"I'd like to take a fire hose to the whole goddamn street." She was reading a paper, which she flipped over as I mounted the stool next to her. Not quickly enough; I saw the headline. "Every year it's the same thing." She climbed down off the stool. "What'll I get you?"

"BLT." I glanced at the clock over the door. 12:10 P.M. "And a Stroh's."

She poured the beer and trundled back to the kitchen. The pounding in my head doubled at the first taste but then quieted down again. I tried to ignore the paper at my elbow, though it shone like an ember. The Dixieland music was faint and far away. I was alone in a silent universe with nothing to hold on to, just endless open space all around me, and it was not so bad. I flipped over the newspaper: SCHOOL BUS DRIVER CRIES CHILD ABUSE. I continued to float in endless black where there was nothing, no consequences or repercussions, no gravity, no barometric pressure, just weightless drifting.

"Mary?"

"Hmm?"

Marion stood at the kitchen door. "You okay?"

"Yeah."

"You want it on white or wheat?"

"White."

Marion disappeared back into the kitchen. There was a brief account of the conflicting testimony from the day before. There was also a quote from Patricia Colby's sister, claiming hysteria and sensationalism on the part of "one witness," calling Jen a perfectly normal kid, and her death a tragic accident. Mad Dog had barred me from talking to the press. As if I would. I flipped the paper over and pushed it away.

Someone fed the jukebox and David Bowie began to sing about an astronaut who hit orbit and never came back. The summer I was eleven, Dad called me to the garage. He was rebuilding the engine on the riding mower he'd bought at Montgomery Ward. Monkey Wards, he called it.

"Listen to this," he said. "Listen to this song." I'd heard it plenty of times before, but I listened: the conversation between ground control and Major Tom, the outer space voice of David Bowie, the electric chill of the guitar.

"Do you think it was an accident?" Dad said. "A mistake?" I shrugged. Hadn't thought about it. "Or did he just cut the line and float away?"

"I don't know."

Dad stopped turning his wrench and gazed at me for a moment. "It's the damnedest song, isn't it?"

I took a long hit off the Stroh's and stretched my hand flat on the cool surface of the bar. I didn't remember the rest of the conversation. I know about a half hour later he lost his grip on that same wrench and cut his finger right to the bone. Most of those rebuilt engines had his blood on them somewhere. These days when Mom needed a new hose on the washer or maybe the furnace was acting up, she called Harold Tucker. I noticed that he'd usually tinker longer than he strictly needed to. So Mom wouldn't see that what took Stu Culpepper two hours, Harold Tucker could do in twenty minutes?

Sitting there in Marion's, the song drifting above my head, there was no doubt in my mind; he had just cut the line and floated away. The Stroh's was taking the edge off the day. Maybe I would sit there on the bar stool until it was time to head to the ballpark. I wasn't up to sidewalk sales or raffles or family fun. Like Amy had said the other morning, run home and have a drink.

"Hey," said a voice to my left. Carl landed on the bar stool next to me. The thought of Amy had conjured him like a curse.

"I didn't hear you come in," I said into my empty glass.

"Your mom said I'd find you here."

Mom had never let go of the hope that Carl and I would one day reunite. She considered Amy a troublesome blip in our marriage.

"And here I am," I said.

"You look tired."

I didn't answer. Marion came in from the kitchen with a little halt when she saw Carl. It was barely noticeable, but I knew she must've heard some version of my fight with Amy. She slid my BLT onto the bar and asked Carl what he was having. He asked for a Jack Daniel's double and a Bud back. Inside, I lifted my eyebrows. Outside, I was a stone.

"You doing good business so far?" Marion asked as she poured his drink.

"I must've had a hundred people in and out since seven."

"Bastards are running you ragged, huh?" She refilled my Stroh's without asking, God love her.

"How you doing?" he asked her, looking around the empty bar.

"I'm doing great. Keeping 'em the hell out." Then she picked up her paper and a pack of Marlboros and settled herself in a booth a discreet distance away.

I stayed quiet and let Carl screw up the courage to say whatever he was going to say. Mostly I pretended he wasn't there and ate my BLT. Marion had laid the mayonnaise on extra thick like the real cook that she was.

"Good luck this afternoon," he ventured.

"Thanks," I said through a mouthful of bacon. "You too." I kept my eyes on the mirrored shelves behind the bar. Carl shifted on his stool and sent the Jack Daniel's down the hatch. Then he reached for his Budweiser and knocked it flat across the bar. Beer rushed past my plate and foamed onto my lap as I jumped off the bar stool.

"Jesus Christ, Carl." I grabbed my napkin and tried to block the beer's path. He reached across the bar, picked up a stack of cocktail napkins, and threw them down here and there. "What the hell's the matter with you?" I asked him.

I was soaked. My shorts would be clammy the rest of the afternoon. Goddamn Carl, ruining a nice quiet lunch. The three of us sopped up the worst of it, Marion with the mop, me and Carl with dishrags. Marion returned to her booth after pouring another beer for each of us. The natural, normal thing for me to say next was, "How's Amy?" I finished my sandwich in silence. He could sit there and rot before I'd bring it up. The BLT was gone and my cigarette half smoked when he broke.

"Amy's wondering why you aren't calling her back," he said. "She thinks you're annoyed with her." I stayed quiet, looking at the tiny cuts on my hand. "What's up?" he asked finally.

I turned to look him in the face, expecting to see the usual avoidance, the bland easygoing emptiness that seemed to be all that was left of a Carl I once knew. But he was hunkered over with his elbows on the bar, head tilted down and turned to me, waiting to hear whatever I had to say. I saw an old Carl from way back before we were married; so far away that I'd forgotten him. I averted my face and drained my beer. I would get up and walk out before I'd let him see how much I missed him. This time he let the silence stretch out. He was waiting for an answer. I opened my mouth, cut the line, and floated.

"It finally sank in," I said. "I can't forgive it."

We swayed in the brief balance where he could pretend not to know what I was talking about. I wished he would, wished he'd prove himself once again the coward I'd said good riddance to. He took a breath to bolster himself and said, "Why didn't you stop me?"

"I didn't think I could."

"Bullshit," he said, pushing his beer away. "You weren't willing to put up a fight and find out."

"I shouldn't have to fight for my own husband." It sounded like an unpleasant echo of Mom. "It was too late by then anyway."

"You made sure of that."

"How, Carl?" I banged my open hand on the bar. Marion kept her nose buried in the paper. "Go ahead and tell me how it was all my fault."

"You shut your eyes at the first sign of trouble," he answered.

I turned on the bar stool like I was about to hit him. "Is that how you've lived with yourself? Convinced that I didn't care?"

"You don't care about anybody—"

"Go to hell."

"—so long as you can protect yourself."

The air hummed like the silence after gunfire. I blinked in the bright clarity of one honest statement bumping into another. The front door opened and Sharon entered, followed by Mom and a newly made-over Mrs. Richardson. Sharon walked pointedly past the bar with barely a nod to me and settled into a booth behind the jukebox. Another chance to remind Carl that he was a traitor and a bastard and a son of a bitch as far as she was concerned. Carl's two mothers-in-law stopped on either side of him.

"Hi sweetheart," said Mrs. Richardson, resting a hand on his shoulder.

"Oh, you found her," Mom said, letting Amy's mother know that he'd been looking for me.

"Yup," Carl grinned. "Holed up and hunkered over a beer."

"That's our Mary," Mom answered, to chuckles all around. I closed my eyes, fingered the small gash on my forehead.

"Mary, I just want to tell you I heard all about what you did yesterday," Mrs. Richardson began. "And I'm telling you right now, I think that woman should be put away until she rots. I told Howard up to the bakery that if you say you saw something, then you saw something. And if that means other folks weren't telling the truth, then they weren't telling the truth."

"That's exactly what I told Jeanine Brickham this morning," Mom said quietly, as if it were a dirty subject. I slid off the bar stool, leaving Carl to juggle them alone. If he was embarrassed, wedged between my mom and Amy's, he didn't show it. I went behind the bar and refilled my glass. Marion was taking lunch orders from the foursome that had just arrived up front.

"Hey Mary, bring me a Miller Lite." It was Sharon, calling carelessly over her shoulder.

I set my pint glass down on the bar. Carl and Mrs. Richardson were talking about Sasha's puppies. Sharon was punching buttons at the jukebox. Mom was watching me. She'd been watching me all morning.

John's desertion landed like a fist in my stomach. He'd left me to this, surrounded by all the people who loved me, sucking the slow poison of my resentment, distracting myself with the occasional married man so I didn't see my loneliness and the long years stretching out ahead. A little rough sex on the side to let off steam so I don't . . . what? So I don't what?

I closed my eyes and saw my bathroom at home. Water was running low in the bathtub, barely more than a trickle. The shower curtain was closed. Frank sat on the toilet seat, meowing, hungry. A razor blade lay on the windowsill above my head. Ribbons of red ran lengthwise down my legs, my arms. Breasts sagged, defeated. The water trickled from the faucet onto my foot, staining it clean. And the look on my face: Behind the loose flesh, the blood congealed and the blood still dripping, there was a look on my face, a look of desolation. I'd always expected peace or serenity; here was just bleak disappointment. One eyebrow was drawn down as if not believing it, not believing that this could be it.

"Mary, you getting that beer?" said Sharon, still at the jukebox.

I stepped out from behind the bar. I walked out the front door of Marion's into a white haze of Labor Day delirium. The heat and noise absorbed me, magically erasing the people left inside the bar. Cars oozed by slowly; people's mouths moved in exaggerated chat, banter, laughter. The sidewalk heaved up to meet me as I walked down Main Street to the First Presbyterian Church. I climbed in the Merc and drove.

18

Didn't think, just drove. Had my bank card, my credit card, a full pack of cigarettes. Wasn't any reason in the world to stop. Didn't have anywhere I needed to be, no place I was going, but I was going anyway. The road was choked with campers, cars towing boats and jet skis, with bikes on the roof that pedaled upside-down in the wind. Everybody was on their way some-where, and I was too. I hit the silver button on the dash and the rear windshield slid down. Hot wind filled the car. I kept the radio off and let the traffic sounds keep me company. I was going south where no one knew me. If I got hungry I'd stop at one of those Cracker Barrels, or maybe a Denny's. No Lake Crest Café where everyone knows your name, your face, your story. Everywhere I went from now on, I'd be a stranger. If I had to I could learn to waitress, or work in a library with lots of quiet and solitude. I'd rent an efficiency with a stovetop and a minifridge. No one would know that I was from up north. No one would know about my part in the Colby trial. Not an inkling about Amy or Carl or a single member of my family. And all of them in Riverton, they'd never hear from me again. "She walked out of Marion's in the middle of the sidewalk sales, and was never seen again."

Now I was in freefall. Nothing above, nothing below, nothing to grab hold of. I thought about the home I would never see again, about Frank's empty food dish on the kitchen floor. I would send for him once I was settled. There was my quilt neatly folded on the back of the couch, my toaster cover with the embroidered birds singing away, half a pot of chili just hitting its stride in the fridge. A strong lake breeze blew the curtains above the kitchen sink like it always did this time of day. A few bowls and a coffee mug were rinsed and sitting on the counter. I wasn't going back there, back to the homey prison I'd made for myself.

My tires hit a gravel driveway. I stopped the Merc, looked up through the windshield. The bikes that once leaned against the side of the tree were gone. No car in the driveway. The crocuses in the corner of the yard were gone as well. A sheet still hung neatly over one window. Heat shimmered up off the yard, a yard without police cars or emergency trucks or people in uniforms milling all around. Just a trailer home like a hundred others around here.

I knew the house was empty. Pat Colby had spent the last seven months in the county jail; no one could afford bail. The other kids were with their dad in Manistee. No one had lived here since last winter. I pulled the Merc behind the house out of sight of the road, then came back to the front porch. Climbed the cinder blocks to the front door. I opened the screen and knocked, leaning against the doorjamb, knowing no one would come. I knocked again and tried the doorknob; locked. Rested my forehead against the screen for a moment then came down off the porch. A robin called out from the silence behind the house. In the backyard was a swing set with a little slide attached to it. Didn't remember it being there before. From there I could see the window of Jen's bedroom. Tried the back door. It opened easily. I stepped back in dismay. Then I entered the kitchen and called hello to the empty air. The chill was gone but the stillness felt the same as ever, as if the house had held its breath all this time. Someone had tidied the kitchen. The avocado-colored refrigerator had the same soccer schedule taped in the same place. I walked into the living room, a place I'd not actually seen before: couch and chair in matching plaid, TV and VCR with children's videos stacked nearby. In the far corner a vacuum cleaner leaned against the wall. I followed the same path I'd tread that day last winter. At the bathroom I flipped on the light. Spotless. A plastic bottle of *Pocahontas* bubble bath sat on the rim of the tub. In the mirror I saw my reflection flicker like a ghost.

All the doors in the hall were closed but no doubt in my mind which one was Jen's. The sister's bed came into view first, neatly made like before. Then Jen's bed with her toys all picked up. The closet door was closed. I thought of the Night Visitor and his tyrannical images, the fear that that door had held for me night after night. I opened it wide. The floor was bare. Someone had tidied up in here as well. Even now I felt the urge to pick her up, pull her out into the light. I stepped inside the closet and sat down on the floor. Left the door open just a little and leaned my back against the wall. I could get no closer to her than this.

No sound anywhere in the house except my quiet breathing. Outside in the world people were getting ready for the final tournament games, soaking up the sun and the holiday atmosphere. There were no more thoughts of running away, no more thoughts of a life surrounded by strangers. If I were found here, it would earn me another stay at Munson Medical, but I didn't feel crazy.

It wasn't that a parade of unexpected memories flooded back to me. There were no revelations, no surprises. What I saw was the same old family, the same people we'd always been. But now my life was turning on a pedestal, revealing facets that I'd ignored. I saw the past from the eyes of the Baptist ladies who cold-shouldered me and Mom because they'd heard stories about Dad. I saw it from my teachers' eyes, who repeatedly wrote in my report cards *withdrawn, has difficulty making friends.* I saw it from Sharon and Stacy's eyes, who hardly knew Dad at all. They were eleven and ten when he died and he'd never been home much in those years. I saw it through the eyes of Dad's women, who looked ashamed when they saw me bleary-eyed in my pajamas, stumbling after Mom as she yanked my arm and told me to look, look. It had not been normal at all. It had not been okay.

And it was not okay now: the cutting jabs among Mom and us girls, the kid I couldn't have for fear of the damage I'd do, the sad silent death of my marriage, and Amy's betrayal. I'd had a lifetime of looking but refusing to see, until finally I closed my eyes altogether; so blinded that I didn't see a little girl on my bus.

You don't care about anybody, so long as you can protect yourself.

I curled up on the closet floor, one arm forming a pillow for my head. I looked up at Jen's clothes hanging above me. The pain in my heart was harder, much harder than the brilliant burst of rage last night. Anger makes you invincible; grief leaves you small and helpless. But the sorrow came finally, quietly. Tucked inside that closet, nowhere else to go, I had forever to cry. Tears rained down on the dry cracked life that was mine. "I'm sorry," I whispered over and over.

■   ■   ■

When daylight was gone I sat up, bones aching. It had to be after 9:00 P.M. I sat rubbing my shoulder, then carefully made my way through the dark and silent house. Once in the Merc I took a deep breath. I was home. I felt something small and tender beginning inside me. There was one thing I needed to do now, one person I needed to see.

Miles fell under the Merc's tires with small sighs. Came up behind a camper poking along in the darkness. Swerved over to pass and met a blinding light and a roar like a tornado. I couldn't swerve back into my lane; the camper was in the way. I veered harder to the left, onto the opposite shoulder. Whoosh! A truck tore past with his horn scolding. I came to a stop and calmed down a little before climbing back onto the road. My hands shook as I gripped the wheel. Thought maybe I should just drive straight home. But I didn't turn onto Tomford Road and home to a quiet night alone. I turned on Route 108 and drove through Riverton to the fairgrounds.

The lights of the Beer Tent glowed against the sky. The music swelled around me as I climbed out of the Merc. Closed all the windows and locked the doors. I had a couple of bucks in my pocket, my keys. I had gone a long way into outer space, into the dark. Now I was back on earth, where people flowed past me, warm and alive. I saw Harold Tucker returning to his table with two plastic cups of beer. He handed one to Mom and sat down beside her. The way she took it from him, offhanded and no fuss, made me look at both her and Harold in a new way. For the first time it dawned that maybe they were more than friends. I moved on without Mom seeing me, into the crowd where I heard lots of voices and laughter, lots of "where you been?"s and "what happened to you?"s. I kept on moving, smiling, nodding. Every alcoholic in Kassauga County was in full throttle by now. Port-O-Potties stood off to the side of the tent like rooks on a chessboard. The band was a country band from over to Cadillac. I remembered them from last year. I stopped to get a beer so I'd have something in my hand, so I wouldn't stand out like a circus freak. Marion shouldered her way up and planted herself in my path. "Where the hell were you?"

"You got a cigarette?"

"You tell me where you were," she replied.

"I ran away from home."

One thing about Marion that set her ahead of the common herd, she recognized the truth when it cropped up.

"Well, we lost." Her voice was neutral, purely up to me whether I wanted to take the blame for it or not. "I guess you know he's looking for you," she went on.

My throat went dry and I asked, "Who?"

"Carl."

"To hell with him," I answered.

"That's my girl," Marion said, smiling. For seven years she'd been waiting for me to take a beer bottle to Carl's head. "Sizemor won the men's tournament," she continued. "That good-looking friend of yours hit a home run."

I smiled, wished I'd been there to see him take that swing. "I'll see you later," I said.

"You be careful." She was gone before I could ask her what she meant. Somehow I'd killed my beer, so I went back for another. Couples whirled and bobbed on the dance floor. People were having a good time. There was nowhere on earth I wanted to be except smack where I was. Everything was going to be okay. For once in my life I was going to do something right. No hiding, no running away, no rolling over and going belly-up at the first sign of trouble. Starting tonight—

"Mary," cried a voice I knew. "Wait up." Julianna was ducking and dodging the dancers, making her way over to me. A large stuffed leopard lay across her shoulders wearing her fishing hat. He stared at me with glazed green eyes. Donna was behind her. Julianna bounced on her toes so the leopard's head nodded up and down. "Look what I won."

"Juli-Wuli, how you doing?" I gave her and the leopard a big squeeze.

"Are you gonna watch the fireworks?"

I nodded, smiling. "What are you doing up so late?"

"I'm spending the night with Donna. This is Donna," she reminded me. "We rode our bikes up here. How's Frank? Is Frank home yet?"

"Maybe in a few days."

"We got sparklers," Donna said. "We're gonna light 'em when the fireworks start."

"Where's your father?" I asked.

Julianna didn't bat an eyelash. "He's getting more beer for him and Nana." The idea of Nana drinking beer had them in giggles.

"Come on," Donna said to Julianna. "We gotta save us a spot."

The two of them disappeared into an anonymous tangle of arms and shoulders. At the confirmation that John was nearby, I drained the last of my beer. I had to find him.

"There she is." A hand clamped around my wrist like a handcuff made of cold bone. "I found her," Amy laughed as if I were the last Easter egg. I had walked right by the table where she and Carl sat with Jeff. My field of vision widened to include Suzanne O'Dell and her fiancé, then Harley and Toomey Sherman. I looked at each old familiar face.

"Hey," Amy said, nudging me with the silver flask that she kept for occasions like this. "I said, where've you been all day?"

Her face was framed by earrings that hung down and sparkled in the light. Only Amy would wear dangling earrings to the Beer Tent and drink gimlets from a silver flask.

"Well?" She smiled. We were both aware that the table was watching us, aware that they'd all heard about the argument we'd had, aware that Carl was sitting right behind her staring into his empty plastic cup. I felt as if I had flown far away from her, but here she was again, half forcing and half begging me to fall in line and rejoin the ranks. It would be easy to return to my half of the friendship, easy to hide in that proud isolation that Amy admired and resented so much. Emboldened by my silence, she said, "Toomey's been looking for you. Haven't you, Toomey?"

He nodded and smiled at the end of the table, too goddamn stupid to know she was ridiculing him. I wanted him to stand up and tell her to go to hell. He sat fingering his wristwatch while Harley leaned over to say something in his ear.

I looked back at Amy, who had dropped my hand, who wanted so badly to continue as we were. How could I tell her all that was wrong with this? Nothing would get through to her except maybe a good knock upside the head. Amy hated violence. Said it was the stuff of daytime talk shows and ignorant thugs. I outweighed her by forty pounds and besides, a sock in the jaw never solved anything. A quarter century of friendship unspooled in my brain.

"Oh hell," I thought, and punched her in the face.

She flew backward over the chair behind her. Earrings flipped upside down, the silver flask leapt out of her hand. The blow knocked her eyelids closed, so I had no idea what was going through her mind as she fell back through the air. Both of her eyebrows were arched this time; genuine surprise at last.

The rest of the table was caught in delayed time. Then they all woke up at once. Carl and Jeff sprang for Amy as if she'd fallen overboard.

"Oh for Christ's sake," said Suzanne O'Dell, who got up and walked away in disgust. Suzanne had an ounce of class to her, so I couldn't blame her. I straightened my fingers, the knuckles bruised. I'd made contact with her cheekbone, which was hard and sharp like a little concrete block. I grabbed her Virginia Slims off the table, lit one carefully, and stuffed the full pack in my pocket.

"Hey, Toomey," I said. "How you doing?"

"Okay," he answered with a nod. We both looked on the ground to see how Amy was doing. All I could see was one slender foot in a straw sandal, toenails painted scarlet. A mob of do-gooders obstructed the rest of her. People were rushing over to the table, appalled and excited. In the contagion of hysteria surrounding the fallen Amy, no one paid much attention to me. You would have thought I'd killed her.

19

I set down my empty beer. Started to work my way out of the crowd. After two steps I was blocked by someone's chest and an arm went around my waist.

"Let's go," he said close to my ear and led us to the outskirts of the tent. He kept hold of my arm as we walked past the Port-O-Potties into a field of dark and quiet. The stars let out a million distant sighs. The weeds around our legs waved back and forth in relief. We sat surrounded by goldenrod and milkweed.

"You're here," John said. He was the better part of drunk, but he was happy to see me, no doubt about that. "I couldn't find you," he said. "I called all day. I drove by your house."

"I can't see you anymore," I told him.

"I know," he said. Then he stopped and looked at me, frowning.

"And Julianna's never going to find out," I continued. "She's my friend."

"All right." He pulled up a long blade of grass and chewed on the end, watching me from under his lowered eyebrows. "But we're here now." He looked and sounded so much like Julianna in that moment, I had to laugh. "You have a good left," he said.

"You saw?"

"If there was any doubt that you were the woman of my dreams, you erased it with that punch."

That must be the perverse allure of religion; the idea of someone or something loving you at your worst, loving you *for* your worst. Maybe God had finally woken up and taken notice. Maybe God was here now, looking out through the blue eyes of this man and saying, "I'll forgive you if you'll forgive me." I wouldn't have minded dying in that moment, sitting there in the scratchy weeds with God's bare arm draped across my knee. A nearby boom bounced up to the sky and exploded in colored lights.

"I have to go back," I said.

"Not yet," he answered. He flopped back on the grass and laughed out loud, drunk and happy. "Look."

The fireworks shouted overhead. I lay on my back beside him. A gulf separated us now, but I was happy. Flowers of light bloomed and faded above us. Their deep thunder mingled with the rumble of the logging trucks down the road. It drowned out the voices that had wandered into the weeds past the Port-O-Potties. John and I were far enough afield to be invisible. Luminous swirly ghosts chased their own tails like puppies across the sky. John said, "Those are my favorites."

"I like the weeping willows," I told him. He nodded. The last thing I saw before the world tore apart was that long blade of grass still in the corner of his mouth.

"I told you," said a young voice. Two figures stood not far away, black silhouettes rising up out of the tall grass. Both John and I sat up. It was Donna who had spoken. Julianna stood next to her. She was looking past me at her dad. A third figure appeared behind them and said, "Go with Donna."

"But it's just Mary," Julianna replied.

"Go with Donna," Doreen repeated, this time sharp and angry.

"Dad?" Julianna's voice, one word traveling across the twenty feet that separated us. She hadn't looked at me.

"Do what your mother says," John replied. Donna grabbed Julianna's arm and pulled her backward. "Come on," she said. "Come on, Juju."

"What's the matter?" Julianna said over her shoulder. "They were just talking."

Two young girls walked awkwardly through the high weeds, lit by the explosions that continued in the sky. The breeze rippled the grass like waves in a silvery green lake. The girls disappeared.

"John," Doreen said with a torn and ragged tenderness. "You swore you wouldn't do this again." A dozen denials came to my tongue, halfway between truth and lies. "Would you leave us please?" she said to me.

The simple tone of it, the naked request for privacy, made me start up to leave. John's hand came down on mine, an unthinking reflex. Doreen saw it. She turned in the grass and walked away. He called out to her.

"Stay away from me, John," she yelled as she kept walking. "Just stay away from me."

He rose up and ran after her. I was alone. The fireworks grand finale was in full tilt above me. The sky convulsed with color and movement. Boom! Boom! Boom! A handful of duds let out their thundering cracks one after another; bright white flashes dotted the sky like machine-gun fire. I lay back in the tall weeds alone, pummeled by the violence overhead. It went on for a good long time. I lay there until the last puff of dying smoke had drifted into the dark. The weeds rose up on either side of my vision. An inch-worm crawled up and over my ankle. I didn't brush him off. The night sky leaned over me, stars held me pinned and helpless. There I lay, the murderer of innocence, the destroyer of all joy.

"It's okay," I whispered out loud. "It'll be okay." Time just gave up and quit. I couldn't imagine ever getting up again.

A noise caught my ear, one that I'd heard many times before, the roar of a logging truck coming past the fairgrounds. It bellowed and clamored, as if it were about to unload a platoon of avenging angels. A horn blew like a ship at sea, a horn that blared in protest. It went on too long. It sounded like panic.

I sat up to see what the problem was. I saw the truck come out of the darkness and plow into the green Cutlass that had pulled recklessly, stupidly, unbelievably, out into the road. I rose to my feet as sound exploded like in a movie when the train derails. But the clumsy sideways leap of the car, that wasn't like a movie at all. Or the accordion-like crunching against the side of the huge truck cab. There was no slow-motion graceful arc, no glass flying in a thrilling fantail; just an ugly, awkward confusion of jolts and slams, violence too fast and too real to take it all in. The cab of the truck slid sideways, steering away and pushing the Cutlass across the pavement with a metallic scream. The weight of the logs followed its own momentum and shoved the cab back on itself in a jackknife. Then the entire thing went over, this time in slow motion, this time beautiful, the truck turned over onto the Cutlass and spilled its wooden guts across both lanes.

The drunken crowd went silent and unmoving. It took them to a count of four to absorb that the accident had really happened; there was no mistake, it wasn't part of the fireworks, not a joke someone was playing. Then the mass surged toward the road. I heard a couple of voices rise in fear, a tangle of question marks. *What? What?* Hands were pointing, children were swung up in their parents' arms. People began to run and then I was running too.

I'd memorized every inch of that car. There was no chance of pretending it wasn't his. I ran with a savage and sickening hope that Doreen had left alone, that it was her in the car and not her husband or her daughter. In the far field a human tide gushed between the rows of parked cars. Once at the road they climbed over the scattered logs to get closer. The back of the Cutlass was pinned under the truck, and its roof slanted upward toward the front. I couldn't see inside, I couldn't push through the crowd. Got a glimpse of the shattered driver's window. Voices penetrated, questions and shouts. I shoved and wedged myself past shoulders, through arms waving pointlessly, until I saw him. It was just an upstretched neck rising out of the collar of his Sizemor Septic T-shirt. His face was mostly hidden by the roof pushed low over his head. Nothing inside the car was moving. Doreen and Julianna were nowhere in sight.

An argument erupted near the driver's door. "Don't move him. . . . Check to see if he's breathing. . . . hurt him worse if you try to drag him out."

I saw blood, but I couldn't tell where it was coming from. I was no more than fifteen feet from him. I couldn't tell if he was dead, and the world went into a sort of limbo where he may as well have been taking a nap; any moment now he would wake up.

A few half-drunk volunteer firemen swarmed up the cab of the truck, where the driver lay awake. No one could do much except wait until the flashing lights arrived with expertise and stretchers and sober magic.

"Mom?" A girl's voice rose uncertainly from the shifting crowd. "Mom?"

I pushed my way toward the sound. Donna and Julianna stood at the edge of the crowd not far from the front of the car. Donna was calling for her mother, who was somewhere in the crush of bodies behind her. She finally pushed back into the crowd, leaving Julianna standing there alone. She was looking in through the broken glass of the front windshield. The spotted leopard stared with its glassy eyes reflecting the headlights. No one paid her any mind. All those people, and none of them connected this twelve-year-old girl with what lay inside the wreck. Why wasn't someone doing something? Where was Doreen?

The slow moan of a siren started up out of the darkness. Julianna disappeared. I tried to push my way after her, but too many people blocked my path. A red glow grew and reflected off the crowd. Folks stepped back so the police could pull up closer, the ambulance right behind. I stopped where I was. Everything was going to be okay now. Someone would take care of this.

A policeman leaned in John's window for forever. Then he looked all through the car to see if anyone else was there. Finally he joined the others at the truck, where lots of hurried activity surrounded the driver. At the Cutlass two medics worked slowly, methodically, to remove the body from the car. They covered him with a blanket and loaded him into one of the ambulances. I watched until they drove away without a siren.

Some folks were standing in bunches, some heading for their cars. The road was clogged by spilled logs. No one was going anywhere for a while. I stayed where I was, watching the empty Cutlass and waiting for it not to be true. As the crowd thinned out I heard a voice behind me.

"Don't let her up there," he said angrily. "She doesn't need to see that."

Uncle Ted stood near Doreen, holding on to her and listening to someone in a uniform.

"Where's Julianna?" Doreen kept asking.

"They went to find her," Uncle Ted told her.

"Where is she?" Doreen looked all around. I backed away so she wouldn't see me, but she wouldn't have seen anything that wasn't John walking toward her, safe and whole.

"Where is she?" Doreen repeated over and over.

Where is she? I looked all through the crowd. I shoved and searched and even called her name, but no one answered in a sea of people who meant nothing to me. No one would ever find her in this mess if she didn't want to be found. Somehow she had vanished, just instantly disappeared. Then suddenly I knew where she was.

I made my way to the Merc. Drove slowly through rows of cars all glistening in the flashes of red light. It was a graveyard of ghost cars, and me moving among them silent as a forbidden thought until I was at the edge of the field beyond the fallen logs. Between me and the road there was a wide ditch. I went in on an angle. Reached the bottom, moving carefully, the grass rising up in both side windows. Coming up the opposite bank, it was like driving into silence and distant planets and peace forever. Out crept the Merc onto the shoulder, grasping at gravel before it reached firm pavement. Then I was moving and the lights of the Beer Tent and the police cars disappeared in the rearview mirror.

I could hardly grip the wheel. John broke into my awareness, blotting out the dashboard, the headlights, the darkness all around. Wanted to scream but swallowed it. The Kools had slid from the dashboard into oblivion. My hands shook so that I had trouble pulling Amy's pack from my pocket. I rubbed my eyes to erase the fact of his face covered and taken away. Drove slowly north of the fairgrounds but saw nothing. I turned onto the darker roads, no traffic at all this time of night. I cruised up and down the darkest stretches, trying to undo all of it in my mind; trying to back up a couple of hours and start the evening over again.

Twenty hollow minutes passed before I saw her. She'd put six miles between her and the accident. I came around in front of her and pulled onto the shoulder. She tried to take a wide swerve as I got out of the car. I caught hold of her and brought her and Eleanor Prudhomme to a stop.

"I'm going to the North Pole," she said. "I have to go."

"Your mom wants you."

"I hate her," she yelled, kicking me away from Eleanor. "I'm going."

I got a firm grip on the bike, and Julianna climbed off it, away from me. I put the bike in the trunk. Julianna remained where she was. The stuffed leopard was gone.

"Get in the car," I said to her.

"I'm not going back," she said to the black trees surrounding us.

"Please get in the car."

She did. The Merc sat on the side of the road with just the yellow flashers on. I made no move to start the engine. Crickets roared all around us.

She said, "He died."

I said, "Yes."

"I'm not going back."

We sat like that for a long time. I looked out the dark windshield and waited.

"I was supposed to spend the night with Donna," she said at last. "I lost my hat."

"I'm sorry."

"Why?" she snorted, looking out her window. "You didn't do anything."

Not my fault. He was drunk, he was angry, who knows what happened. I had done the right thing.

Suddenly Julianna kicked at the dashboard. "What'd she get so mad for?" Vicious, violent kicks. "Why'd she tell him to leave and never come back?"

Oh no. Had Doreen said that? Had she really said that? I could see them standing in the shadow of the tent, the anger and hurt spurting out of her mouth. *Leave and never come back.* And him, drunk and cornered, leaving her there and going to the car.

Julianna's foot kept hitting the glove compartment. "I hate her. Why'd she do that?" she yelled. "You were *just talking.*"

I didn't cause this. I had done the right thing. I had opened my eyes in time, and Julianna never needed to know. She was too young to understand. He and I were just talking.

"No, we weren't," I told her.

"Yes you were," she yelled louder at the dashboard. "Yes you were."

"I'm sorry—"

"Shut up!" And she was out of the car. I stepped out on the shoulder and watched while she kicked the side panel of the Merc over and over. Even in gym shoes, she was going to break every bone in her foot if she didn't stop.

"Liar! Stupid bitch! Dyke!" Each word now punctuated by a rock, or a broken bit of pavement that she picked up off the shoulder and hurled close range at the growing dents on the side of the car. I stood and watched. Watched and saw. Somewhere there was chaos, pandemonium, folks rushing up and down. Somewhere a body was lying at the morgue. Somewhere there were people looking hysterically for a lost twelve-year-old. But we were here.

You betrayed me. You broke my heart. You have done the ab-solute worst thing in the world. Just overused words that Julianna would not say. A large chunk of asphalt flew through the Merc's back window. The sound of breaking glass was a relief. A moth beat against the car's flashers. An old story came to mind, but all I could remember was the last line. Something about "I wish I wanted something as bad as that moth wanted to fry herself." Something like that. Where was that from?

"Were you fucking?" she screamed in a nasty, hate-filled

voice. "Is that what you're saying? You were fucking each other out there?"

She hadn't looked at me since she and Donna arrived in the field earlier. Now she glared at the Merc, waited for an answer with another rock in her hand.

"No, we weren't fucking out there."

"Make up your mind," she said. The rock made sharp contact with my knee. "Tell me the truth."

"Do you want to hear it?"

"No! Yes. I don't . . ." Fury and frustration balled up tightly together. Tears came to her clenched face. "Damn damn damn damn hell!" she hollered, sitting down in the dirt. "What did you *do*?"

She broke off and sobbed into her dirty hands. There was too much she needed to know, and no words to ask for it. Too young to understand. Not my fault. I was gutted: heart, lungs, liver all scooped out in a heap on the side of the road. Don Marquis. That's who wrote the story about the moth and the flame. *I wish I wanted something as bad as that moth wanted to fry herself.*

I sat down next to Julianna. There in the dirt, with the small islands of yellow light blinking on and off, I told her. Told everything I could remember about Number 34, about the Colby trial, and how I tried to run away from it. I told her about the two of them, her and her dad, sitting in my living room that Sunday afternoon when Ruther was born. I talked about Uncle Eddie's truck stop, the gumball ring, how he had talked a lot about her. I told her about me and Carl, about my own mom and dad, about Amy. I didn't spare either Julianna or myself. I let her know where her father was, and what he had been doing, the night he didn't come home. Maybe she only heard half of it, but all of it had to be said. She listened through sniffles part of the time, cried harder than ever when I described Thursday afternoon with the two of them at the fair. I didn't keep anything from her: not the selfish need, the shaggy mane of guilt, or the deadening despair of the Night Visitor. And her dad: the fistfights at the ballpark, playing with Frank on the kitchen floor, his drunkenness, his tenderness, his desertion Friday night, and how the whole thing had ended in that field just before the world blew up.

My voice trailed off down the black road. Julianna leaned against the side of the Merc. Her eyes were closed against the sight of me. She looked as gutted as I felt.

After a punishing silence her voice came formal and hard. "Did he love you?"

"No," I told her. "He loved your mom. He loved you."

"Did you love him?"

If I said yes, would that make it okay? Would she find a way to forgive me if I couldn't help myself? "No," I said. "He just made me feel a little better."

Try to understand that someday. Try to live with that forever. Moonlight tore itself on the ratchety tips of the pines. It was almost September. The night wind was wild and chilly, carrying hints of all the small deaths to come in the months ahead. I looked at Julianna sitting next to me. The hands covering her face were shaking with fatigue, loss, shock. *Someday, please God, let this do her some good.*

"You were my friend," she said.

"I am your friend." I laid a hand on her arm. "I'm sorry."

She shook my hand off in disgust and stood up. "I want my mom."

■　　■　　■

The lights of Riverton were bright and dreamlike after the dark of the woods. Cold air blew through the broken window. Julianna gave me directions to her house as if I were a stranger. I prayed that someone would be there as we pulled into the yard. Uncle Ted stood on the front porch talking to two cops. When he saw Julianna get out of the car he yelled, "Where have you been?"

She took a step backward. Aunt Sophie appeared behind Uncle Ted and came across the yard toward us. She held on to Julianna without a word. Her resemblance to John tore a hole through me. I unloaded Eleanor Prudhomme. Police uniforms fell out of my vision as Uncle Ted approached.

"Where'd you find her?" he asked in a voice like rusted barbed wire. He and his wife stood looking at me, waiting.

Remorse constricted my throat, choking off all explanation. "I'm sorry."

"I'll tell Doreen she's here," he said, and disappeared into the house.

Sophie looked at everything but me. "We thought we'd lost her too."

I laid my hand for a moment on Julianna's shoulder. It was ice cold. "She's okay now," I said. Julianna didn't move, didn't look at me as I got in the car.

The drive home was a series of precise motions. I started the engine. *Now I am starting the engine.* I steered carefully toward the cottage. *I am moving the wheel to the left. I am braking lightly.* With Julianna safely home the rest of the night came flooding back. Parked in the driveway, I saw John seated in the passenger seat, felt the heat of him just a few feet away. *I am getting out of the car. I am standing in the yard.* I looked for Frank in the front window before the bullet of memory lodged in my brain. Frank was not there. Maybe he was never coming home again. All I had was a grave out back with someone else's lost pet lying in it. I walked around the outside of the cottage several times. I couldn't go inside. Couldn't go in the kitchen, where the Yahtzee game still sat on the kitchen counter, Julianna's scorecard beside it. Couldn't face the living room, where John sat with Frank on his lap a week ago. There was no comfort, no fur to bury my face against while I mourned the friends I had lost. *I am walking in circles around the cottage. I can never go inside again.*

I felt for the pink plastic ring on my finger. Found nothing but clammy flesh. The thick stench of burning plastic returned to me. I ran to the burn barrel and dug through piles of debris. Maybe there was some pink fragment, some little plastic relic left for me to hold in my hand. I choked on the ash rising into my face. My eyes blurred and closed up. *Please, please. Just one small piece of comfort.* But it was gone. I began to cry, an ugly and wrenching sound. He was gone, he and Julianna both.

A car door slammed in the driveway. I came around the side of the cottage believing believing believing that John was standing there beside the Cutlass, hands in his pockets, smiling at me under those eyebrows. Julianna would be there beside him and we would laugh at this awful night, at this terrible thing that hadn't happened after all. We could go back to the way it was when he was only Number 34.

But the figure standing on the porch was Amy. I stopped short as she turned toward me. One eye was blue and swollen.

"I've been calling and calling," she said, coming off the porch. I went to her, crying because my heart was breaking. Amy put her arms around me and held on. How could I find the words to tell her? Julianna. *You were my friend.* John lying in the silent ambulance. Gone. Amy stood for a long time with her head pressed against mine, her hand rubbing my shoulder.

"Come on," she said, and we went to the cottage.

20

John was buried the following Tuesday. I didn't go to the service. I have kept away from Julianna and her family.

Amy stayed with me for three days until the funeral was past. All that time I didn't stop talking. It was a form of delirium, talking about Fritos and Little Debbies in the boat with John, about Julianna's stuffed leopard staring into the headlights. Told her about waking in the backyard the day after her and Carl's wedding, and the hidden wound that had never healed. She sat huddled at one end of the couch, stripped of her façade and miserable, but listening.

"That sock in the eye," she said at one point, "I had it coming."

She and Carl decided to try a separation. He moved into the Pineview Apartments. I didn't ask for details, so she didn't give them to me except to say that they were going together to "see someone" once a week in Cadillac. I don't know if they'll work themselves out or not. Finally, it no longer concerns me.

When Sharon heard about the accident she came to the cottage, she and Amy striking a tacit truce. Sharon spent a lot of time at my place during the following month. If Mom knew, she kept her mouth shut and waited for me to speak of it. I didn't. Our Sunday night dinners have tapered off. For now, I don't miss them.

Patricia Colby's trial lasted eleven days. I wasn't called again. The defense didn't want a loose cannon on the stand, and Mad Dog was afraid they'd move to impeach her best witness and strike out all of my testimony. Besides, two other witnesses reported "not wanting to admit" their own suspicions, including the elementary school principal.

Patricia Colby was found guilty of second-degree murder; life, with possible parole after fifteen years. She maintained that it was an accident even in the face of mounting proof. Jen's brother and sister remained in Manistee with their father and his second wife. No amount of questioning had ever gotten anything but a wooden "I don't know" from either of them. Blind love and loyalty, or fear that their mother's anger would turn on them, I don't know. For a few days it was all over the headlines, Jen Colby's picture smiling up at me again from the front page. But she no longer haunted me; the Night Visitor was gone.

The *Gazette* described Patricia's testimony as inconsistent and evasive. Out-of-town papers painted her as a monster. But the image that has stayed with me is a tired woman with her hair in a ponytail, not so different from any other mother on my route.

September came and I went back to work. I was still flayed

with sorrow, moving in a dream, but I was no longer afraid of the tiny bodies that filled the bus. It's a different route now, a new load of little responsibilities.

"Who are you?" a chubby boy asks as he bangs a book bag against his knee.

"I'm the bus lady," I tell him. "I'm Mary." I look at the children on my bus. I see each one.

In late September I received a postcard, plain white with no picture, in Julianna's handwriting. "I've reached the North Pole. There's nothing but cold and dark, no one for miles and miles. I'm not coming home." It was unsigned. I keep it propped up on my dresser.

How I love October: wool jackets, apple cider, crisp blue skies. Trees shake off their blazing coats with gleeful abandon. Clouds hurry along as if pulled on a string. I love the quickening in the autumn air, the energy in the woods now that the dogged haze of summer is past. There won't be many more days of this sunshine, so I have the front door open. Down the road the Millers are burning their leaves. The smell causes my heart to stir.

It's Saturday afternoon and Michigan football is on the television. The Wolverines are destroying Indiana, so I'm smiling despite the tobacco cravings. Later tonight I'm going to catch a movie in Cadillac with Suzanne and Peg. For now I'm putting the finishing touches on little Ruther's christening gown. Stacy is bringing him over for me to baby-sit tomorrow. One corner of the living room is given over to a rocking chair, stuffed animals, a mobile of flying elephants. He's turning out better than I expected. He adores his Aunt Mary.

Frank is curled up with Sock Buddy on the rocker. He moves much slower now, but all four legs are working and there's no pain. He still terrorizes a cricket or two. His coat has thickened, ready for another winter.

"It's third and goal for the maize and blue with less than a minute here in the half."

I look up from my embroidery to watch them score. The faint sound of tires on gravel brings me slowly off the couch. I stop at the door. It's the first I've seen her since that night. She wheels her bike up to the porch and leans it against the railing.

"Hello," I say through the screen door, through my happiness.

Her amber eyes are solemn, looking at the ground. "Hi," she says.

"Come in."

I grip the door handle tightly. She looks just like John, who is never farther from my thoughts than a breeze. She wears a denim jacket that she leaves on as she comes inside. Her hair is a little browner, a little longer, the curls tucked behind her ears. She seems older. I wonder if her mother knows where she is, and my heart hurts all over again. I turn off the television as she looks around the cottage, noticing the baby things. We sit at the kitchen table. She takes a long breath and lets it out through her nose, frowning.

"Well," she says to her knee. "I'm home."

"I got your postcard," I tell her. "I'm glad you came back."

She gazes at the wall, taking a minute to steady herself. It's taken her months to get this far.

Finally she says, "I got lonely."

Frank leaps carefully down from the rocker and pads over to rub against Julianna's leg. She lifts him into her arms and lays her cheek against his head. Outside, fire-colored leaves fall to the ground.

About the Author

LISA REARDON is the author of a half dozen plays and one novel, *Billy Dead*. She received her M.F.A. from the Yale School of Drama. Ms. Reardon conducts a writing group for adolescents at St. Luke's–Roosevelt Hospital in New York City, where she lives with her husband, actor Mick Weber.

About the Type

The text of this book was set in Aster, designed by Francesco Simoncini in 1958. Aster is a round, legible face of even weight, and was planned by the designer for the text setting of newspapers and books.